BLOODSTAINED
Beauty

ELLA FIELDS

Editor: Jenny Sims, Editing4Indies
Proofreading: Allison Riley
Formatting: Stacey Blake, Champagne Book Design
Cover designer: Sarah Hansen, Okay Creations
Cover model: Anthony Kemper
Photography: Regina Wamba

Be unhurried in giving your heart
For there is always another counterpart

For those who still believe in
fairy tales.

T HE COOL BREEZE KISSED MY CHEEKS AND UNFURLED MY hair but did nothing to dry the stinging pools of fear that had welled in my eyes.

Shining bright, but not bright enough, the half-moon mocked me from where it sat pressed into the deep, dark sky. Even the stars had abandoned me, winking out of sight the moment I plunged into the dense woods.

Perhaps that was my own fault for stepping into the cover of trees. But I'd like to think when running for one's life, the obvious thing to do wouldn't be to hide in plain sight. Better to make it harder for them, even if it made it harder for me at the same time.

The obvious thing.

I choked back a wet snort.

How many fucking things had been obvious since day one? Since the moment these monsters waltzed into my life?

I'd been oblivious. I'd been too trusting. I'd been a fool.

I'd been in love.

Well, love did you no good when your heart, that fucking traitor, was pounding at an ungodly speed as you tried to outrun certain death or worse.

Adrenaline spiked my pulse higher, made my feet move faster, and spread my thoughts wider.

Don't you dare give up on me now, you asshole. You got us into this mess, and I'll be damned if you give out before we've seen the sun rise one more time.

Time.

I couldn't remember anything past my visit to the local grocer. It all became a blur, a cacophony of vague memories. Tires skidding, screams, grunts, and cursing filled the air and then … quiet.

Nothing but me and the sound of my feet snapping twigs and scuffing over rocks, and my labored breathing.

Then another sound.

His voice echoed through the trees as though he had all the time in the world. As though he was walking languidly, strolling lazily behind me, uncaring of the fact I could get away. "You may as well stop, Jemima. We both know it's useless."

I would've scoffed if I didn't have better things to do.

If I wasn't so fucking petrified.

Too busy tossing a glance into the gloom behind me, I tripped over a fallen, hollowed out tree trunk.

No, I screamed to myself. This wouldn't be how it ended.

My ankle panged in protest as I forced myself onto my hands and knees. The sound of leaves and twigs crunching filtered into my panicked brain, and my stomach heaved.

Before I could stand, a hand wrapped around my elbow, wrenching me from the damp, mildew-scented earth.

I acted on instinct, my knee rising to his crotch as I spun, then I stumbled away when his hand fell loose.

Again, I ran.

I ran, ignoring the pain in my ankle and the fear that had

me wanting to bang my head against one of the blurring trees to wake up from this nightmare.

I ran from the pain in my heart.

I ignored it all and managed to smile when I saw the headlights of a lone car through the curtain of trees and foliage.

I could make it. I could run along the road until someone passed. Never mind it was late and we lived on the fringes of society, it would happen eventually.

Air escaped me in a rush. A scream tore itself from my lungs, echoing into the silence as a sharp bite penetrated my skin.

"Fuck," I whimpered, slowing and reaching around to pluck what looked like a dart from the back of my arm. With my heart trembling, I staggered back into a tree as warmth spread from the stinging prick and oozed into every limb of my body.

Losing control of my legs, I fell to my ass. Hard. Yet I couldn't feel it. I couldn't feel a thing as I stared up at the sky and searched for the moon through the giant treetops, for one last source of light.

I found it, clung to it as my breathing slowed and my vision frayed.

"I told you it was useless."

The moon disappeared, his calm words following me into the dark.

CHAPTER
One

Eight months ago

I T DIDN'T SEEM RIGHT THAT EVEN WITH THE BOXES, BED, dresser, entertainment unit, TV, and an old couch, my apartment still looked bare.

Though coming from a house filled to the brim and threatening to overflow with memories, it was bound to.

"Are you sure about this?" my dad asked, his voice gruff as he stacked a large box on top of another by the door. "It's not too late to change your mind and come back home."

Tempting. It was so damn tempting.

My excitement since getting the callback for my first ever teaching position was fading fast. Spending the previous month apartment hunting and shopping for cheap necessities had helped battle the nerves. Nerves that were now curling sharp talons into my chest and threatening to make my voice shake as I said, "It's time, Daddy."

Dad's nose scrunched in that way it did when he thought I'd said something ridiculous.

"Besides," I continued as I waded over the scuffed wooden flooring to the window and parted the dust-marked checkered curtains, "it could be worse. I could've been accepted for the three jobs I'd applied for out of state or that last one in Tennille, which would mean a three-hour drive." I fought the urge to sneeze as my hand stirred dust while gliding over the white painted windowsill. Turning to Dad, I wiped my palm on my jeans. "As opposed to twenty minutes." I quirked a brow.

He waved a hand, marching over to inspect the smoke alarm with narrowed brown eyes, much like my own. "I'm just saying that living in the real world is tough, baby girl. I wouldn't judge you if you changed your mind."

Smiling, I left him to his inspections and went to grab the last two suitcases from the stairwell that led out to the busy street below. The apartment was open plan, but thankfully, it had a bedroom. The fact it was situated above a twenty-four-hour drugstore made me pause, but I'd tried to look at the positive side. Easy, quick access if I ever ran out of toiletries and it would be handy if I got sick, which was likely seeing as I was about to start teaching first graders.

I tried not to think about that.

Positives. I needed all the positives, or else the emotions that made my hands clammy around the suitcase handles might just get the better of me.

I was close to home, I reminded myself. So close, I really could be there in twenty minutes.

Our home sat nestled on the other side of the river that divided the concrete and suburban from the trees and wildlife. Glenning was a small, rural area often bypassed due to its size and dirt roads, but it owned a huge piece of my heart. That I got to work and start my venture into full-blown adulthood within reach of home was a dream, really.

Ugh. The way I was finding reasons to reassure myself grated.

I thought graduating college and landing a job my first year out meant I'd automatically mature into the woman I saw myself as in my mind.

Strong, fearless, capable.

You are, I tried to remind myself. *You can fire a gun, milk a cow, read five novels a week, juggle a part-time job while studying, and ace your finals with one hour of sleep.*

All were true.

Confidence snuffed out the fear at the reminder, and with it, that familiar excitement returned.

I dumped the suitcases in the middle of my tiny apartment and planted my hands on my hips as I released a huge breath. Who knew what this adventure would bring? The thought thrilled as much as it terrified.

The sun had shone all morning, so I'd slipped on my new cream gauzy dress.

It had ruffles spilling over the neckline, stopping beneath my breasts. Elegant, understated when paired with my favorite black flats, and professional.

It was my second week working at Lilyglade Prep, which was a little more esteemed than I'd have guessed before the interview process. Nevertheless, I was thankful for being forewarned. Jeans, a T-shirt, nice cardigan, and Chucks wouldn't cut it.

They paid well, so shopping for a new work wardrobe didn't hurt too much.

My new dress fluttered around my knees as I stepped out from the stairwell of my apartment and onto the street. As I was stuffing my keys and phone into my bag, someone bumped into me, and I grumbled beneath my breath, "Rude."

Rain had started to fall, and I cursed my decision to park

behind my apartment building rather than wait for a vacant spot in front of it the day before. I turned, thinking I'd run back inside to fetch my umbrella.

My heart jumped, and I stopped.

It couldn't be…

Deciding to forgo the umbrella, I looked forward again, shaking away the absurdness. But another glance over my shoulder as I was about to turn the corner at the end of the street said my first crazy assumption was correct.

A sexy madman was chasing me down the street.

Clearly, this living away from home and becoming a full-fledged adult thing was off to a climactic start.

Okay, so he wasn't *chasing* me. He was walking. Kind of fast. And he definitely wasn't a madman, I realized as he gently tapped my elbow outside the bakery to get my attention.

"Hey, you dropped this." In his ginormous hand sat my phone.

Hesitantly and without meeting his gaze, I reached out and took it, slipping it into my bag. "Thanks. I didn't even know I'd dropped it."

Those big hands sank deep into green cargo pockets, and his large chest barely moved as he shrugged. "Lucky I saw then. I'm Miles."

"Okay, hi Miles."

"And your name?"

"Um." Nerves tinged my laugh, my eyes daring to creep up his chest to his face. "Jemima."

"Jemima," he repeated, trying it on with a smile. "Well, Jemima, I'm sorry if I spooked you." His voice was deep and held a roughness that felt like sandpaper brushing over my arms.

"That's okay. And uh, thank you," I repeated, my eyes stuck on his chin. A chin that was covered in thick, dark stubble.

Stubble that peppered his rugged jawline and wrapped around a set of decadently plump lips.

"You said that already." He laughed, and the bell over the door to the bakery chimed, prompting him to grasp my shoulders and gently urge me to the side for someone to pass.

Droplets of rain splattered onto my cheeks and chin, courtesy of being moved beneath a gap in the awning. I swiped at my face. "Sorry. I find it hard to communicate like an intelligent human being before my morning caffeine consumption." My eyes widened after that little bit of verbal vomit.

God, *shit.*

He chuckled good naturedly, and I tucked some hair behind my ear as I finally met his gaze.

Eyes like honey stared back at me; a golden brown so rich, they almost glowed. Dark lashes that matched his thick, unruly dark hair fanned over them as he blinked down at me, then licked his lips. "Well, this is kind of awkward. I'll just—"

"No," I blurted, then cringed, wanting to back into the bakery behind me and disappear. "I should get going before I'm late." I smiled and shifted on my feet. "New job, can't be late."

Fucking hell. *Shut your trap, woman.*

When I chanced another peek at his face, his eyes were smiling, his teeth flashing. He was all predator, and I felt like a timid little mouse. "Congrats. And I hope you don't mind, but I, well …" He rubbed behind his head, seeming unsure all of a sudden, which I already knew was a rarity for this man. "I kind of, maybe, called myself on your phone."

"Kind of, maybe?" Breath lodged in my throat as I stepped back into the brick wall.

He nodded, lips pinching.

My stomach flooded with flutters. "Why?"

Another devastating grin. "Because you and me, we're

having dinner."

I watched as his eyes dropped to my chest—later realizing my beautiful dress was see-through when wet—snared in a web of confused exhilaration as he turned and went back the way he'd come.

I wasn't that girl. The one who thought she wasn't good enough and plagued by insecurities. But this guy, Miles, he had to be thirty. At least. He held an air of maturity sprinkled with mischief while I'd only just started paying off my student loans.

And there was no way I wasn't going to dinner with him.

CHAPTER
Two

Seven months ago

LIGHTNING STREAKED ACROSS THE SKY, AND THUNDER had us both jumping and laughing in the seats of Miles's truck as we shoved the last of our cheeseburgers into our mouths.

We'd made a habit of frequenting McDonalds for most of our dates, even if that meant sitting beneath a storm dark sky as rain pelted the truck roof and cascaded down the windshield in tiny rushing rivers.

If someone had told me that I, some small-town girl with medium sized dreams, would be sitting in a strange guy's truck three times a week, a guy who was at least ten years my senior, I would have laughed and said I knew better than that.

But he wasn't a stranger or just some guy. Talking to Miles, even just sitting with Miles, was like being with a friend you'd known all your life but had been separated from for years. And now, we were simply catching up.

"First time was outside on a park bench."

"Too impatient to find a bed?" I prodded.

His top lip tilted, and I wanted to bite it. "More like there were no better places. I was sixteen, and so was she." He paused, his gaze moving outside the truck window for a beat. "We couldn't exactly do it under our parents' noses. They weren't the type to let us get away with that. So, park bench it was."

I laughed, shaking my head.

"What?" he asked, reaching over to poke my cheek. "Never been that adventurous?"

I took a sip of soda, then stuck the cup back into the cup holder. "Nope, beds only."

Miles was quiet as his eyes dragged over my face. "How many times?"

Shocked by his bluntness, I laughed again. "Well, lots. Mainly with my high school boyfriend."

His brows furrowed. "You still talk to him? What happened?"

"He went to college out of state, and we eventually broke up when we realized it wasn't going to work out."

Miles forced a pout, and I reached over to slap his upper arm but only hurt myself. "Ouch." I rubbed my fingers, and he took them and kissed them. "Are you eating cement for breakfast?"

His laughter sprang sharp and sudden, filling the truck with its rough, loud volume. He had a nice laugh; the kind that said he did it often and unrestrained.

Taking my fingers back, I finished answering his question, "We don't talk anymore. I had another boyfriend in college, but it only lasted a few months. That's it."

Miles nodded. "So you've always wanted to teach?"

"That or own my own bookstore."

His lips quirked, his finger rubbing his brow. "I could see that."

"One day, maybe. What about you? Did you always want to mow people's lawns?" I waggled my brows.

He chuckled. "That's not all I do, you know." At my shrug, he continued, "Actually ... when I was a kid, I wanted to be a cop."

"Yeah?" I said, unable to see that with the easygoing, tatted up giant sitting next to me. "What stopped you?"

His phone rang, and he fished it out of the center console to inspect the screen, then shut it off.

"You can take it." I gestured to the phone he'd tucked into the driver's side door.

"It can wait. Work." He turned fully to face me. "Where were we?"

"Cop?" I asked.

His mouth twisted, then he pulled me over to sit astride him, and held my face. "I was too much trouble to head down that road."

"I don't know if I believe you," I breathed.

"Believe it, baby," he whispered, lips meeting mine.

Six months ago

"You liked the Care Bears?" Miles snorted, placing Funshine Bear back on his home atop my dresser. "Why am I not surprised and kind of turned on?"

"Because you're a freak," I said, laughing and refusing to feel embarrassed about my inability to let go of some of my childhood.

He pouted playfully, going through more of my belongings on the dresser.

"Kidding. And give me a break. Other than college, this is my first time living away from home."

"Didn't you attend college in Riverstone?"

I tried to remember when I'd told him that, assuming it was probably during one of our many takeout dates or over the phone. We were still in that sickly stage of talking most nights until we were ready to pass out. "I did, yes." My book shut with a thwack, and I placed it on my nightstand. "But still, I stayed in the dorms for a bit."

"A bit?" he questioned.

"Okay." I flopped back onto my bed, smiling up at the white ceiling. "I lasted a semester."

Miles's laughter bounced off the walls of my bedroom and could probably be heard from the street.

His red Henley covered his inked arms, the muscles on his back flexing as he reached up high to a bookshelf and plucked one down. "*Little Red Riding Hood*," he read aloud.

"A favorite."

He scrunched his nose at it, then carefully pushed it back in its place. "Not worried about being a little old for fairy tales?" He paused, taking in the Care Bear and then the old ragdolls I had sitting in an armchair by the window. "And toys?"

A sting jolted my heart, but I masked it with a smile. "Not worried at all."

Returning my gaze to the ceiling, I heard something softly hit the floor, and then he was crawling over me. Shirtless. "I'm a dick," he said, arms flexing as he rested his forearms next to my head.

I gave him my eyes and nodded. "A little, but I've heard it before from my sister."

"That's different." His head lowered, lips whispering over my cheek. "You shouldn't have to hear it from me, someone who loves you in a much different way than your family."

My breath froze in my throat, my lungs and eyes swelling. "So you love me, do you?" I tried to say it mockingly as if it didn't mean anything.

It meant everything.

"I tried to stop it," he said, his forehead coming to rest on mine, the scent of cherry gum caressing my lips from his breath. "But it happened anyway."

We'd been dating a couple of months. And even though it seemed like a relatively short time, especially when it came to dropping the L word, it didn't feel rushed. It felt like a natural progression. I'd come to expect Miles in my life the way one expects the sun to rise. Every day.

"Why would you try to stop it?" I asked, unsure why. Maybe I was stalling. Maybe I was just too damn curious.

A puff of warm air hit my neck as he lowered his head, using his nose to nudge my chin up and allow him better access to the column of my throat.

I moaned, my thighs clenching, when he said, "Because you're too good for some bastard like me. But I want you in every fucking way I can have you, and I'm no good at staying away from what I want. What I need."

My legs lifted, toes pushing at his jeans. Soon, our clothes were in a pile on the floor, and he was dragging his lips over my tight nipples, his large palms swallowing my breasts.

When he reached the apex of my thighs, his mouth and nose were on me, inhaling deeply. The rush of his exhale set my thighs quivering and opening farther as he began a brutal assault with his tongue. I was instantly climbing high, my hands fisting the brown strands of his hair as his tongue dug at my opening.

"Miles," I panted.

He sat up and leaned over the bed, snagging his jeans and then unwrapping a condom.

Apricot light was fading fast outside my bedroom window, casting his tanned and inked skin in half shadow. He looked like bad news, and when my eyes reached his swollen cock, he looked like he'd split me in two.

Yet I greedily wrapped my legs around his waist, impatient to impale myself on him anyway.

"Fuck," he spewed as the head breached my opening, and my hips rolled, desperate to pull him closer, to connect, to fill myself.

"Please," I said, my voice unrecognizable. I was already out of breath. I liked sex, sure, but I'd never felt this burning lust to have it. This feeling consumed me every time we'd gotten close, and now that we were finally doing it, it was dizzying how badly I needed to combust.

His nostrils flared as he steadied his weight over me with one arm while the other grabbed the side of my face. My lips caught his as soon as his head descended, and then he pushed forward, swallowing my garbled cry into his mouth with a groan.

He fucked me slow, his hips rocking as though he could do this for days, but I soon learned his control only extended so far. Within minutes, the sound of our skin meeting echoed through the room, accompanied by the sound of my panting and his cussing.

His nose came to rest on mine, his eyes squeezing shut as he whispered, "Come. Holy shit, please come."

It took a minute of my hips meeting his to search for that perfect friction. I only needed a little, and then my head fell back. My thighs became a vise that made it harder for him to maintain the pace he seemed frantic to keep.

A strangled curse filtered into my hazy brain, and then my thighs were wrenched open. Miles rose onto his haunches, using my body to milk himself with a bruising grip on my hips.

I watched in rapt fascination as he came, his head angled toward the ceiling, eyes half open, and every muscle seizing.

His corded throat bobbed as he swallowed, and slowly, he relinquished the harsh grip on my hips.

With my thighs resting over his and my ass half on his knees, I listened to his heavy breathing as my own heart rate slowed.

His eyes hit mine what felt like a full minute later, and I smiled, wondering what thoughts were swirling in those brown depths. "You're quite a sight."

He laughed, lowering me to the bed and moving to sit on the side of it, his fingers running through the messy strands of his hair. "I could most fucking definitely say the same thing about you." His voice was strained as though he'd exerted a lot of energy just minutes ago. I grabbed the blanket from the end of my bed and pulled it over my rapidly cooling body as he disposed of the condom in my bathroom.

Miles returned wearing his briefs and bent over to grab his jeans. "Did I hurt you?"

I hummed. "Nope."

He inspected his phone, frowning as he looked at the window for a minute, then pocketed it after stepping into his jeans.

"You're going?" I sat up, the blanket falling around my stomach.

He nodded, walking over to me after pulling his shirt back on. "Sorry, someone needs me to quote a job. I thought I could do it tomorrow, but apparently, they're expecting me to start tomorrow." He rolled his eyes, something he rarely did, which made me laugh. "I'll see you tomorrow night?"

Though my heart wanted to protest, I nodded. "Sure."

He kissed me, light and quick, then straightened and marched for the door.

"Wait," I said, wrapping the blanket around me and almost stumbling over it as I hurried after him to the front door of my half-empty apartment. I grabbed his hand, then grabbed the side of his face, rising on my toes to whisper against his lips. "I forgot to say I love you too."

His eyes shut briefly, and a ragged breath coated my lips before he kissed me. Our tongues met, and the blanket fell away, his body melding mine to the wall by the door.

"What about the job?" I said between breaths.

"Fuck the job." Bending, he gripped my thighs and wrapped my legs around him, then carried me back to my room.

CHAPTER

Four months ago

"**K**EEP THEM CLOSED."

"Why?" I whined. "This isn't as fun as it looks in the movies. I'm going to face plant or something."

A hearty chuckle sparked every one of my available senses. "Where's the trust, Jem-Jem?"

"Up your ass, courtesy of my foot if I get injured."

He stopped, turning me to the side, and lifted the blindfold. "Is that anyway to speak to your fiancé?" He dropped to one knee on a paved driveway.

My gasp shook my lungs, and I looked behind him to the red and cream home. Quaint, new, and surrounded by tiny hedges.

"Miles …?"

"Down here." He laughed.

"Shit." I exhaled, returning my attention to him and the ring that glinted in the afternoon sun. "You're …?" I swallowed over the tears invading my throat. "You want to marry me?"

"It's not a question," he said, voice quiet but resolute. "I *am* going to marry you. You're going to be Mrs. Fletcher."

I sniffed, my head bobbing uncontrollably. "Okay." I nodded

again. "Oh, my god, okay."

Miles laughed, shaking his head. "This isn't going how I planned. But Jem, I love you. I want you with me all the time. In that house behind me, in my bed beside me, and if you agree to take this ring, I promise I'll cherish you for the unexpected gift you are."

I was full-blown crying by that stage, unable to see his face or anything around me through the blur of tears. "Stop it," I said, sniffing and roughly wiping my hands over my wet cheeks. "I said okay."

He pulled me to his lap, where I straddled him in the middle of the driveway in the middle of the afternoon and let him slide the glittering diamond ring onto my finger.

"Sorry," I said once I'd finally calmed down a little. "I kind of had an emotion explosion."

"If you hadn't, I would have wondered who I was asking to be my wife." Some unnamed emotion skittered across his face as I smiled down at him. He kissed the ring on my finger, then lifted his T-shirt to wipe my cheeks with it. "I've got you, Jem-Jem. I swear."

"Dad, could you please just give him a chance?" I whispered in the kitchen.

The same one I used to slide into in my socks every winter when the floor was cold and extra slippery.

He sighed, taking the towel from me and hanging it up. "He didn't ask my permission."

I groaned. "We don't live in that kind of world anymore."

He stabbed a finger at me after popping the tab on his beer can. "Exactly. And we're all doomed because of it."

I crossed my arms, leaning back against the kitchen counter with a brow raised.

Dad sighed. "Jesus Christ. I'll try, okay?" He looked out the small window in the kitchen, the one that granted a view of the dining and living room beyond, and didn't even try to lower his voice. "I don't trust him."

That wasn't the first time I'd heard that. Miles met my dad briefly when we'd invited him out for lunch not long after we'd started dating, and Miles had been called into work halfway through.

"A man who gives a damn puts his woman's needs first. Always," he'd said after Miles had apologized profusely before jetting out the door of the coffee shop.

He had a backward, old-fashioned way of looking at things. Always had. He'd never liked my high school boyfriend, and he didn't even know about the one I had in college, but he had no problem with Hope's husband, Jace, or the many boyfriends she'd had before him.

Hope said it was because I was the baby, which I found ridiculous. I might've been a dreamer, but I'd always been far more responsible than my older sister.

Being that she was four years older than me, my early teens were filled with memories of her sneaking out, sneaking back in, and ditching school to hang out at the local skate park on the outskirts of town. Kind of stupid, if you asked me, seeing as Dad was Lilyglade's sheriff at the time, and word always got back to him.

He'd retired two years ago to concentrate on the small farm we had. Maintaining it became a full-time job when he let go of the help he'd had while working.

I thought it would keep him busy enough that he wouldn't grow more cynical, but I should've known better.

"Everything okay?" Miles asked, walking into the kitchen with some empty plates.

"Fine," I said, taking them from him with a smile.

He leaned down to kiss my forehead, inhaling a deep breath and whispering on an exhale so low I almost didn't catch it, "Let it go, babe. He'll come around in his own time."

My dad watched Miles leave the kitchen with a twist to his lips. "Look, Jemmie." He took a large pull of his beer, then looked at me. "I'll wait for this shitshow to blow up, and I'll be here when it happens. But in the meantime, he's not getting any of my fucking beer."

He left the kitchen, muttering something that sounded like, "Bad enough he eats my god damned food."

CHAPTER
four

Three months ago

I INSPECTED THE PRICE TAG ON THE WOODEN CHOPPING board. "Holy fuck."

Miles chuckled. "Shhh." He glanced around, then took the board and set it down. "Not the best place for people with potty mouths."

I scowled at him, and he wrapped an arm around me and kept us moving. "You're way worse than I am."

"True, but I don't have a job where I need to tone it down. You should know better," he teased.

I inhaled the crisp, clean scent of his cologne, then pressed a kiss under his jaw as we stopped at a selection of dining tables. "Now I'm hungry."

His hands landed on my hips, squeezing. "Dirty girl, not here."

I stepped away, smacking him lightly in the chest. "For actual food, smartass."

An older woman a few feet away, wearing her hair in a tight chignon, frowned at me before scurrying off. I shrugged, plucking out a white dining chair and taking a seat.

The wood of the table matched the chairs, the surface smooth beneath my palms as I ran them over the paint. My ring stole my attention, something that had happened often in the weeks since Miles slipped it on my finger. I'd dreamed of happily ever afters since I was a little girl, using books as a crutch to liven my sad soul after Mom died.

It worked, so much so that the love and the way I depended on them never left.

Had I imagined a more elaborate proposal than what I got, I couldn't remember. It was finding love and being in love that held my complete and utter fascination when I thought of happy endings. Not the ostentatious gestures.

"I've gotta say, I love how much you stare at that."

My lips thinned as I tried to hold back a grin, then rose from the dining table. "It's too big."

"The ring?" he asked, his voice raised from shock.

I laughed. "No, that's perfect. I meant the table." A look at the price tag attached to it had me adding, "And too freaking expensive."

Miles took my hand after I'd tucked the chair beneath the table, steering me toward a smaller one that seated four but extended to seat six.

"We'll need it for visitors." My shoulders slumped a little. "Not that we have many."

Miles chucked me under the chin, then sighed as he slipped his hands into his jeans pockets and glanced around at the almost empty store. "We'll invite your dad and sister over."

He said it so casually as if he didn't care one bit that my dad hated him and my sister had yet to even meet him.

"When will I meet your parents?" I asked again. He rarely spoke of them unless prompted, and when he did, it was always the basic facts. They lived in a small town two hours north. His dad was a carpenter, and his mom ran the local library. For that fact, I really wanted to meet her, certain we'd have loads in common.

Miles's shoulders tensed, his eyes moving to the dark oak dining table. "Soon, I hope. I should call them." He nodded as if making a mental note to do that. "It's been a while."

Humming, I brushed a hand over the wood, imagining a cute lunch spread sitting atop, smiles and laughter from those helping themselves. "Does your mom like to cook?"

"Um, yeah. I guess." He shook his head, some of his hair falling to his forehead before he pushed it back. "She likes to read and listen to my dad in his workshop."

That made me smile. "I can't wait to meet her."

A tattooed arm slid around my shoulders, pulling me against his hard body. "She'll love you," he murmured to the top of my hair.

A saleswoman approached, asking if we needed any help. I was about to shake my head and say no thank you when Miles stopped me. "This one. We'll take it."

CHAPTER
five

Present day

"YOUR ASS IS MINE TONIGHT."

"Uh-huh. Hey, pass me my brush, would you?"

Miles huffed but did as I requested, watching as I dragged the brush through my dark brown hair. He was wearing his gym shorts and a white band T-shirt that wrapped snug around his huge chest.

I loved the way I felt tiny next to him, even if I wasn't tiny at all. Something about it made chills spark over my skin and caused my heart to swell with anticipation.

His wavy brown hair was damp, and I watched him rake a tattoo covered hand through it as I applied a nude gloss to my lips.

"Stop it," I said, tucking my gloss away and smacking my lips together while inspecting the rest of my face.

"Stop what?" His chest met my back, thick arms banding around my middle as I tried to leave the bathroom.

"I'm going to be late," I whined as he pushed my hair aside for his lips to glide over the sensitive skin below my earlobe.

"Live a little, babe."

I rolled my eyes. "I'm trying but living requires working in order to pay for living. Necessities and all."

He chuckled, tilting my chin up to stare into my eyes. "Fuck work. We could live off the grid, or hey, I have a chunk of savings left. Let's take a year off and travel. Live like nomads."

"Tempting."

"Yeah?" His voice lowered as his lips did, hovering over mine. "The only necessities we'd have to worry about would be the primal need to fuck." His lips pressed into mine. "All day." Another kiss. "Every." And one last lingering one. "Day."

Seconds later, he'd put a condom on, and I was against the wall. My dress was around my waist, one of my shoes kicked to the tiled floor as he pushed my panties aside and invaded. One glorious inch at a time.

"Oh god," I hissed through my teeth.

Miles's hands clenched around my thighs, fingertips bruising. "That's it, baby. Take my cock."

His breath fanned hot over my mouth as he slammed into me. Slow at first, then unrestrained when he heard those telltale cries whimper past my lips.

"I'm …"

"Fuck yes, you are."

I let go, my head rolling into the wall as his teeth dragged from my chin down my neck, stopping at my pulse. "I want another one before I explode."

"No," I croaked, unable to control my voice or my breathing as waves of bliss assaulted me. "No more." I'd be a gooey mess all day.

He grumbled what sounded like, "Fine," then sank deep, grinding as he worked himself in and out of me. "God damn, nothing has ever felt this good."

I smiled, stars blinking into my blurry vision. Mesmerized, I watched his Adam's apple bob as he grew closer. I still pinched myself at times, amazed by the fact this rugged, warm, giant man wanted me. That I could make him curse like a drunken sailor when he came, latching onto me for dear life.

His forehead fell against the wall next to my head, and I listened as his rough breathing started to slow.

"I love you, Jem." His head dropped to kiss the skin between my shoulder and neck. "So fucking much."

He lowered me to the ground, and I frowned as he stepped back while I put my shoe back on. "Then why are we still using condoms?" I fluffed my hair as he knotted the condom and tossed it into the small trash can beside the vanity. "You know I'm on the pill now."

He tensed, then lifted his hands to run them through his tousled hair before meeting my eyes with stormy ones. A smile was quick to make them gleam.

Annoyed at the ease he could rid my worries with just a fucking look, I righted my panties before inspecting my reflection in the mirror.

Without touching, he edged in behind me. I could feel him studying me and cursed my liquefied limbs for being too relaxed to walk away.

"I've never gone bareback before," he finally said.

"Never?" I asked, lifting my eyes to meet his in the mirror.

His hands settled on my hips, then righted my dress. "Never ever."

Knowing that pensive look, I dropped my eyes to the sink, giving him time to conjure his thoughts into words.

"In high school, there was this wild party in senior year." He laughed, shaking his head. "I was so drunk, and I banged this chick." Noticing my scowl, he squeezed my hips. "I didn't remember much of that night or any of the nights I spent drinking in my youth. But a couple of months later, said chick tells me she's pregnant and the baby's mine."

My mouth fell open, and I turned to stare up at him. The questions sailing through my mind evident in my eyes.

He brushed a finger over the bridge of my nose. "I wasn't her baby's daddy; some other prick was. But I believed it for a month and even went to a damn ultrasound with her. Until one of her friends eventually told me the truth."

"Shit, Miles."

He shrugged. "Guess the guy who knocked her up was more of a screw-up than I was."

"You're not a screw-up."

His lips twisted. "Jem, I mow lawns for a living."

I laughed with disbelief. "But it's your own business, and look around …" I swung an arm around the bathroom. "It's enabled you to buy your own beautiful house."

Nodding, he grabbed my hand, placing a kiss on it. "Our house. Anyway, when I confronted her about it, she said she was sorry, and that she remembered I'd worn a condom." He chuckled. "No matter how plastered I was, I always remembered the condom, which was why I was shocked as shit when I thought I'd knocked someone up."

"Condoms break."

"They do." He shrugged. "But I guess I'm a lucky bastard because that's never happened to me."

"I love you," I said after a long minute had passed. "But I really need to go."

After placing a kiss on my forehead, he released me, and I left the bathroom to grab my bag and keys.

I was almost out the front door when he called out, "Babe?"

I spun around, and he smiled as he leaned against the wall at the other end of the hallway. "I want that. With you. I just need time to … wrap my head around it for a bit."

I laughed, waving at him before shutting the door on his grinning face.

∾

Lilyglade Prep looked like an old museum.

Maybe it was. I hadn't ever bothered to research much of its history.

The long structure stood on almost two acres, ivy crawling over the discolored sandstone exterior and trailing beneath the arched windows. The lawns and rose gardens manicured to perfection, curtesy of Miles, who worked there two mornings a week.

I parked in the far end of the lot reserved for teachers and quickly flipped my visor down to check my appearance, hoping I didn't look nearly as disheveled as I felt.

After smoothing some hair back, I grabbed my bag and climbed out of my Corolla.

The teachers' lounge was empty, and I tucked my bag away, grabbing the planner I'd prepped for this week before hightailing it down the hall and up the first flight of marble stairs to the second floor.

I had fifteen minutes before class began and used it to sharpen pencils, make copies of today's spelling test, and straighten tables and chairs. We had cleaners that came in twice a week, but the parents still held us accountable for anything they could.

Not today, I thought as I returned to the teachers' lounge to make a cup of tea as the second bell rang, signaling the children to start making their way to their classrooms.

We managed to make it to lunch before any altercations happened, and Jerimiah, a boy with a smile that'd warm the coldest hearts, was the culprit once again.

"What happened?" I asked Lou Lou.

She sniffed, spine straight and shoulders back as she stared at Jerimiah with clear distaste. "He's a bully; that's what happened."

Lou Lou wasn't overly chatty and often only played with Rosie. But when she opened up, she just about blew me over with her vocabulary, and that trace of importance to her innocent eyes. I wasn't sure if she was just spoiled like many of the other kids at this school, or if she wasn't like them at all.

The latter tugged at me.

"She said my hair smells like wet dog," Jerimiah sputtered, pointing an accusing finger at Lou Lou.

I lowered to their eye level, my gaze drifting from the calm and collected six-year-old girl to the flushed faced, fidgeting, and close to tears boy. "Lou Lou, why would you say that?"

She looked taken aback for a second before saying, "Because it does."

I tried to contain my snort by pinching my lips together. If I had a dollar for all the times I'd wanted to laugh at the wrong moments since starting this job, I would've had enough money to buy myself a better ride.

"Okay." I stood when they just stared at me. "If there's nothing else to add, we'll have to leave a red circle on your behavior card for saying mean things, Lou Lou."

Her eyes bulged. "What?" She shook her head, her ringlets dancing. "But he's always saying stuff to me. Why can't I defend myself?"

Jerimiah frowned and got busy staring at the table next to his. "Jerimiah."

He looked back at me, shrugging. "I didn't do nothing, not this time."

"You didn't do anything," I corrected. With a sigh, I told

them to return to their seats to finish up their math worksheets.

When the dismissal bell rang, I did my best to stop them from stampeding out the door, but ended up jamming my back into the frame, making me wince.

"Are you okay, Miss Clayton?" Lou Lou had stopped outside the door, her rosy cheeks pinching as she studied me.

"Fine," I told her. "You should hurry along. You don't want to miss your bus."

"I don't catch the bus," she said. "My dad meets me out front, but I forgot my behavior card."

I winced again for different reasons. There was something to be said about being put in your place by a six-year-old. "Right, I'll grab it."

She took it from me a minute later and deposited it into her bag as I watched and pondered what to say. "Lou Lou, I'm sorry. You know we have zero tolerance—"

A gentle yet deep baritone interrupted. "Lou Lou."

In the time I'd been teaching at Lilyglade, I'd never once met her dad. As a few others had done, he'd turned down the opportunity for a parent-teacher conference before Christmas. I hadn't thought anything of it given how bright Lou Lou was.

Yet now, staring at the suited man who was slow to approach as he removed a feathered fedora from his head, I was glad for different reasons.

Talk about walking intimidation.

He towered over six feet. Lean, long limbs moved as though he had the grace of a leopard beneath the luxurious fabric that enveloped them. Hair so dark, it made you look directly to his cobalt eyes in hopes of a reprieve. A reprieve that stole the breath from your lungs and forced it back down your windpipe with savage intensity, for they were the coldest blue I'd ever encountered.

"Ready? You didn't come out with the rest of your class."

"I forgot something," Lou Lou mumbled, which made both her dad and me frown as she was not one to mumble.

Cold eyes shot to me. "I see."

My smile wobbled with nerves as I reached over and offered my hand. "You must be Lou Lou's dad. I'm Miss Clayton, her teacher."

"I know," he said, eyes steadfast on mine, unblinking, before he dropped them to my hand.

When it trembled, I cleared my throat and pulled my hand back. "Okay, well, have a nice afternoon."

Slightly shaken and slightly embarrassed, I didn't wait for them to walk away before I retreated into my classroom.

CHAPTER
Six

"**N**OW, REMEMBER, YOU DON'T CATCH FLIES WITH ..."

"Cookie jars!" the kids hollered, then filed out the door.

Laughing, I put the book we'd been dissecting that week back on the stand and watched them go, tucking in chairs and collecting sweaters once the door had shut.

I was bent over, picking up a rogue pencil, when a sharp knock had me straightening so fast, I felt something pop in my back. "God, I need to start working out."

Framed in the small oblong window of the door was a black covered shoulder and arm, and a tan profile. My heart rate stalled momentarily.

Lou Lou's dad walked in as soon as the door opened, and he instructed her to wait in the hall. I smiled at her, hoping it would ease the worry marring her tiny brows, then shut the door.

"Mr. Verrone, how can I—"

"It's Dr. Verrone. And there seems to be a problem with Lou's behavior card."

I blinked, then remembered yesterday. The incident with Jerimiah. I folded my hands together, straightened my shoulders, and calmly explained what'd happened.

"The child is a nuisance," he said.

For a moment, I thought he was referring to his daughter, then I realized that wasn't so. "Well …" I hemmed.

"No false pretenses. You know I'm right. I've watched him skip in and out of this school every morning and afternoon since Lou Lou told me about her first run-in with him. I can peg them when I see them."

A bit shocked, a small, incredulous laugh slipped free. "He's not so bad." He could be trouble, yes, but even then, he was a beautiful boy. "He's just in need of direction, not harsh discipline."

"I disagree."

My brows nearly met my hairline.

He waved a hand dismissively, then leaned against my desk with a sigh. "But I suppose that's too much to ask from schools nowadays."

"Nowadays?" I questioned before I could think better of it.

He nodded, and I realized then that I still didn't know his name. I was sure I'd seen it in records and could look it up, but I thought it'd be better to ask. "I'm sorry, I didn't catch your name."

"That's because I didn't give it to you." Blue eyes collided with mine, making something skitter down my spine before locking into place. Something was definitely wrong with my back. "It's Thomas."

Huh. "Well, I'll be sure to keep a close eye on things with Jerimiah, as always, Thomas."

He wasn't looking at me anymore, well, not exactly. His gaze had dropped to my cream-colored ballet flats that had tiny satin bows on the toes. "How old are you?"

I coughed. "I'm sorry, what?"

His lip quirked, those glowing eyes glinting as they traveled over my legs and stopped at my chest. "You heard me."

Those eyes lifted, crystal blue grabbing mine and refusing to let them look elsewhere. And I really needed to look elsewhere. He hummed. "You're just shocked, but that's okay. I'll wait."

A twitch pinched my stomach as he held my eyes prisoner. "Uh …" I laughed, my head shaking as I finally looked away and pretended to get lost in some pencils in a jar at the craft station. "I don't know if that's exactly, um, appropriate?"

A question? *Really?* I couldn't even muster the steel to end a sentence properly.

Dark and vibrating, the timbre of his voice reached my ears as his gaze singed my back. "Do I make you nervous?"

I scoffed, turning and crossing my arms over my chest. "This is kind of"—I threw my arms out, my finger gesturing between us—"weird. Yeah, let's start again. You're Thomas, Lou Lou's dad, and …"

"And you're Jemima, Little Dove, her first-grade teacher."

Blinking again, I asked, "How do you know that?"

A shoulder tilted, barely perceptible, but I saw it. "You must've mentioned it around Lou Lou."

"Right."

The clock behind his head ticked.

Once, twice, three, then four times.

"Are you going to tell me?"

I frowned. This had to be the most awkward encounter I'd ever experienced in my life. "My age?" I sucked my lip into my mouth, pondering the odd request. "Is it because of the shoes?"

I met his gaze as his lips twitched. "A little, yes. But I'm mostly just curious."

"Why?"

Another almost smirk. "Why indeed."

"Fine. I'm twenty-three."

"Twenty-three."

"Twenty-three," I repeated slowly and rocked back on my heels.

When I glanced over at the door, I saw Lou Lou had her head tilted up to the window, brown ringlets sprinkling over her shoulder. Painting on a smile, I held up a finger, indicating we'd only be a minute, then looked back at Thomas. "So am I not going to be treated to the same courtesy?"

His eyes widened, then he chuckled, a sound so rough and abrasive it was clear he didn't do it very often. His thumb glided over his bottom lip. "That wouldn't exactly be appropriate, now would it, Miss Clayton?" A heavy pause filled the room as he stood and then adjusted his jacket, eyes boring into mine. "Until next time, Little Dove."

Outside, he took Lou Lou's hand, and she shot me a small wave as they disappeared down the hall.

What in the name of strange?

Miles walked in the door just after seven.

I watched from my perch on the couch where I was painting my toenails a lime green as he scarfed down the steak and vegetables I'd prepared earlier.

"Not even going to sit down?"

"Can't talk," he mumbled around a mouthful. "Too hungry."

I snorted, my smile softening as I took in his chaotic appearance. His shirt was sweat stained and his hair damp with the day's work, and I had no doubt that dirt sat beneath his fingernails.

"So something weird happened today." I capped the polish and wiggled my toes.

"Yeah?" He lifted his plate, licking, actually licking, the

gravy from it.

I laughed, spinning the ring on my finger absentmindedly. "Could you quit and listen to me?"

"Listening," he said, moving to rinse the plate.

I waited until he'd tucked it into the dishwasher and grabbed a bottle of water from the fridge before saying, "I met this dad. One of my kids, Lou Lou ..."

Miles smirked and leaned against the doorway to the living room. "I love it when you call them your kids."

"They spend a lot of time with me, so they're not just any kids," I defended.

He waved a hand. "I know, and I love you." Dark eyes glued themselves to mine as he waited for those words to penetrate and hit their mark. They did, each and every time.

"Love you too." I sighed, straightening my legs, my toes scrunching in protest over the cold tiles. We'd yet to buy some rugs, as well as many other items, for the house. "Anyway, he came in to speak to me about Lou Lou's behavior card, which is understandable seeing as she's pretty much perfect."

"No one's perfect."

"Wait until you meet this girl," I said, unable to stop from smiling as I conjured Lou Lou's sweet face to the forefront of my mind. "I'm giving her work from the second grade most weeks."

Miles shifted, eyes shooting to the ground. "So her dad?"

"Right, yeah." I stood, stretching my arms above my head as I yawned. "Funny guy, in a way that's not really funny at all."

Miles's brows furrowed. "How so?"

"He's just ... hard to describe, but it was weird."

Miles waited, but I realized I didn't have much more to tell him, a way to relay all the details in their entirety, so I just shrugged. "Guess it was one of those times when you had to be there. I'll do him no justice trying to describe it."

"No justice?" Miles asked with clear humor as he followed me down the hall to our bedroom. "What, is he some kind of comedian?"

"Ha, no." I put my nail polish away in the en suite bathroom, walking right into Miles's chest on the way out. "Ugh, you'll break my nose one of these days. You need more cheeseburgers."

Arms captured me, hands smoothing up my back and trailing around to my chin to tilt it up. His eyes narrowed as he said, "I don't know if I like you talking about some kid's dad for longer than two minutes."

"Two minutes?" I asked, a little breathless as his thumbs moved to my mouth, teasing the skin under my bottom lip.

"Yeah. Way I see it, anything longer than two minutes, and you're curious."

I leaned into him, nipping at his thumb. "Jealous, are we?"

"Hell fucking yes, I am," he groaned out, dropping his lips to mine.

"You have nothing to worry about," I said between kisses. "He's not you, so he's not my type."

"Prove it."

I pushed him back, which only served in pushing me back. Whatever worked. "You stink. Come find me after you've showered."

I ran out of the bedroom before he could catch me, and the sound of the shower turning on a few beats later had me smiling as I opened the fridge.

I'd just taken a sip of bottled water when I heard Miles's phone ringing from the bedroom. I ignored it until I heard it start again, then I walked back to the bedroom to grab it in case it was a client. Winter had been slow to leave, so Miles said he was taking on any work he could get now that things had thawed and started growing again.

The ringing started again, but I couldn't see where he'd put his phone. I followed the sound to his nightstand and opened the drawer. There it was, with unknown caller flashing across the screen. I stared at it a second, then decided to answer it.

"Hello, Miles's phone?" Yeah, I couldn't think of anything better to say.

A loud silence infiltrated my ears and made my brows lower, then whoever it was on the other end hung up.

Still frowning at the screen, I tossed it back into the drawer right as a set of headlights flashed through the sheer curtains of our bedroom window, which faced the street.

I walked over, shifting them just in time to see a black car drive out of view.

It wasn't until Miles had thoroughly reminded me why he was the only type I had, then passed out beside me, that I realized the phone I'd answered earlier …

It had a different screen saver and case.

CHAPTER
Seven

"O NE SEC." My sister hissed something at one of her kids, then came back. "Hey, what's up?"

"Just wanted to check in." I stared through my windshield, the sun highlighting how overdue my car was for a wash.

Hope laughed. "Sure. Still not made any friends in that big city of yours?"

She knew the answer to that. It wasn't that I hadn't tried; it was that I was either working or with Miles. Come to think of it, Miles didn't hang out with the few friends he'd mentioned having either. And my colleagues, as nice as some of them were, were mostly over thirty. Our lives were at different stages, we had little in common, and I was still the new chick on the block.

"I wanted to ask you something."

"Okay," Hope said. "So ask."

"Has Jace ever lied to you?"

"Sure, I guess." Hope was quiet a minute, the sound of my nephews laughing over something in the background reaching my ear. "But I'm guessing this isn't a 'no, I didn't leave the toilet seat up or feed the dog your leftover cereal which in turn gave him diarrhea' kind of lie?"

My nose crinkled. "He gives Ziggy your cereal? Dogs can't have dairy."

"Right? That's what I said. Anyway, what happened?"

I watched as the last staff members drove away, leaving only the principal's and janitors' cars in the lot with mine, and a sleek black Bentley. My tongue trapped and glued to the back of my teeth, the words I needed to say to answer her question wouldn't budge.

Yes, I was pretty certain Miles had two phones, but no, I still hadn't broached that fact with him. Maybe it was for work, but I'd never seen it before.

And the car … it was probably just someone driving down the street. The timing of it is what shook me.

I knew I'd sound paranoid. The first thing Hope would say would be to speak to Miles. I needed to, but I couldn't find the words or the right timing. He'd been so busy with work that when he'd get home, he'd eat, shower, fuck me senseless, and then pass out only to repeat it all over again the next day.

Letting out a shaky exhale, I said, "Don't worry, I think I'm due for my period maybe."

Hope asked, "You sure? You can talk to me, you know. God knows how many secrets you kept for me growing up."

"I know." I smiled, saying the words. "It's fine, though, really."

Hope sighed. "Okay, but if you feel like this again anytime soon, call me. I mean it."

"Will do. Tell the boys I said hello."

"Come visit and tell them yourself."

I laughed, feeling nostalgic for just that, then hung up and slumped back in my seat, closing my eyes.

I startled at the sound of light tapping next to my head and straightened up, taking in my surroundings. Lou Lou's dad was standing stock-still outside my car, and I quickly glanced at my dash, noting it was almost five. I must've dozed a few minutes.

Thomas stepped back when I opened the door. "Do you

often fall asleep behind the wheel?"

"I wasn't driving," I volleyed, closing the door and folding my arms over my chest. I looked around, finding no sign of Lou Lou. "Where's Lou Lou?"

"At home. I had a meeting with Mrs. Crawley."

Trying not to let that rattle me, I nodded. "Everything okay?"

He picked a non-existent piece of lint from his black suit sleeve. "She'll be moving Jerimiah to a different class if he keeps bothering Lou."

A part of me was relieved he didn't rat me out in any way, yet I was still kind of pissed on Jerimiah's behalf. "That's not exactly fair. He really is a good kid."

"A good kid with terrible outbursts, I'm sure." He retrieved a set of keys from his trouser pocket. "Are you going to answer my question?"

Still reeling from his last statement about Jerimiah, it took me a beat to catch up. "Huh?"

His face crumpled with clear distaste. "I think you meant to say excuse me."

I couldn't help it, and a laugh escaped.

His lips twitched, but otherwise, he waited for me to gather some self-control. "Uh, well, I don't believe you asked a question I haven't answered, Dr. Verrone."

"Thomas." He tilted his head, eyeing my well-loved Corolla before pinning those freezing blues on my face. "And I believe I was enquiring about why you were sleeping in your car two hours after the children have left." He paused. "You have a home, do you not?"

Who was this guy?

And more importantly, why was I still entertaining him by standing there?

I was too frazzled to answer that, but I did know that, weird guy or not, I wasn't rude. And the parents here paid a lot of money for their children to attend. I'd have my ass kicked back home if I didn't watch my attitude and play nice.

"I was on the phone," I finally relented. "Then I guess I lost track of time."

Thomas stared, his eyes piercing my browns as though he was trying to look inside my thoughts to find the truth. "You don't talk on the phone when driving." He shifted, and I glanced down at his expensive looking shoes. "Good."

Smiling a little, I looked at him once more, taking in the clean-shaven lines of his strong jaw, the lightly tanned skin molded over stark cheekbones, and the thick dark brows that matched his perfectly combed over hair. Pulling a pocket watch out of his jacket, he inspected it, and it was then I noticed he was without his hat.

"Where's the fedora today?"

He tucked the watch away. "It's Thursday. Too many things to do on a Thursday."

"I see, and it'd probably wreck what you have going on"—I gestured with a wave to his perfect hair—"up there."

A wrinkle of confusion appeared between his thick brows, and he puckered his full lips as he stared at me. "Going on?"

"Your hair," I said, feeling my cheeks heat. "It's, um, nice is what I meant to say."

"You went to college?"

His hard words had me stepping back into my car. "I did, yes."

"Yet you like to abuse the English language."

I forced a mock gasp, and he tilted his head again, eyes inquisitive.

"I'm kind of offended. Words are my drug of choice."

"Drug of choice," he murmured as if tasting the words to see if he liked them.

"Are you foreign?" I asked. He didn't have an accent, but curiosity over his distaste for common slang got the better of me.

"Absolutely not," he said so quickly I almost laughed.

Lifting my hands, I relented. "Yeesh, just asking."

"You're a peculiar woman, Little Dove."

The threat of nightfall had painted the sky orange, pink, and blue. The combination was so striking behind the enigmatic man that I wished I had a camera handy to capture what I saw in front of me.

"As are you." I quickly amended, "Though not a woman, clearly."

He smiled. He actually smiled, and the sight was enough to have my bottom lip disconnecting from the top, my mouth agape and heartbeat skipping.

His teeth were perfect, every single one of them, and a glowing white. But it was how his eyes changed from ice to lukewarm pools of water that seized me, imprinting on my retinas.

"You look like you've been kicked in the stomach," he commented, his smile slipping away as fast as it'd appeared.

I shook my head, unable to muster conversation with this fascinating stranger anymore. It was bound to get awkward again, so I chose to bail on a good note.

"I like your pocket watch," I told him, then climbed back inside my car. "My grandpa had one just like it." I winked as I closed the door and started the engine. Once I'd backed out, I told myself not to look in the rearview.

Naturally, I did.

He was still standing there, statue still, his blue eyes watching as I sped out of the lot.

CHAPTER
Eight

THE SUN HID BEHIND FEATHERED TREETOPS, AND I swore my lungs were about to collapse.

Miles pressed on ahead, carrying a large stick in his hand that he used to whack at the brush and thicket. He looked as though he'd only been walking two minutes instead of almost thirty.

"Seriously, why are we doing this again?" I wheezed as we neared the top of a small crest where rocks sat in a small cluster off to the side.

Slumping down onto them, I scrambled for my water bottle. Miles had woken me at dawn, saying we were going on one of his beloved hikes. He'd made me tag along once before, but hiking wasn't for me. I'd only said yes to this particular excursion because it meant we'd have breakfast with my dad. But after he'd eyed Miles with so much scorn and distrust as he scarfed down runny eggs and soggy toast, I was kind of relieved to leave and hit the woods.

Was.

Miles, not realizing I'd stopped, kept walking, then backtracked. He grinned, tugging at a piece of hair that'd curled around my hairline, no doubt from the exertion I could feel heating every inch of my out-of-shape body. "You said you did this all the time as a kid."

I swallowed and capped my water bottle, shoving it away even as my tongue and throat ached for more. I'd need to save it, considering we definitely weren't done yet. "Correction," I said as I raised a finger, my heart rate finally resuming a normal rhythm. "I wasn't allowed in this far. I'd get in trouble every time I dared."

He motioned for us to keep moving, and at the roll of my eyes, he laughed and grabbed my hand in his, heaving me up from the rock. I gave it a longing look as Miles hauled me down the hill and deeper into the forest that bordered my dad's property.

"You know, couples can have healthy relationships without making one another indulge in each other's hobbies."

"We haven't been hiking together in months," he said, then stopped, looking east before continuing north again. "I thought you'd like it after hearing you mention playing here as a kid."

I removed my hand from his, not wanting him to feel the moisture that would no doubt reappear soon. "My lungs and legs didn't hate me as much as a kid."

Miles huffed, holding a branch out so it didn't smack me in the face, and I had to say, if nothing else, it was kind of nice to see those calves of his working. He was like a lion, every movement fluid and powerful, and I was but a meager bird in comparison.

Sighing, I redid my ponytail as we approached a familiar clearing. My feet halted, my heart dunking into my stomach as memories resurfaced.

"You okay?" Miles asked, stopping farther up ahead to stare at the faint cream outline of the castle through the trees. "You look like you've seen a ghost."

"I'm fine, but we should head back. This is private property."

His eyes narrowed, then dropped to the ground where we were standing as he walked over to me. "We're already trespassing; let's just take a little peek."

"Peeking leads to trouble," I said, then groaned. "Ugh, I sound just like my freaking dad."

Miles gently gripped my chin, searching my face. "You've been through there, haven't you?" He smiled as if I was some deviant, and it thrilled him.

I stepped back, causing his hand to fall to his side. "Once or twice."

He hummed thoughtfully, and my dry throat had me reaching for my water again.

Screw it. If I ran out, I'd drink Miles's for making me exercise on a Sunday when I could've been watching *Keeping Up with the Kardashians* or, even better, reading.

"Story time," he said, rubbing his hands together. "And what better time than now."

Taking a long gulp of water, I slumped to the dirt. "Not much of a story, really."

Miles joined me, wrapping his arms around his bent knees as he stared through the trees, the May sun unbearably hot on our heads as it blazed through the clearing.

"Tell me anyway."

Birds called from high above, and I inhaled the scent of damp earth from this morning's rain. Closing my eyes, I let my mind free fall back, then reopened them and followed his gaze to the castle.

The castle appeared through a gap in the trees up ahead. A soft cream with one milky turret, just like the one in my book.

I snapped the book shut and put it away, excitement carrying my feet faster over the fallen logs. I leaped over holes, ditches, and slinked by thorny trees that snagged my dress.

This was the farthest I'd ever been into the woods that ran alongside our small farm. Daddy always said I couldn't go in and to only play on the outskirts because there could be snakes and other horrid things inside. Not to mention, I could get lost.

But Daddy was working a double at the station, and Hope had friends over, so she was distracted. No one would even know. Besides, I wouldn't get lost. I could see the tip of the castle from my bedroom window each night when I counted the stars to help me fall asleep.

I knew the way.

My mom had taught me that. Counting stars. Not that it was hard or anything, but it helped my imagination quiet down, enabling me to fall asleep easier.

She died a year ago, not long after my seventh birthday. I'd cried. A lot. But I had to stop crying after a while because Daddy didn't like it. Hope said it was because he couldn't cry. He couldn't get sad like us, so we had to be tough and help him by keeping our tears quiet or by turning them off.

I learned to turn them off, but it took a while.

And my mommy … Before someone crashed into her car, she would always tell me made-up stories about the castle next door. About a prince who lived there with his parents, a gentle king and a wicked queen.

And finally, finally, I got to see it for myself.

Stopping in a small clearing, I wiped drops of sweat from my forehead with the sleeve of my sweatshirt and got my bottle out of my backpack. I took a huge gulp and almost choked when I saw a boy appear from behind a giant, moss-covered rock.

"Go back, little girl."

"Who you calling a little girl?" I eyed the boy, who couldn't have been more than thirteen or fourteen years old. Though he was really tall and thin. So maybe to him, I was little.

One side of his mouth lifted as I put my drink bottle away. "You're the only other human here. Well, of the female variety."

His voice was croaky, but it wasn't deep. Hope said a boy became a man when his voice got deep. That made him just as much of a kid as I was. Yet his words sent a bite of fear zooming through my chest. My heart pounded as my throat dried.

His eyes were so bright, and he stood so still, even his hair, as though the breeze floated around him.

"Who are you?"

His head tilted just a fraction. Then he blinked. "It matters not who I am, what matters is that you're trespassing."

My hands landed on my hips, one cocking to the side as annoyance melted any fear I had. He was just a boy. A weird, statue-looking, bossy boy. "This is my daddy's land too."

He made a tutting sound, which brought back long-lost memories of my mother. She'd make the same noise whenever I was doing something she didn't approve of or was about to. Like walking inside with muddy boots.

"Your daddy's land ended a mile back. You've come too far, turn around."

No. No way. My eyes stung, and my feet hurt. I'd walked for what seemed like two hours to see the castle.

I turned the tears off.

"I just want to see the castle, and then I'll go." I tried to compromise. Who was he anyway? I asked him as much.

"Castle?" Another tilt to his lips, and then he folded his arms across his chest, which was covered in a black polo shirt. "I'm the owner of said castle."

My eyes bugged out as I dropped my backpack and dug out my book. Without thought, I marched over to him, opening the book-marked page as I did, and stabbed my finger at the illustration. "Is *it just like this? I've always wondered."*

He took a step back, his nose scrunching as if he'd sniffed something foul. I lifted my arm to check my armpit, wondering if it was me.

Not yet, *I thought. My sister's floral spray kept the smellies at bay. Hope said the smellies arrived in the summertime first, but they'd stick around once you reached a certain age.*

I wasn't a certain age yet, but still, I didn't want to stink, and I liked the floral smell.

"It's nothing like that."

My heart sank to the soles of my worn sneakers. "Oh." I stuffed my book away, then shouldered my backpack again.

The boy sighed. "But I guess, seeing as you walked all this way, you can see that for yourself."

My smile stretched so wide, my cheeks hurt. "You mean that?"

His brows crinkled. "I don't say things I don't mean."

Such serious words for a young boy.

I ignored them and moved past him through the clearing, wading through undergrowth and clumps of leaves until I reached the tree line.

A gasp emptied my lungs and filled the air. The boy laughed, an oddly musical sound, as I took in the beauty before me.

It was gigantic.

A perfect monstrosity.

The cream exterior shone beneath the sun's rays, covered in ivy and other serpent-like vines with tiny flowers on them. The windows were oblongs that curved at the tops, and the doors were huge and wooden, polished and gleaming and surrounded by large potted plants.

Water gurgled from a fountain in the courtyard, and as I dared to step closer, I saw orange and red inside the water. Fish. Carp, maybe.

"It's magical," I breathed. "The only thing that's missing is a moat. But still ... magical. You live here? You really live here?"

The boy kicked at some rocks where we stood on the pebbled path by one of the rose gardens. "I don't say things—"

"You don't mean," I finished for him, then smiled to show I was just messing with him.

He didn't return it, and instead, a look of panic washed over his face when he heard an older man's voice.

My daddy's voice.

"Crapper jack." I spun back to the woods. "I gotta go."

I didn't wait to see if the boy waved as I ran into the woods, following the sound of my dad's voice until I met up with him in the middle of the tree-shrouded landscape.

He was dressed in his work uniform, and his face was a mottled red, lines of concern creasing his forehead. "Fucking hell, Jemima. What on God's green earth do you think you're doing out here?"

Out of breath from running, it took me a moment to answer. "I was just exploring. I didn't mean to go so far."

He looked behind me into the trees, a frown wrinkling his ageing face further. "You know you're not allowed. Your sister called the station in tears saying you were missing, and I almost crashed the truck speeding home."

"I'm sorry." I swallowed, my shoulders slumping. "I got bored and only wanted to look."

"Looking leads to trouble, Jemmie."

"It's okay. I was fine. And I met a boy in the woods."

Daddy was quiet a minute, then said, "They're a bunch of rich, entitled snobs, that family. They wouldn't want you trespassing on their turf, got me? If I say don't do it, I say it for a god damned reason."

"Okay, Daddy."

"No TV for a week, and you're making dinner tonight."

I sighed with relief that my punishment wasn't worse. He could've taken away my books.

That night, I sat on the window seat in my room, scrubbing my hands on my nightgown to rid the smell of raw potatoes and onions from them. But the moon was too weak, and I couldn't see the castle through the trees. And even when I broke my promise to Dad, venturing back to the castle over the following summer, I never did see the boy again.

A few years later, after one last daring venture, I discovered the family must have moved.

Nothing remained.

Only empty beauty.

"It looks even worse now," Miles said as he crept closer, using the pair of binoculars he'd brought with him. The ones meant for bird watching, of which we'd done none of.

"It's been abandoned for years." Chills shot down my arms, my exerted body shivering. "Let's head back."

He stared a full minute longer, his shoulders loosening with a long sigh. Then he turned and took my hand in his, allowing me to walk a much slower pace than the one he'd set out for us to get there.

Except I didn't want to walk slow, so I picked up my feet.

Thirst and exhaustion forgotten, I tried not to run and power walked until the feeling of something crawling over my skin melted away into the shaded gloom behind us.

CHAPTER
Nine

MILES REJECTED THE INCOMING CALL BEFORE IT could even connect to the Bluetooth, then shut his phone off.

"Who was it?" Normally, I wouldn't ask, but something about the unknown caller from last week was still niggling at me.

Miles grabbed my hand, turning onto the off-ramp to join the line of traffic exiting the highway. "Probably just my mom or something," he mumbled, then kissed my hand. "How long do we need to stay at this thing again?"

After months of being engaged and living together, I still hadn't met Miles's parents.

And some quiet part of me, the one that had started making more of an appearance lately, wondered if they even knew about me or that we were engaged.

Wouldn't they want to meet their son's future wife? Congratulate us? Hell, maybe his mom would even want to plan an engagement party with me.

Pondering the night ahead, I rubbed my bare arms as the A/C blew ice over my skin. "Two hours should do it."

Miles heaved out a breath and remained quiet until we'd parked among the half-filled lot of various luxury cars.

The pungent scent of money and misery saturated the city's

concert hall where parents, teachers, and waitstaff intermingled. The dress code was above my pay grade, but I hoped I'd hidden that well with a secondhand black Versace gown. A hundred dollars had bought me a dress that clung to every curve and dip of my body, the bodice bunching and pushing up my breasts. Paired with strappy silver stilettos from my high school prom and my straight hair falling over my shoulder blades, I felt good enough to fit in.

Even if it was only on the outside.

Miles had been tugging at his suit since he'd thrown it on as though it were a winter coat and not fine clothing, complaining of it itching.

Despite his clear discomfort, noticing the way the material threatened to burst over his bulky arms had my legs shifting, my thighs tempted to rub.

He returned from the bar with a glass of champagne for me and a beer for himself. Smacking his lips together after he took a sip, he grimaced.

I laughed, grabbing the lapels of his jacket to hoist my mouth up to his. "You're cute when you're uncomfortable."

"Yeah?" he whispered back, an arm looping around my waist and climbing my back. "You're cute all the fucking time." After placing a kiss on my lips, then the tip of my nose, he straightened his back and shot his eyes around the room.

I decided it was time to make the rounds and introduced him to some of my colleagues, waving and smiling at any parents I recognized as we passed. Their eyes seemed to swell, lips popping, as they took in the man beside me who had his hand glued firmly to my hip, my side melded to his, no matter where we ventured.

"So fucking stuffy," Miles grumbled after an hour of making small talk and sipping on expensive drinks. "Thank fuck the food looks good."

He nabbed any finger food that flew by us on shining silver trays, inhaling them and making me laugh as a few onlookers gawked at him licking his fingers. Tracey, our school's principal, came over to gush over his fabulous work on the school's landscaping.

I looked around as she blushed under his gaze, and when my eyes landed on the far corner of the room, my quiet laughter vanished, my smile sinking.

Thomas Verrone stood by another man, talking with empty hands and his eyes firmly fixed on me.

Quickly, I maneuvered the smile back into place, lifted my hand in a small wave, and ignored the way his eyes traversed the length of my body.

"Who's that?" Miles broke me from my shiver-inducing spell when Tracey walked away to mingle.

"Hmm?" I took a sip of my drink; the same one I'd been nursing since we arrived.

"The guy in the corner who's looking at you."

Dammit. "That's Thomas Verrone, Lou Lou's dad."

Recognition lit his eyes, and he glanced over at Thomas, who had now turned his back to us as he talked with his companion.

Miles looked back at me. "The strange one you were telling me about?"

I hushed him, thwacking his arm lightly. "Quiet. Jesus."

Miles chuckled, taking my chin and tilting it to meet his gaze. Swirling questions stared me down. "You never said he was good looking."

My eyes widened. "What?"

He tipped his shoulders, the seams of his jacket protesting the movement. "Just because I'm straight doesn't mean I don't notice the obvious."

Shaking my head out of his hold, I stepped back, nerves pulling a laugh from me. "No, no." I smoothed a hand over my already smooth hair. "It's not that; you just caught me off guard."

Miles grabbed my hand, and I stepped into him as he grinned down at me. "Admit it then."

"That Thomas is good looking?" I glanced back over at where he'd been standing, but only empty space remained. Remembering his cheekbones, the dark hair, ice blue eyes, and that jaw, I acquiesced, "He is, I guess."

Miles laughed, drawing countless eyes with his usual loud and abrasive tone.

I didn't care. I reveled in the way my stiff shoulders loosened at the sound, and then I wrapped my arm around his back to rest my head on his chest. "Are you done with the inquisition? Because I now fear everyone knows how good looking *you* are."

He squeezed me to him, inhaling deeply before pressing a kiss to my head. "Fuck, I love you."

I smiled up at him, and the humor left his face, leaving only a seriousness that rendered my limbs useless and made my heart thump.

The musicians took the stage, and the slow strum of an acoustic guitar entered my ears.

Miles tucked a piece of hair behind my ear. "Let's watch this shit, then go home and get naked."

"I like that plan." I pressed my empty glass into his chest. "But first, I need to pee."

After doing my business, I dried my hands and checked my reflection, eyeing a woman with glowing red hair and a shimmering golden dress who stepped out of a stall behind me.

She froze, then smiled and continued forward to the sink, quickly washing her hands and leaving me in a cloud of Coco Chanel.

I hissed with annoyance when I realized I'd forgotten, yet again, to use one of the many perfumes I'd collected over the years. Blowing out a breath, I eyed myself in the mirror, failing to see the grown-up woman with angular cheekbones, a some-what passable hairdo, and designer gown. Outside packaging couldn't hide the inadequacy I still felt as I floundered in this city. Most days, I felt fine, secure in my relationship and my job, but during times like this, surrounded by people who were the very opposite of what simmered in my soul, I longed to run back home.

Not to hide from responsibility, but to feel the fresh air on my skin as it carried familiar, comforting scents on the breeze. Apple blossoms, hay, and pasture ... *home.*

Shaking off the melancholy, I resolved to put a smile on as I left the bathroom. We'd go home soon, and I'd be able to believe I was adjusting just fine, thanks to the love of a good man, a job I enjoyed despite feeling as if I didn't belong, and the escape of good books.

"Little Dove." Thomas stepped out of the half-shadowed corner beneath the emergency exit light.

I jumped. "Shit." My heart screeched in my ears, my hand flying to my chest. "Warn a girl before you go all vampire hiding in the shadows."

To my amazement, he chuckled. A rough and rusty sound that was quick to fade.

Adjusting his cufflinks, he stepped closer, and I sucked in a razor-sharp breath as his teeth slid over his plump bottom lip. He watched me, studied me, waiting ... but for what?

"Erm, are you having fun?" I inwardly rolled my eyes at my awkward question.

"Hardly," he said, sounding as though he wanted to follow it with a scoff. With his eyes pinned on my mouth, he murmured,

"You have something on your chin." I slunk back against the wall as he reached a hand toward my mouth. His thumb was smooth, and his touch was ghost-like in its gentleness.

I struggled to breathe as the scent of mint and cinnamon filled my nose and caused something to stick in my throat.

I was too transfixed by the blue of his eyes to move. Too distracted by his next words.

"You didn't tell me you were engaged."

Not a question, but a statement. His voice was clinical and curious at the same time.

He took a step back, but not far enough. As my gaze dropped to his lips, I realized if someone walked down this hallway, we'd appear to be in a rather compromising situation.

My stomach turned. I didn't know him, and what I did know of him set my teeth on edge and had my heartbeat dancing wildly with apprehension.

"I don't recall you ever asking if I was." Nerves sent a soft laugh rattling out of me. "It's not the kind of thing I just announce to strangers."

"Strangers?" His dark brows gathered. "I thought we were past the point of being called strangers."

"What …" I licked my lips, ignoring the way he watched, and directed my gaze to the column of his long throat. "What would you call people who'd only met a handful of times then?"

His hand lifted to touch a strand of my hair, his brows furrowing further as he rubbed it between his fingers. His Adam's apple shifted as he said, "Acquaintances."

It was the smack in the face I needed to step aside and move away from him.

"What's wrong?" He turned. "You don't agree?"

"It's not that." I pretended to fuss with my dress to keep my eyes averted.

"Then what is it?"

He sounded impatient, which made honesty coat my tongue and drift past my lips. "I'm engaged, and you were …" I cleared my throat. "Well, invading my space."

A noise resembling a humorous huff left him, and I kept my eyes trained on the exit. "Interesting choice of words."

I didn't know what he meant by that, and I didn't care. He unnerved me in a way that shocked me into freezing in place, further allowing him to do so. It alarmed me to think I was naïve enough to let that happen.

"I need to go. Have a good night, Thomas." Without looking at him, I traipsed down the cool hall, the music growing louder the closer I got to the room full of people. To warmth.

"Until next time, Little Dove."

I swallowed, tripping over my next breath as I tried not to stumble, and frantically searched the crowd for Miles.

I couldn't find him inside, and after getting stuck in a conversation about vegan lunch menus with Principal Crawley and Monica, our librarian, I resumed my search.

The sun had descended past the horizon an hour ago. Stars painted the sky, glittering next to a full moon behind tall buildings in the distance. After pressing by a few chattering groups, I finally found him over by the back railing of the deck, talking to some woman in a hushed voice. Not just any woman, though; she was the same woman I saw in the bathroom.

She saw me first, staring a long moment before a smile lifted her red lips.

"Hey," I said, touching Miles's arm as I walked up behind him.

He flinched, cursing softly as he turned around with a drawled, "Hey, babe." He wrapped an arm around me, then introduced me to the redhead, whose eyes kept bouncing back and forth between us. "This is Amelia; we went to college together." He chuckled after a quick pause. "Haven't seen her in years."

"It feels like it," the woman said, then held out her manicured hand to me. I shook it as she said, "We used to date. You must be the fiancé he's just told me about." She grinned when I took my hand back, then sniffed and looked away.

I frowned. "Yeah, nice to meet you." My phone chirped, and when I realized Miles clearly wasn't done talking to her, I decided to step away to check it.

Unknown number: Little Dove, you smell good enough to eat.

With my next heartbeat screeching in my ears, I spun around, expecting to find Thomas. All I found was a black Bentley exiting the lot.

In a trance, I watched it drive away and disappear.

Against my better judgment, I gave into the burning need to know and texted back.

Me: Thomas? How did you get my number?

Somehow knowing I wouldn't get a response right away, I tucked my phone into my purse and walked back over to Miles, who was staring into the distance as if he'd watched Thomas leave too.

The woman was gone.

"I don't know about you," I said as I grabbed his hand, willing it to stop the tremors in mine, "but I'm ready to go home."

"I agree. More than ready."

The drive home was quiet. And I would've been more

worried about Miles if it weren't for my own desperate need for silence. Thomas had rattled me, sure, but it was the red-haired vixen who'd pushed me into a tailspin. Something about her nagged at my subconscious, but nothing came forward to answer that nagging.

The house was dark, and I hurriedly switched on the hallway light before blitzing down the hall and kicking off my heels in the bedroom. I scrubbed the makeup off my face and brushed my teeth as Miles locked up and went straight to the shower. In the bedroom, I undressed and slipped on a long T-shirt, then waited for him to come to bed.

I was nearly asleep when the sheets whispered over my bare thighs and the bed dipped with Miles's weight. His hand came to rest on my hip, his lips brushing over the back of my hair for a quick kiss. "Good night, babe."

There'd be no sex tonight, which I was okay with. Miles had a big appetite, so I didn't complain when he decided he wasn't in the mood. Though it was rare, and it only took a few heated touches to pique my libido, sometimes it was nice to just be.

Gazing out the window, I realized I'd forgotten to shut the curtains and stared unseeing at the street beyond. "Good night."

Exhaustion smothered me, but the night wouldn't remove its teeth from my psyche, and even when it did, it stalked my dreams.

And my phone.

Unknown number: I'll never tell.

CHAPTER Ten

"Tracey," I called as I saw her about to slip inside her office at the start of recess.

I wasn't on duty, so I'd tried to prepare for our papier-mâché-filled afternoon but kept getting sidetracked.

I needed to know.

She raised her brows, coming to a stop outside her open door. "Jemima, how are you?"

"Good, thanks." I motioned to the door. "Do you have two minutes I can steal?"

"Of course. I'll even give you five," she said, waving me inside and taking a seat behind her large steel and glass desk.

Traipsing over the plush rug, I tried not to collapse into one of the two comfortable red leather armchairs and gingerly adjusted my plaid skirt over my knees as I crossed my legs.

"What's up?" Tracey asked, switching on her monitor. She plucked her glasses from her blouse and slid them on. Her hands moved deftly over the keyboard as she logged into the school's server.

With the woman's name sitting on the tip of my tongue, I thought to hell with it and asked the question as though I had every right to. "There was this woman who attended last night. Do you know her? Long red hair? She goes by the name of Amelia."

When Tracey continued to look puzzled, I did my best to describe her dress, hairstyle, and asked if she was a parent perhaps.

She studied me over the rim of her glasses, hands poised above the keyboard, then slumped back into her seat and removed them. "I remember the woman you're talking about." She looked behind me to the closed door, then leaned forward, her voice quieting. "But between you and me, I had no earthly idea who she was." Wrinkles bunched as she sniffed haughtily. "So I chalked it up to her being one of the fathers' new girlfriends. There are a few single dads with kids here, after all."

Not a parent then.

"Thank you," I said, not sure what to say now that I'd gotten some confirmation. For what, I didn't know. Something about the woman made me want to dig a little deeper.

Rising from my chair, I paused as Tracey asked, "Everything okay? Did you know her?"

Lie. I needed to lie, and so I did my best to sound like I was merely curious. "I could've sworn I'd met her before. Years ago. It was bugging me."

Principle Crawley stared a full six seconds before nodding with a slight smile, her glasses returning to their perch on her nose. "Very well. I hate it when that happens."

"It's rather annoying," I agreed, vacating her office with more questions than answers.

The darkening sky chased me on my drive home.

Thoughts of a shower, dinner, and bed with a book sounded all too appealing after the day I'd had. Something about impending rain seemed to make some kids hyperactive.

I parked in front of the garage, noticing Miles's blue truck in the drive, then grabbed my bag and hopped out. In the doorway, I kicked off my glue-covered shoes, lamenting the fact I'd probably need to throw them out rather than try to save them. Craft glue was a bitch to peel off.

That'd teach me to spend more than thirty dollars on a pair of work shoes.

Tossing my keys on the entry table, I fished my phone from my bag and took it to the kitchen, plugging it in to charge just as Miles appeared, freshly showered and with a stony look in his caramel eyes.

"Well, hello." I waggled my brows at his shirtless chest. "As much as it kills me to say it, I wouldn't come near me. I'm covered in a layer of glue."

He said nothing. Just stood there with his arms crossed over his chest and his feet planted apart as if he was bracing for a standoff.

We'd had plenty of fights over the course of our relationship, but I wouldn't exactly call them fights. More like skirmishes or bickering and mainly over stupid things that annoyed me. The milk carton being used as a drink bottle. The mail being dumped on the counter everyday instead of opened. Dirty clothes sitting around the hamper rather than inside it. You know, the usual.

But now, well, he looked pissed. And not the *quit be annoying* kind of pissed. But *pissed*.

"What's wrong." I didn't say it as a question even though it clearly was because it was evident I'd done something.

My mind skipped backward, then forward, rolling inside out in the span of one minute, trying to find what it was he could possibly look that angry—oh.

"Why did you keep your apartment?" His voice was deceptively calm but layered with the type of warning that meant he could possibly lose his shit, depending on my answer.

But no explanation was good enough, and I didn't want to lie. So I settled on the truth. "Because the lease wasn't up. I'd lose money, and I ..." He waited, bare feet shifting slightly on the tiles as I blew out a breath and admitted, "I guess I like knowing it's there."

He stormed down the hall, headed for the front door.

Shit.

"Miles, it's not a big"—the front door slammed shut—"deal." I sighed.

I didn't know how long I stood in the kitchen after the rumble of his truck faded away. It could've been two minutes, or it could've been thirty. The talk I'd had with Tracey and the questions that arose from it vanished. Nothing seemed more important than this hollowing feeling in my stomach.

Eventually, I forced my bottom lip and hands to quit trembling and went to shower.

By the time I'd gotten out, dried my hair, and dressed, he'd returned. The sound of his truck had never sounded so good, and I bounded down the hall, entering the kitchen just as he did with two pizza boxes in hand.

"Now," he said, placing them on the counter, then grabbing two water bottles from the fridge. "Don't mistake the food for forgiveness. I'm fucking pissed, Jemima."

The use of my full name had me nodding slowly, my heart pattering harder as I watched him grab some paper towels, then take a seat beside me at the counter.

"I'm sorry." It was all I could say. I wouldn't get rid of the apartment. The lease wasn't up for another few months, and what I'd said was true. We'd gotten together so quickly that it seemed like a stupid idea not to have a safety net of some sort, and I couldn't always rely on my dad for that.

A tiny part of me bloomed with pride even as a bigger part shriveled with guilt. It was what it was.

"Will you terminate the lease if I ask you to?"

I opened my box of pizza, forcing a smile as I picked up a slice of pepperoni with extra cheese, my favorite. "It's up in a few months."

Miles exhaled, running a hand through his still damp hair, then tore off a huge chunk of his Hawaiian pizza, chewing hard as if he wanted the pizza to suffer.

Tension rolled off him in hot waves, and it was all I could do to keep eating as I tried not to cower beneath it.

"Why?" he finally asked, then cursed. "I mean, I know *why*. But what can I do to make you feel more secure?"

I stared at the ring on my finger. "It's not so much about you as it's about me. But maybe …" I licked sauce from my lip, trying to ignore the way the heat in his gaze changed from anger to hunger. "We could set a date for the wedding." We hadn't really discussed it beyond the point of agreeing we wanted time together to enjoy one another before settling down even more.

His hand froze. The heat in his eyes dissipating.

He pushed his stool back and marched to the sink, his back hunching as he shook his head. "You want to set a date, but you don't trust me? I don't get it."

I got up then, my patience starting to fray. Couldn't a girl try to protect herself without getting ridiculed for it? I wouldn't budge. I was keeping the damn apartment until I was ready to let it go.

I stopped beside him, carefully reaching out to brush the inked roses and thorns on his arm with my fingertips. They reached the leaves that scattered into twisting flames around his elbow when he recoiled a little.

He wouldn't even look at me.

"Miles, I do trust you. It's …" I couldn't figure out how to say it without sounding like a scared little girl, but I decided to do my best. "It's life I don't trust. We moved fast. I'm not saying I wasn't okay with that. I'm just saying I was okay with it because I still had my own place." Quiet stained the air between us. "Even though I prayed I would never need it."

Finally, after a long two minutes, he ripped his gaze from the sink and gave it to me. "You want to set a date? Will that make you feel better?"

I stepped closer, my arms looping around his waist as I rested my chin on his chest, staring up into his face. He stared down, brows still etched with concern, but slowly, he relaxed and wound his arms behind my back, raising a hand to tangle in my hair.

"I want to set a date because it's what you want, not because you feel backed into a corner about it."

His eyes said so many things, yet all that left his mouth was, "Let me think about it."

"'Kay," I said, laying a kiss on his chest, his shirt carrying undertones of sweat. He must've grabbed a shirt from his truck before running in to pick up the pizza.

I went to step away, and he grabbed my hand. "Is there any other way to make you feel better about this? About us?"

"Miles." God, this sucked. "If I didn't feel like you'd taken ownership of my heart, then this ring wouldn't be on my finger, and I wouldn't be here."

His eyes shuttered. "You fucking slay me, Jem-Jem."

Relieved, I smiled at that and tugged him toward the bedroom.

There were no protests as I slid off his shirt. His eyes hooded as I stripped, then he got rid of his pants. He reached over to the nightstand, snatching a condom and rolling it on as he sat on the side of the bed.

Right before I impaled myself, I whispered against his lips, "Also, you could finally let me pay for some of the mortgage." I knew it had to be expensive; this house was practically brand new when we'd moved in, and it sat outside a suburb that cost a fortune to live in.

Miles coughed, his grip on my hips burning as he blinked up at me. "No, babe. We've already been over this."

Gripping him, I paused with the tip at my entrance. A shiver raced over my skin, raising hair and gooseflesh as he groaned in torment. "It would make me feel better." I rocked my hips, and he slid over my center. "Much better."

"Fuck," he spewed, then grabbed my hips, slamming me down. He threaded his hands into my hair, tugging, and growled against my lips. "You can pay twenty-five percent."

"Thirty." I grinned, even as my eyes watered from the sting radiating over my scalp due to his rough hands.

"Deal."

CHAPTER
Eleven

THE WEEKS TUMBLED FORWARD.

Flowers bloomed in our garden that I didn't even know Miles had planted or tended to. Though it shouldn't have surprised me he would, being that was his job and all.

I was pulling sheets off the line, cursing beneath my breath as clothespins fell to the grass and I tried to carry my load without a basket, when the faint sound of talking echoed from the garage behind me.

Curious, I moved to the door attached to the back, adjusting my hold on the now rumpled bed linens to turn the handle. What I heard next had my hand stilling.

"Don't you think I know that?" Silence, then, "I can't." A pause. "No, I know what I promised, but you're asking the impossible of me right now, Shell."

Shell? Who the hell was Shell? Shell as in Shelley?

With my eyes smarting and my head spinning with questions, I stayed on the small patch of grass behind the garage, unable to move even if I wanted to.

"You know that's not true," he continued. "But it hasn't been that simple for a while now."

A passing car, young children playing out on the street, and birds calling to one another in the trees beyond our backyard filled the gaping silence.

"No, I can't. You know why." He groaned, hissing something I couldn't quite make out, and then the seconds kept ticking until I realized whatever conversation he'd been having, obviously on the phone, had ended.

And still I couldn't move.

Not until I heard his truck reversing out of the drive, then fading in the distance.

"Hope," I whispered, unable to form the word over the panic weighing down my tongue.

"Jem? What's up? Shit, hang on." A few seconds later, I heard a door closing. "Sorry, just locked myself in the pantry. The boys are screeching at some TV show."

A laugh sputtered from me. "The pantry?" I sniffed, swiping at my nose with the edge of my sleeve. "You couldn't walk into another room?"

"I was thinking quick, and besides …" A rustling sound hit my ears. "I want to snack in peace."

Peace.

I wanted that, which was precisely why I'd left the pile of rumpled sheets on our bed and dinner uncooked on the counter, then drove until I'd reached Glenning. Until I'd reached home.

But the peace I sought and had always found here hadn't arrived yet, hence my phone call to Hope.

I'd had some friends in college, high school too, but I guess those bonds weren't strong enough to maintain after going our separate ways. So Hope was often saddled with my problems. Though I didn't think she cared as she often called me to vent about the boys, Jace, or sometimes just to fill the time while she folded laundry.

Our relationship now was different than it had been when we were kids, but it was better.

After our mom died, Hope seemed to grow three feet taller in every way. As though she couldn't be a kid anymore and needed to grow up faster. It made me sad for her now. For those years she'd jumped between the role of something she wasn't ready for to acting out as teenagers were meant to, only worse. Though, back then, I was just sad she refused to play with me.

I now knew that without her taking the role of big sister to a whole new level, I probably wouldn't have met the world with such an unguarded heart. She'd shielded mine by sacrificing hers, and it was sickening that I'd never noticed it much until hurt—all the things she'd tried to protect me from—started slithering into my life.

"I love you," I told her.

"Oh, my god. Are you dying?" She laughed, then stopped abruptly. "What's wrong? Tell me. Now." Her mom tone had come out to play.

I smiled out the grimy window of my old bedroom. "I just thought you should know. You're strong, and selfless, and awesome, and I love you."

She was quiet a moment, her voice rougher as she said, "Love you too, baby sis."

We sat in silence as memories infiltrated, and I knew she understood why I was suddenly being so affectionate when she said, "I have no regrets, Jem. None. Even if Mom hadn't died, I've always been headstrong. I've always craved to be in charge and to have independence."

I knew that, and it made me feel marginally better.

After a few minutes of her regaling me with a description of the mess the boys had made at dinner and how Jace was going to have to clean it because she was declaring herself off duty for the day, she got back to the matter at hand.

"Speak. Tell me what's going on." She paused as it sunk in. "God, is it Miles? After your phone call the other week, I've done some thinking, and I think I should meet this shithead."

I laughed. "There might not be a reason for that soon enough." It killed me to say it, but something was going on, and after the phone call I'd overheard … well, it only made my suspicions morph into something real. I could feel it crawling closer when he was near. Taste it when he kissed me. And hear no other sound whenever his phone rang.

"Shit, Jem," Hope whispered, followed by the sound of crunching as she snacked on something.

"Has Jace ever cheated on you?"

She coughed and cursed, then croaked out, "Warn me before you ask stuff like that. Holy mother of hairy, I almost died." She'd never outgrown her dramatic tendencies, so I waited until she finally breathed normally again. "Okay, let's back up a bit."

I told her about the phone, the woman at the school's fundraiser, and how comfortable she seemed with Miles, how Tracey had said she didn't know her, and finally, about the phone call that afternoon.

"It could be because they dated, like she said," Hope chimed in after a long stretch of quiet.

I twirled a tassel on the blanket beside me. "Could be, I guess." I sighed, returning my gaze out the window to the greenery that sat on the edge of our land. "Do you think I'm overthinking it?"

"You're not one to overthink." Hope snorted. "No offense, but you're kind of oblivious to most things in the real world."

"Thanks," I muttered. She was right, though; no matter how much the truth made me frown with indignation.

"But," she said on an exhale, "the sheer fact that you are usually oblivious means there could be something. I mean, I'm not saying there is or isn't, but your gut is telling you to listen."

"So," I mused, "I suppose all I can do is keep listening." I stood, pacing the round blue woven rug as my free hand dug into my hair. "That doesn't help."

Hope cursed. "I've been discovered." The sound of my nephews' laughter as they no doubt opened the pantry to find their mother made me smile. "I know it doesn't," she said quickly, "but that's all you have for now. Rely on it, but don't freak out until you have to. You don't wanna drive a wedge between you guys for no reason."

All true.

I tugged at my bottom lip as the boys screeched, and then one of them started crying. "You go, but thank you. I'll talk to you later."

"'Kay, make sure you keep me updated."

The line went dead, and I dropped my phone to the bed, eyes drifting over my bedroom.

A photo on my dresser caught my eye, tugging at my heart and feet until I stepped closer and picked it up.

Hope and I both looked like her with our dark brown hair and dark eyes. But whereas Hope had gotten Dad's button nose, I'd inherited the strong bridge of Mom's, one that stood proudly on my face. Such a thing would normally irk most girls, but I'd gotten a piece of her, and for that fact, I could only love it. Love what I saw every time I looked in the mirror. Not in a vain way; though I wasn't insecure or self-deprecating, I knew I wasn't bad to look at. No, it warmed my heart even as it squeezed it to see some of her staring back at me whenever I saw my reflection.

"What would you do?" I wondered aloud to the picture of a woman with long brown hair and a glowing smile that she directed to the two girls on her lap. "I'm so fucking confused."

The picture stayed still. The perfect moment captured in time and sealed behind a wall of finger smudged glass was both unhelpful and soothing.

I placed it down, sighing as I went back to my perch by the window.

My phone chirped with a new text from Miles. He was probably asking where I was. I'd answer him. And I'd go home.

I looked at the woods.

Just not yet.

I arrived home in the dark.

No lights were on except for a lamp in the living room. The uncooked food no longer sat on the countertop.

My tongue wrapped around excuses for my whereabouts the whole drive home, yet even as I thought to hell with it, I'd just ask who he was talking to, I realized it wouldn't be that simple.

Miles was asleep, his muscular limbs sprawled over our duvet as if he hadn't meant to pass out, the moon highlighting the dips and valleys of his broad back. His snoring was the soundtrack I needed to brush off the events of the day and get undressed.

I'd shower in the morning, not wanting to risk waking Miles after I'd been given an out.

But as I laid next to him, not touching and staring out the same uncovered window to the night sky beyond, I couldn't sleep.

I'd been given an out, but I didn't need one.

He did, and I'd unknowingly handed it to him.

CHAPTER
Twelve

"EVERYBODY PICK FIVE THINGS EACH FROM YOUR activity station to pack away."

I returned to tidying my desk as the kids scrambled to grab five items and return them to their rightful homes. The fact I only needed to make it a game and they'd snap into action, no matter how grumpy, tired, and hungry they were, made a giddy smile appear on my face every time.

After they'd left, I finished tidying what little hands and eyes had missed and printed off fresh spelling tests for Monday.

Glowing sunshine lit the world outside Lilyglade Prep, and my eyes watered as I blinked at the brightness, almost stumbling down the steps with my folder and bag to the parking lot.

After offloading my stuff onto the passenger seat and closing the door, I turned and screamed.

Thomas scowled as if my fear was a pest he wished he could swat away. "Honestly, Little Dove."

"It's Jemima," I said, my hand fluttering to my face. I hastily raked it through my hair and looked over his shoulder to his car, where I could see the top of Lou Lou's pigtails through a dark tinted window.

"Same thing," Thomas said, following my gaze. "She's playing an iPad, and the A/C is on, so she'll survive."

I coughed over the laugh that tried to barrel free. "Okay then."

Looking him over, in his pressed suit and dress shirt, I decided to kill one of my many questions. "What happened to her mother?" I waited for the anger, the scolding sure to follow such a personal question.

Thomas merely lifted a brow. "So she finally asks."

"I know she's not in the picture," I muttered. "School records and all."

Thomas nodded once, but otherwise, no part of him moved.

My fingers curled at my sides as I let my eyes meet his.

"She's dead." His voice held no trace of emotion, neither did his eyes.

Still, I said, "I'm sorry."

His head tilted. "There's no need to be sorry. She was a rotten woman."

Well, shit. I couldn't help it, and an incredulous laugh slipped past my lips. "I'm sorry," I said again, breathing in a steadying breath. "That's just …"

"It's the truth."

"It's shocking."

Thomas rubbed his lips together, and my eyes followed the movement. His bottom lip was fuller than the top but not in an overly noticeable way. No, you had to be standing close enough to see, which had me sliding along my car, heading for the driver's side.

"Anyway, I better get going." I had no idea why he'd hung around after picking Lou Lou up. Perhaps he was running late after work. Lou Lou waved when I glanced over at their car, and I waved back. "Have a nice evening."

"Wait," he said in a tone that conveyed no urgency, only gentle command. "My text messages."

With my back to him, I let my eyes shut. Then slowly, I turned, acting about as nonchalant as a bumbling elephant. "Oh yeah, about them …"

"Don't contact me."

I wasn't planning to, but his quick words pulled me up short. "What?"

"Trust me when I say it was a foolish move on my part. I've since discovered the error in my ways, and you can't contact me."

A little bit stung, yet unsure why, I felt like saying I didn't even want to. But meeting his gaze again, I couldn't bring myself to say anything. He exuded professionalism, a little too much, yet beneath that hard exterior, something simmered that I didn't trust, something I feared to upset. Whatever that was.

"No worries." I opened my door, watching as he turned for his car. "Hey, but you never did tell me how you got my number."

"And I never will," he said, then climbed into his car. I was about to do the same when his window wound down, and his next words stunned me. "Are your eyes open, Jemima? Because things are never as they seem."

"Babe," Miles cooed in my ear as I prepared a salad at the kitchen island. "I missed you. Where'd you go last night?"

He stole a piece of carrot, pecking me on the cheek and chomping down as he leaned his hip against the countertop.

"Went to Dad's." I drizzled the dressing in, then tossed the salad.

The sound of his chewing, even with his mouth shut, grated like nails down a chalkboard.

My skin prickled.

"Where'd you go?" I asked before he could drill me on why I went home.

Home. Funny how that hadn't changed even after I'd been living here with Miles for months.

"Got called out to a job. Someone found a snake in their yard, and I wasn't about to turn down five hundred bucks."

"A snake?" Grabbing two plates, I set them down before removing the chicken from the oven.

"Uh-huh."

Miles would probably gripe that this wasn't enough food for him, but I wanted chicken and salad, so that was all I cared about. His eyes danced hot on my profile as I readied our plates.

Once served, I dumped the oven tray in the sink, snatched some cutlery for myself, and went into the living room to eat.

Miles followed a minute later, carrying half a loaf of bread in one hand and his dinner in the other. He sat on the other couch and kicked his feet up onto the ottoman.

I'd just about finished eating before he finally asked, "Are you going to tell me what's bugging you yet?"

"You are," I said, shocking myself and him.

Ignoring his pinched expression, his mouth stuck mid chew, I took my plate into the kitchen and began cleaning up. He wisely let me be, or maybe it wasn't so wise as my frustration only grew.

I slammed plates into the dishwasher, almost cut myself on a knife, and when I tossed the food into the trash, half of it landed on the floor in front of it.

Fuck it, he could pick it up.

At that moment, I could barely discern what was eating at me so much. Miles and his lies, or Thomas and his weird vibes.

An odd combination of both.

I stomped down the hall, ripping off my dress, panties, and

bra, then tore open the shower and stood under the cool spray until the water warmed, hardly feeling it.

Miles came in as I was working conditioner through my hair, his arms looping around me and pulling my back flush with every hard part of his chest.

Sliding his tongue over my shoulder to my ear, he breathed, "Talk to me."

"I don't know if I can." And the truth in those words hadn't registered until then. I didn't know if I could talk to him. I didn't know if I could handle knowing, or if I could survive the frustration and anxiety of not knowing.

When his hands glided over my stomach and wrapped around my breasts, he started rocking his hips and sliding his hardness over my ass and lower back.

"Do you need me?" His teeth plunged into my neck. I squeaked, and not totally in pleasure, but in pain. "Let me fuck you better."

A coil wound tighter than any knot unfurled in an instant, fraying and snapping as I spun in his arms, shocking him enough that I was able to shove him back into the shower wall.

"Who is Shell?"

I watched his eyes, watched the way his pupils dilated and the whites shrank even as he kept his expression tight with confusion. "The fuck? *Who?*"

"I heard you on the phone yesterday." I was past the point of wondering if I sounded like a crazy, paranoid fiancé. If it would quell the shaking terror that quaked higher every day my worries festered, I was giving myself a pass to be as crazy as I needed.

Miles seemed to fade into the tiled wall, his gaze turning down to where the soap-clouded water swirled around our feet.

After a minute of only the running water to drown out my stalling heartbeat, he met my eyes again. "She's my sister."

"Your sister."

He nodded, and I stepped under the spray to rinse the conditioner from my hair, my eyes never leaving his as I digested his blatant lie.

It wouldn't go down easy, no matter how much I longed for it to.

And so I left him in the shower, dried myself off, and retreated to the living room.

CHAPTER
Thirteen

Thomas

L ITTLE DOVE'S EYES WERE REMINISCENT OF A PAIR I'D
seen before.

As soon as I saw them in person, I'd faltered.

Her lithe little body was innocence swathed in guilt, though she had done nothing to warrant that guilt in the first place.

She was merely a fly tangled up in a web of retribution.

Then she looked at me.

Smiled at me.

Talked to me.

Laughed with me.

Unknowingly, she began to flatten my precariously erected plans.

Then, even though it took more time than I'd care to admit, I became aware of *his*.

Now we were all tangled up.

Did she blind me to the obvious? Or was my mind playing tricks on me to keep me sharp?

Either way, it was as clear as a cloudless sky now.

It was just too bad, really. Too bad that I never could've predicted how difficult this would be. And not for the reasons it should've been.

Was this what happened when you were controlled by your dick?

I mean, I'd heard it countless times before, but I'd never been ruled by lust. No matter how pretty the Little Dove was. Lust was incapable of fooling me and thwarting my schemes.

No, it was something else. Something unnamable yet smothering. The way it took up space in my brain. The way she did.

I wasn't equipped for this.

I didn't foresee this.

I couldn't walk away from this.

As much as it didn't bother me—they'd *never* fucking bothered me—it did involve me.

Everything and anything to do with her very much involved me.

In fact, everything that'd happened and would likely happen was because of me.

CHAPTER
fourteen

MILES WENT TO BED AFTER I'D LEFT HIM IN THE shower, and he woke early for work the next morning.

Are your eyes open, Jemima?

Armed with a plan and riddled with tension, I ignored the usual chores I'd do around the house on a Saturday and decided I could take a day for myself.

And I made good use of it by tugging open drawers, ripping away blankets, and searching between the mattress and bed frame. Though if Miles had a second phone as I thought he did, then I guessed he'd likely taken it with him.

It was lunchtime when I forced myself to set everything back in the right order and take a time-out.

After eating a whole bag of peanut M&M's, I washed them down with half a bottle of water, resigned to the fact that I'd either need to be more persistent in getting him to tell me the truth, or I'd need to quit this witch hunt and chill the hell out.

I went to the study where my books still sat dust covered and lonely in boxes.

Miles had bought shelving for them, which sat in flat packaging by the wall, but he'd never gotten around to setting them up. I'd thought about doing it myself, but Hope had warned against doing such things when I'd whined about it, saying it made some guys feel like less of a man when we took tasks like that from them.

Well, fuck his manhood.

I ripped open the packaging, more so for something to do than anything else, and froze when something clattered onto the white pieces of wood inside the cardboard box.

Peering into the dark interior, I saw a black lump near the bottom, and sent my hand in to fish it out. It latched around a familiar shaped object.

A phone.

My heart raged, in both triumph and despair, as I stared at the phone I'd first seen weeks ago.

I sniffed back tears, turning it to its side to see it'd been set to silent, so you couldn't hear it buzzing or ringing.

So I couldn't.

The screen lit up, displaying a new message from six this morning.

S: I'll be there in ten.

My hands shook, my chest inflating as I took a deep breath and investigated further, opening a stream of messages.

There weren't many, but the few there were all from someone named S.

Shell.

His supposed sister.

S. It feels like this will never end.

S: I miss you.

S: Don't you dare forget about me.

The last one had me throwing the phone at the wall.

After leaving a dent, the casing flew off the phone, and all of it fell to the beige carpet between two boxes of my books.

Time passed in eerie stillness as I stared at the phone and tried to comprehend everything it meant. As I absorbed the reality I'd gone hunting for.

Once it registered with the force of a sledge hammer to the chest, the tears arrived, and I curled into myself against the wall.

⌒〜〇

"Jem?"

Dragging my eyes open, I wiped beneath my mouth, almost smiling, almost forgetting, as Miles knelt in front of me, concern crinkling his features.

"Hey, what happened?"

I scooted away and stood, my legs jelly from having been on the floor too long. Miles tried to steady me, and I snarled at him, "Don't touch me."

"Babe." He took a measured step back, hands raised as if he was dealing with a feral animal. "What the hell is going on? Talk to me."

His eyes skimmed the room as he waited.

It was either tell him, or leave him, or both. Or … I didn't even know what to do. There was too much happening inside me to decide a damn thing.

"I found your phone," I said. "The other one." Dragging my wrist beneath my mouth again, I sniffed. "I was going to set up these bookshelves, finally, and what do you know?" My hand waved at the dent in the wall, his eyes following and seeing the phone and its case in pieces on the floor. "A phone appeared."

"Jem," he started. "This isn't what you're thinking."

"Don't you dare." I stepped forward, hissing, "Don't you dare tell me I'm crazy or that I'm wrong, when for weeks, *weeks*, I've been slowly losing my mind, wondering if I'm insane." A crazed laugh left me, which only made me laugh harder at the ironic timing. "I don't want to be fed any more lies, Miles. I want the fucking truth."

He opened his mouth, more lies about to spill, and I scoffed, heading for the door to the room.

His next words stopped me. "It was after we'd first met. We'd only been on the one date …"

My hand shot out, clenching tight around the doorframe.

The one date.

He said it so clinically as if that time spent together, no matter how small, meant nothing to him. Not in the way it meant to me.

Turning, I raised my hand, not hearing anything else he was saying, and asked with more calm than I thought I'd ever have in this kind of situation. Not that I'd ever expected to be in this situation, though I guess I'd gone looking for answers. I couldn't lose my shit or complain too much about finally getting them. "How many times?"

With his brows pinching, he took a step toward me.

"Stop right fucking there." He did, nostrils flaring and hands fisting. "How many times, Miles?"

"Once. Fuck, I swear. But it's more complicated than—"

"What did you do?" I couldn't believe my own question. Why did I want to know specifics? I couldn't answer that, but I just had to know. "Kiss, just touch, or …" I swallowed, eyes closing briefly as I said the last word. "Fuck?"

The drooping of his shoulders and the hesitant step he took said it all.

"You fucked someone when we first got together?" I

batted his hands away when he tried to reach for me and moved back out of the room and into the hallway.

"Jem, please. At the risk of sounding like a fucking moron, I can explain."

My arms folded over my chest. "Go on then. Explain. I'm sure it was some huge mistake. People accidentally have intercourse all the time."

Ignoring my sarcasm, he shook his head, eyes pleading. "I can't yet. Give me time and it'll all make more sense."

A strange noise sounded, and I realized it was laughter. My own choked, wet laughter. "Not only have you fucked another woman, but you're seriously telling me I have to wait for an explanation as to *why?*"

He bit his lips, more tense than I'd ever seen him before. A strangled sound wrenched from him as he squeezed the back of his neck. "Yes."

"Why is she still contacting you?"

He didn't answer me.

I tried again. "Why, Miles? And is it that same woman from the fundraiser?"

He dug his hand into his hair, tugging and groaning. "Please, Jem."

Tears continued to well in my eyes.

Okay, now I could lose my shit. "Fuck you and fuck off."

"I'm not going anywhere," he said, trailing after me down the hall. "I'm not that guy, I promise. It sounds bad now, but …"

In our bedroom, I whirled on him. "Go away before I kick you in the junk."

His lips dared to quirk.

My knee met his balls, and he went down like a sack of potatoes, groaning on the floor and staring up at me as though he didn't even know who I was.

And maybe he didn't.

After stuffing some clothes into a bag, I marched into the en suite to collect my toiletries and my hair dryer.

He made the decision, however unwise, to let me go.

CHAPTER
fifteen

"J EMMIE?" MY DAD CAME OUT ONTO THE WRAPAROUND porch holding a cup of tea in his hand. "What are you doing?"

Tugging at my duffel, I pulled it out of the back seat. It hit the packed dirt with a thud, and I slammed the door before hauling it and my purse toward the porch.

My dad's eyes bulged, and he set his tea on the steps before lumbering down them to grab the duffel from me.

I thanked him but otherwise said nothing as we went inside.

"Jem," he said, trailing me up the stairs to my childhood bedroom. The same room I sat in a few days ago, trying to find answers. I'd gotten what I'd asked for, so why did I feel even more confused than before?

"Jemima Dianne Clayton, care to tell me what the hell is going on?"

Being that it was Mom's first name, I knew he'd only use my middle name if he was really concerned. "Sorry," I said, sniffing and hoping my eyes had dried. "I'm okay. Miles is a fucking dick, but I'm okay."

Dad blinked, dropping my duffel onto the bed. "He's a dick, and you're okay?"

I nodded, not wanting to talk about it just yet. I hoped he'd understand that without me having to say it.

"Okay," he finally said. "Have you eaten? There's beef stew in the fridge you can reheat."

"I'm good," I said, trying for a reassuring smile. It wobbled and fell. "I just need some time."

After a long moment of studying me, he went to the door. "I'll be watching the game if you need anything."

Exhaling a relieved breath, I started unpacking my bag, hoping my work clothes for Monday weren't wrinkled. I hated ironing.

"Oh, and Jemmie?" Dad called from down the hall.

"Yeah?"

"Is this a bad time to say I told you so?"

My eyes rolled, then watered. "Love you too, Dad."

"Miss Clayton?"

I glanced up from where I'd been staring at the weeds sprouting around the climbing frame and found Lou Lou, her hair in two braids, standing before me.

"Hi, honey," I said, then looked around. "Where's Rosie? She doesn't want to play today?"

Lou Lou sucked her bottom lip, then shook her head. "No, Rosie's fine."

Knowing she wanted to ask me something, I gave her my patience even though I longed to wallow in peace before I had to return to class.

"Are you okay?" she finally asked, peering closer at my face.

Shocked, I smiled and smiled big. "Of course, why do you ask?"

I'd been careful to be my usual self. School was almost done for the year, so I could fake it until summer break. Apparently, I

hadn't been careful enough. Or maybe Lou Lou was as perceptive as I already knew her to be.

"You seem sad."

Oh, boy.

Her little hands wrung together, and leaning forward, I
gently clasped them in mine. "I've just got a lot on my mind. I
promise I'm okay."

"You promise?" She lowered her voice. "Daddy says promises are unbreakable. So you need to mean it."

That made me smile for real. Regardless that it felt like a
lie, people had their hearts broken every day and lived to see
another sunrise. So I knew, no matter how much it hurt to force
the words out, that I wasn't breaking her promise by saying, "I
will be okay, I promise. All in good time."

Lou Lou stared. The innocent worry, the way her amber
eyes searched mine for the truth to my words made me want to
gather her close and squeeze her in a hug. Instead, I squeezed
her hands, then released them, murmuring for her to go play.

She took a step back, eyeing me another breath before running to the playground, where Rosie appeared with a soccer ball
in her hands.

<hr />

I returned home hungry and weary.

Something that was becoming a horrible new normal.

The drive wasn't long unless you tried to make the trip in
rush-hour traffic. But I'd been at my dad's all week and licked
my wounds long enough, so I made plans to head back to my
apartment that weekend.

As I brushed dust from frames and placed books on shelves,
I smiled.

I smiled because even as the hurt bruised every breath I took, I was proud of myself. Not that being proud helped much. But the apartment that I'd kept was a sign that as much as I'd dived into our relationship with reckless abandon, and as stupid as it made me feel, I'd done one thing right.

And I desperately needed not to feel like a fool for a hot minute.

Dad had followed me into the city. His help wasn't needed, but his company was appreciated as he helped me clean, ridding the apartment of dust bunnies and cobwebs. He was silent mostly, which I was thankful for, knowing he was probably seething inside after I'd finally divulged the details of what'd happened with Miles. He'd kept quiet for me, and for that alone, I hugged ten years off him on the sidewalk before he got into his truck and drove back home.

Rain pelted the window as I laid out some laundry to dry over a clothes rack in the corner of the living room. Draping a gray cardigan over the last free row of rails, I peered out the window to the cloud dusted sky. I wondered, a lot more than I wanted to admit, what Miles was doing. I wondered why he hadn't tried to call me, or why he'd never shown up.

Was that other woman taking up all his time now? Had he really moved on that quickly?

I wondered, and I cried, and eventually, both things happened less frequently. It was scary that over the course of almost two weeks, I could already feel the difference in my chest. Feel it loosen more and more. The difference most noticeable when it clenched tight, making it hard to breathe, as thoughts of him knocked me sideways.

Hope had told me the trick was not to think about him after I'd caved and called her last week. But I'd tried that, and the fear of suffocating on memories was somehow worse than reliving them. So I forced myself to re-live them. Every night, in the safety of my twin bed with Funshine Bear and my ragdolls staring at me from their corners of the room, I let out what I no longer wanted weighing on my heart.

Four knocks hammered my door just after eight the following night, and I knew.

I knew it was him.

I wanted to ignore him. To forget him the way he'd seemed to have already forgotten about me, yet I got up off the old scratchy couch and padded to the door in my sleep shorts, a T-shirt, and slippers.

"Who is it," I said more than asked.

"Jem, let me in. Or at least open the door."

"Why?" I knew I would at least open it, but he could sweat first.

"Because I'm a huge fucking asshole who misses you. That's why."

My lashes felt heavy, my eyelids drooping to the scuffed floor as his hoarse words slithered inside my aching chest, burrowing into wounds that were healing, or at least trying to.

I opened the door.

Miles stared at me with assessing eyes and his head hung. He was the picture of torment with his arms braced on either side of the doorframe. Muscles seized, then bunched, and the energy radiating from him made me take a step back. I clung to the door as his gaze raked me from head to toe and back again, holding my stare.

"You weren't here when I came by last week."

"I was at …" I stopped myself from saying home, not

wanting to hurt him even though I shouldn't give a shit. It was then I realized you could hate and love a person at the same time. You could wish they'd never existed while missing them with a tenacity that scorched your insides.

He nodded, understanding. "Will you let me in?"

I shook my head.

He sighed out a long breath, arms falling away from the doorframe as he inched closer. He stopped and leaned into it, close enough to touch, and close enough to smack him in the face with the door if I let it go.

Tempting.

"I know I fucked up. I'll never deny it—"

"But you did," I cut in. "Deny it. You covered it up the whole time we were together, Miles."

He swallowed, his jaw working. "Yeah. The thing is, I was telling the truth when I said there's more to it. More that I can't explain right now."

"I can't wait for that, and if I'm being honest, what good would it even do?" I begged for him to hear me, to understand. "It won't change what you've done, will it? What you might do again, if you haven't already."

"No," he said instantly, moving forward and cupping my chin. "I swear to you, it won't happen again. I meant it when I said I'm not that guy, and I hate that I've made you think I am." His head bowed, and his lips moved fast over mine, taking, prying, pleading.

I pulled away, loosening my hold on the door until it slipped free of my clammy hand.

He took the opening, taking two strides into my apartment and whispering with vehemence, "I love you, and I know you still love me." His gaze dropped to the ring I still wore. The ring I couldn't tug off my finger yet. It was more than just the pain it'd cause. It was saying goodbye to a fairy tale that I wasn't ready to do.

"That doesn't mean I can just forgive you. It doesn't work like that."

"So let's make it work." His voice was still low, rocking me on my feet with his stare and its intensity. "It's you and me, babe. We'll get through this. We just need time."

Need time.

How often I'd said those words myself.

"Go. Please." I grabbed the door. "I don't want to do this."

"I'm not leaving until I know I've still got you." He reached out, grabbing the back of my head and threading his fingers roughly into my hair. "I'll give you space, but I won't give you up. Understand me?"

Words coated my tongue, weighing it down with all I wanted to say, scream, and yell. But I did none of those things. "I can't tell you what you need to hear. And seeing as you can't do the same for me, I'd think you'd understand that." Tears hitched my voice, feathered up my throat, and pricked the corners of my eyes. "We're stuck. There's no moving."

Miles dropped his hand, defeat dragging his shoulders as he retreated a step. "Not true. We'll talk soon." When I said nothing, he pressed, "Okay?"

Wanting him gone, all I did was nod.

After I'd slammed the door shut, I heard a growl of curses in the stairwell.

Seconds later, what sounded like a fist meeting the wall hid the sound of my choked sobs.

CHAPTER
Sixteen

S UMMER CURLED WAVES OF HEAT AROUND THE SPRINGTIME air, warning everyone she was upon us.

I had one week left until I could do what I wanted most—flee back home or go anywhere else that wasn't here.

Thankfully, none of my co-workers commented on my rumpled appearance or sleep-starved eyes. And the kids, besides Lou Lou, were oblivious for the most part as long as their routine stayed the same.

Armed with a bucket of soapy water and a sponge that I kept in the sink at the back of the room for cleaning art supplies and paint mishaps, I got comfortable in front of the marker art drawn on the wall. Well, as comfortable as one could get on hard wood floor.

"You should really try isopropyl alcohol."

The sponge landed in the bucket, drops of warm water jumping up to smack me in the face.

Glancing over my shoulder, I saw Thomas standing in the doorway of my classroom, holding his fedora between his hands. "Huh?"

He closed his eyes and sucked in a hissed breath. When they reopened, they flashed with irritation. "It's excuse me, Little Dove. And I meant rubbing alcohol."

When I still sat there dazed, he continued as though I didn't understand him. I did; I was just speechless. "Nail polish remover, hand sanitizer …"

I got up off the ground, halting him right there. "I know what rubbing alcohol is." I rolled my eyes. "I went to college, remember?" I reminded him of the time he'd all but accused me of being uneducated.

"I suppose they don't teach manners there."

Ignoring that, I waved at Lou Lou, who stood behind him, chomping on an apple.

"What can I do for you, Dr. Verrone?"

Brows furrowed, perhaps over the use of his surname and not his first, it took him a moment to say, "I was just saying hello."

Now it was me who was confused. "Right. Well, thank you?"

"You're welcome. May I walk you to your car?"

I stared back at the wonky smiley face on the wall, then shrugged. "Sure, one second."

I took the bucket and sponge to the back of the room to empty and set it upside down next to the sponge on the sink. When I turned around, Thomas was studying the math equations on the whiteboard. "This is basic."

"Such simple things to us," I combatted. "We forget how intricate it is for the mind to solve at first."

Thomas stared, his eyes unreadable as they stuck themselves to mine.

Lou Lou cleared her throat, and then he said, "Actually, Lou would like to know if you want to play."

I glanced from him to her, uncertain where this idea had come from.

Lou Lou groaned and yanked on his hand. Thomas sighed. "Fine, she said you need to come play because you haven't smiled properly in two weeks."

Ignoring the curious gaze from her dad, I asked Lou Lou, "Is that right?"

"Yep. Swings always make me smile."

With nothing else planned besides ramen noodles and a half-finished book, I locked up and followed them outside to the empty playground.

"We're technically not supposed to let anyone use the play equipment after school hours," I unlocked the gate, and bent low, whispering to Lou Lou, "so it'll have to be our little secret."

Lou Lou mimed zipping her lips, then bounded over to the swing set, little legs kicking as soon as she jumped onto the rubber seat.

I lowered to the wooden buddy bench, and Thomas slowly did the same, keeping a large amount of distance between us. I was on one end, he on the other.

"Do I smell?" I went to check myself, then thought better of it, knowing I didn't. "I might work with kids all day, but I don't think I do."

Thomas slid closer in answer, but there was still enough room to squeeze two bodies between us. I smiled down at the ground.

"Lou says you'll feel better soon." He kept his gaze on her. "I'm guessing trouble with the … fiancé?"

"You guessed right. I've actually been wanting to ask you …" I licked my lips, his words returning. The same words that sent my doubts free-falling in search of the truth. "How did you know?"

Thomas placed his hat on his head. "How did I know what?"

"You know, that he'd cheated on me."

His hands clasped together in his lap. "I didn't know that."

Perplexed, I ran a hand through my hair. What had he been talking about then?

Lou Lou squealed in delight as she whipped through the air, her curls billowing behind her.

"How does it feel?"

His soft words were slow to penetrate, and when they did, I swung my eyes to his profile. "Being hurt, you mean?"

Thomas sat pin straight, leather wrapped feet planted evenly on the bark covered ground in front of him. "Yes. He didn't hurt you in the physical sense." He didn't wait for my answer. "He hurt your heart."

Such candid yet interesting words. "He did."

"So he was having an affair?" There was no hesitation behind his words, no concern for overstepping. It was refreshing.

"Not exactly. But he slept with another woman. We'd apparently just gotten together when it happened."

For the first time ever, I heard Thomas Verrone curse, then mutter in a dry tone, "Apparently."

Lou Lou frowned as if hearing him from her new perch on top of the slide. He waved, forcing a smile that looked as if it'd crack his perfect cheekbones, and she returned it then hurtled herself down the slide.

"You call her Lou?"

"Yes," he said. "Saying Lou Lou too much makes me feel like I own a Chihuahua instead of a child."

I laughed at the usage of *own*. "You're kidding, right?"

His lips twisted, then a shoulder rose. "Of course. So how does it feel?"

"You really want to know?"

"I wouldn't have asked otherwise."

"You've never had your heart broken?" I studied him closer, admiring the way the afternoon light snuck beneath the short brim of his fedora and bounced off the sharp angles of his face. Untouchable. Even to the elements. "Ever?"

"Once," he admitted. "But not in the same capacity as you."

I wished I could ask him the same way he'd asked me, without hesitation, who or what had broken his heart. Maybe I could, but for now, I settled for trying to describe my own pain.

"It's like something is sitting on your chest. Pressing. There's this pressure that affects everything you do. How you eat, how you sleep, how you breathe, how you talk ... everything."

I looked at Thomas, who'd removed his eyes from Lou Lou and was now staring intently at me. Having this man's full attention ... there was nothing quite like it. In an instant, his stare alone chased away every feeling I'd just described. "Go on."

I shook my head, coming out of my stupor.

"Why'd you stop?"

Inquisitive man.

Feeling thrown, I decided to see how he felt when the truth was volleyed back at him without any forewarning or sugarcoating. "Because for a second, looking at you, it all disappeared."

If he was shocked, he didn't show it. He blinked, sweeping long black lashes over ice cold eyes. Eyes that seemed warmer than I initially thought. "Daddy! Miss Clayton! Come climb with me."

Somehow, I knew Thomas would choose not to, and needing away from the warmth of his attention, I jogged over to the climbing frame, singing with Lou Lou as she counted her steps up and down the rope ladder.

Principal Crawley peeked over the roof of her car ten minutes later, and I collected Lou Lou from the swing, taking that as a cue to leave. "We'd better go," I said. "We don't want to get caught and possibly banned from using the playground."

"No way," Lou Lou said, taking my offered hand and swinging it as she met her father, who was standing with his hands deep in his pockets, fedora tilted low over his forehead as he watched us.

After locking up the playground, I helped Lou Lou into the back of their car, making sure she fastened her seat belt. Right before I closed the door, she said, "You smiled a lot more smiles. Are you better now?"

I reached inside the car to tweak her nose, and she giggled. "Almost."

With the door shut, I turned and came face to face with Thomas. He seemed to have no concerns about personal space now and was standing hair rising close to me.

He removed his hat, yet his dark hair remained perfect. "Did you mean what you said?"

I could lie and make myself feel less embarrassed, or I could admit the truth and hope it didn't make things awkward. "I don't say things I don't mean." His eyes sparked. "And yes, for a moment, you made me forget." My smile trembled. "So thank you."

I stepped around him, unlocking my car and climbing inside.

Before I could start it, the door opened, and Thomas climbed inside too.

My eyes shot to his, my mouth about to ask why he was in my car, but I didn't get the chance.

His hand reached forward, settling over the side of my face with his thumb brushing my cheek. Any words I had were now fried and forgotten. "Little Dove, I'm going to kiss you."

And he did.

Before I could say anything or even draw breath, his lips melded to mine. Soft, pressing, and perfect.

My hand moved for his face, fingers burning as they connected with his warm skin. I reached farther, and they tingled with the urge to tug at his soft hair.

A clicking sound reached my ears, and my eyes opened,

but then his tongue separated my lips, moving slowly inside to meet mine.

His movements were hesitant but full of purpose. His thumb still brushing my cheek and his minty taste corroding the shock of having another man's lips touching mine.

Another snap had me pulling away and glancing out the windshield to see if something had hit it.

Nothing was there. Just the swaying of the trees and an empty school yard.

And when I looked over at Thomas, my skin flushed and my heart booming in my ears, he was already out of the car. "Until next time, Little Dove."

Incapable of moving, I sat there, watching as his car left the lot with my fingers on my lips.

I wasn't sure what I felt. Anger over the way he might've taken advantage of my honest words? Guilt for letting another man's lips kiss mine? For even if I was technically single, I still hadn't taken the damn ring off. Or was it excitement from the endorphins that crept through my bloodstream, humming steadily as I left the parking lot?

At home, I paused at the sight of the fist-sized hole in the stairwell, the one Miles left behind after his visit, and decided on guilt.

CHAPTER
Seventeen

Miles

I N A MATTER OF WEEKS, JEMIMA CLAYTON TURNED MY entire world upside down.

And I was still hanging there, waiting for her to tip me right side up.

Except that probably wouldn't happen.

And it was all my fault.

My heart became wrapped up in a woman who was all slender curves, doe brown eyes, and feather soft dark hair. And even though it wasn't meant to turn out the way it did, I wasn't surprised. Not by a long fucking shot.

She was twenty-three and way too young for me. I was almost ten years her senior. Though she acted ten years older in most ways, there was a vulnerability to her that quickly became apparent.

My little Jem had never flown far from the nest. Even with her mother dying while she was a kid, she'd lived a sheltered life. I could've fucking shot someone when I'd discovered exactly who I was ruining.

I guessed it was only fair I'd be ruined in return.

An eye for an eye.

But I thought I could stop it from happening, stop myself

from getting in too deep. And by the time I feared it was too late, I was already a drowning man.

There was no going back now.

CHAPTER
Eighteen

MILES DIDN'T COME BY AGAIN THAT WEEK.
I told myself to be thankful for it, for the space I'd asked for, but I wasn't thankful.

I was mad.

What I was thankful for was the school year coming to an end that Friday. We celebrated with class parties and movies, then followed with a staff meeting to wrap up the year and ensure everyone was on the same page when we returned in late August.

Standing in the doorway to my classroom, I stared at the naked walls as nostalgia washed over me. A room where artwork, coats, bags, multiplication tables, and charts hung, each item desperate for more room, now rendered an empty shell.

The door shut with a click so quiet, it shouldn't have echoed in my ears. I rubbed my bare arms, then grabbed the canvas bags full of my things from the floor and carted them outside to my car.

Swathed in his usual suit but this time with the jacket abandoned, Thomas marched away from my car and toward me. He took the bags from my hands before I'd even had a chance to say hello and walked them silently to my car.

"Thank you," I said. "We didn't see you today." Some of the parents attended on the last day of school, taking part or helping with activities. It was a sugar-fest, and many kids burned out after lunch in lots of fun ways, so the extra help was appreciated.

It didn't shock me that Thomas didn't show; what shocked me was that I was digging for an answer as to why he'd kissed me just days ago. And by the quick side glance he threw me as he placed my bags in my messy trunk, he knew it.

"I had to work," he stated, closing the trunk and placing my purse in my hands.

Heat infused my cheeks as I glimpsed the smooth tan skin above the undone buttons of his dress shirt, and his scent reached me. That cinnamon and mint. It was becoming something I liked, something familiar. Shame spiraled icy tendrils down my spine at the discovery.

"You look constipated."

"What?" I all but screeched.

Thomas, sounding puzzled, explained, "You have a look on your face that Lou gets when she really needs to use the bathroom but can't."

My bag slipped from my hands as I doubled over, laughter howling out of me and causing my eyes to water. I wasn't even embarrassed. I was far from it as wetness trickled onto my cheeks, and I straightened, rejoicing that they weren't my heart's tears. "Jesus."

"No need for blasphemy," Thomas said with such seriousness that I bit my tongue to stop from laughing again. He gathered my bag from the ground, and after dusting the dirt from it, he handed it back to me again.

I took it, my hand clasping his before he could let go of the leather material.

He seemed startled, his blues widening with his quick intake of breath. "Thank you."

"For saying something rather stupid?" He shook his head.

"Or for making you drop your bag? Look, I'm not well versed with, um, women."

"Oh," I said, my heart sinking a fraction, yet I didn't drop his hand.

A current radiated between our skin, mine prickling the longer I touched his.

"That doesn't mean I prefer men." He stopped, looking exasperated with himself, which hitched my lips higher into my cheeks. "It would seem I'm doing it again."

Guilt, anger, and any shame I felt by being near him evaporated, leaving room for me to recognize the steady growing warmth in my chest for what it was. Burning curiosity. Unlike any I'd felt before.

It could've been the striking difference between him and any other man I'd ever met.

Or it could simply just be.

"Have a drink with me," I shocked us both by saying. I wasn't even much of a drinker.

He glanced down at my hand, and I tugged it away, feeling mortified by the suggestion and the fact I'd asked it while still wearing another man's ring.

"When?" Thomas asked as I spun for the driver's side of my car.

Blinking a few times, I swallowed and met his intense gaze over the roof. "Uh, whenever you're free, I guess? I'm as free as a bird all summer." To emphasize my excitement over that, I flung my hands out, and my purse smacked me in the leg, making me jump. "Shit." He smirked. "Maybe tea or coffee? I didn't mean a *drink*, drink." God, my cheeks were likely the same color as my red ballet flats. "Anyway, there's a cute coffee shop down the street from my apartment called Bernie's."

A flash of white teeth held me glued to the spot, his eyes

glinting as he nodded and opened his car door. "I have to go; Lou is at piano a few blocks away." He sank into the car's dark interior. "Tomorrow at ten, Little Dove."

Nine fifteen.

Silver and diamonds sparkled in the glow of early morning sunshine as I sat on my couch. Still in my pajamas and still without any trace of makeup on, I was still unsure.

Time was supposed to heal all wounds. I believed that, losing my mom being proof. I missed her every day for years, and now I just missed what could have been as well as the little snippets I remembered of her.

It all fades. Memories fade. Heartaches fade. But although time makes it bearable and easier to smile, to live, it doesn't erase the pain entirely.

Were we doomed to forever hold a sting in our hearts from those who had left or hurt us?

As I sat there, in the same spot I'd been sitting in since five in the morning after waking up in a cold sweat, staring at that ring and feeling its familiar weight on my finger, I concluded one thing only.

It was entirely up to me how much I let that sting hurt.

I didn't have to let whatever was happening with Thomas turn serious. I didn't have to let the worry of moving on too soon plague me.

I just had to do whatever it took to make time bearable.

Getting up, I traipsed to my bedroom on numb feet as the circulation returned and opened the jewelry box I'd had since I was a kid. The fairies' time-worn smiles both mocked and soothed as I pulled the ring off my finger and dropped it inside.

Nothing happened. My chest didn't cave in. My breathing stayed the same. The only difference was a noticeably lighter hand.

I shut the lid and walked to the shower where I stripped out of my sweat sticky tank and panties, and allowed myself to cry one more time.

Nine forty-five.

Racing through the apartment, I tugged a white cotton dress with sunflowers from the clothes rack where it'd dried overnight and slipped it over my head. I checked and re-checked my appearance, then decided it didn't matter if I wore one layer of mascara or two.

Thomas had seen me covered in paint smears, glue, and worn down by hours spent with children. Still, I had enough time to half dry my wet hair, spritz some floral perfume behind my ears and wrist, then slip on a pair of pink flip-flops.

The gusty breeze that tunneled through the city streets finished drying my hair and any sweat that'd beaded on my skin from walking so fast.

He was already there. Wearing a pair of dark denim jeans with a matching black polo, he sat at a table in the shade with his eyes on his pocket watch.

"I don't think I've ever seen you not wearing a suit." I dragged a chair out, the metal legs scraping over the concrete.

A quick perusal of me had shock muddling with obvious appreciation in those serious eyes.

His expression returned to impassive, and he leaned forward to pocket his watch in his jeans. "It is rare that I wear anything else, yes." Using his index finger, he pushed a menu across the metal surface toward me. "I've ordered a tea for you, but would you like something to eat?"

"You know how I like my tea?"

His expression didn't budge from unreadable, but his gaze was heavy on my lips. "I took a wild guess."

A waitress set our tea down, and to my utter shock, he'd gotten it right. Earl Grey with two sugars. I took the sugar packets, shaking and tearing them open to dump into my tea as I tried to figure out how I felt about him knowing such personal details about me.

"Thanks," I managed as I stirred my tea.

A nod was granted, and then he took a sip of his own. No sugar. Just black. "I figured you weren't too adventurous, then started narrowing down by choice, and—" At my smile, he exhaled a long breath. "And I'll shut up."

"Please don't," I said, lifting the white mug to my lips and taking a sip. "I didn't invite you here so I could do all the talking. What kind of doctor are you?"

"The kind that deals with teeth." I smiled over the rim of my tea cup. "Why did you invite me here?" He didn't sound annoyed, merely curious.

The hot liquid slid down my throat, and I took another sip as I really thought about that answer. "I don't know," I finally admitted. "Why did you come to the school yesterday while Lou was at piano?"

He took a sip of tea. "I don't know."

I blinked, running my finger around the saucer. "Where's Lou Lou?"

"With my assistant at home."

"She's a very bright girl." I relaxed into the uncomfortable, cold seat. "I'm not just saying that either. She's … intuitive too."

Thomas's shoulders seemed to rise, my words pulling his

already perfect posture a notch higher like a puppet on a string. "She's brilliant."

There was more to his words than mere father pride. He knew she was brilliant beyond the ways he loved her, but in ways that'd offer her many opportunities. I smiled. "She could have the world."

"And I plan to ensure that happens."

The gravity behind his words had me laughing, then glancing around the small courtyard to find a couple's eyes on us. They looked away.

Thomas sighed, and I looked over in time to see what appeared to be a grimace cross his features. "I lied."

"Oh?" I frowned at his obvious discomfort. "That's okay." I tried to laugh it off even as I burned with the desire to know what he'd lied about.

The seconds ticked on as he watched me drink my tea over the rim of his mug. His stare was studious as though he was learning, absorbing, and memorizing. It had ants tap dancing over my stomach and made me feel as if I'd never truly had someone look at me before.

I'll give you space, but I won't give you up.

The teacup almost slipped from my shaking hand as I pushed thoughts of Miles away.

This was too soon, and if I had to be honest with myself, I was probably just using Thomas to feel better. Maybe he knew that. Maybe he didn't care.

Thomas banished my thoughts with his next words. "I do know why I went back. It was to see you." He licked his lips, and my eyes tracked the movement, then I parted my own as he said, "And would you believe me if I said it was to ask you out?"

"Strangely enough, I think I would."

His smile made mine appear again, and that steady growing

warmth trickled through my limbs. "Lou says you grew up outside the city."

"Glenning. My father's still there on our small farm."

Thomas sat back in his chair, fingers meeting over his flat stomach. "Tell me about it?"

I smiled. "Okay."

CHAPTER
Nineteen

BANG, BANG, BANG.

"Open up, Jem!"

I dumped my book on the coffee table, slowly unfolding my crossed legs to stand. I'd been home for all of an hour, so the timing of Miles's visit had my head spinning.

Thomas had walked me home, but he didn't kiss me, didn't so much as touch me, and left with a stilted, "Until next time, Little Dove," hanging in the humid air between us.

I'd watched him walk down the street and stood there as people bustled by long after he'd vanished around the corner.

"Hi." My greeting was cautious when I opened the door to find a strung-out looking Miles.

His hair was messier than usual as though he couldn't keep his hands out of it, and his eyes were rimmed in red as though he hadn't slept in days. His shirt was wrinkled, and it was one he often only wore around the house. Never in public.

"Babe," he rasped, collecting me to his chest in two quick strides.

Lost in the smell of him, the sunshine and sweat that lingered on his skin, it took me too long to step out of his embrace. When I did, he scowled and reached for me again.

"What do you want?"

"That's obvious, isn't it?" he snapped, then shook his head.

"Sorry. You, I need you. This is driving me crazy."

"Miles—" I started, but he cut in.

"No, don't say it. Don't say any of whatever it is you're thinking. Just ..." He drew in a loud breath, his huge body shaking as he set it free. "Come home. I've given you space, and you're on summer break now. You can come home. We don't need to talk, touch, or any of that shit. I just want you near me."

The sound of footsteps in the stairwell had him spinning around and bracing.

My peripheral snagged on Thomas, who'd paused at the top of the stairs, assessing Miles as if he'd arrived at the zoo and had never seen such a creature up close before.

Oxygen vanished. My throat constricted. And still, the two males stared.

"Hey," I called to Thomas.

Finally, he removed his gaze from Miles and skirted around him as though the predatory menace radiating off Miles was of little concern.

I forgot Miles. His anger. His betrayal. His eyes on us. Thomas swallowed up the space without even trying, and all I saw was the blue of his eyes as he stopped right in front of me, the tips of his black boots kissing my bare toes.

"You forgot this." He handed me my phone, then bowed his head. Heat escaped his mouth and met the skin of my collarbone as he exhaled out, "Don't let him touch it again."

The words were whispered so low, it took me a few seconds to make out what he'd said, and then he was gone. His footsteps echoed up the stairwell, followed by the sound of the door below booming closed.

Staring at the empty stairs, I wondered if he was talking about my phone or me.

Then I remembered Miles, who seemed ready to chase and

kill. But when he looked at me, it disappeared, and he looked like he wanted to puke as fear rounded his eyes, and they fell on my phone.

After a beat, he cleared his throat. "The guy from your school? The, uh, that dad?"

My head moved, nodding once.

He nodded too, eyes still on my phone. "I've gotta go, but I'll be back."

He raced down the stairs, taking them two at a time by the sound of the thudding.

Then I was left on my own, reeling, barefoot, and more confused than I'd ever been in my life.

∞

The next day, I left the bakery to the feeling of eyes on me, and when I glanced over my shoulder, I swore I saw a flash of Miles's red gym shirt and his unruly hair.

I'd planned to go home for the summer, but something kept me here, so I stayed.

But as the first week of break rolled into the second, the second about to meet the third, I gave up hope I'd hear from Thomas, and Miles's behavior was starting to rattle me. He never came back to my apartment, but he'd decided it was okay to follow me?

In the drugstore with a box of tampons in hand, it might've been my hormones, but I'd decided I'd had enough. The box slipped from my fingers as I ran outside and went back the way I saw him. Some minutes later, I found him half standing in an alleyway.

"You're following me, aren't you?"

He tried to look like he was relaxing against the wall, typing on his phone as though he usually hung out in alleys. "Hmmm?"

"Cut the shit, Miles."

"Okay, maybe I am." He straightened.

I nearly growled. "Why?"

"Because … shit, Jem." He groaned. "I can't explain it all right now, but you need to come home."

I rolled my eyes, about to storm back to the drugstore. I needed the freaking tampons, dammit. And a butt load of chocolate.

"Jem-Jem," he said, his hand grabbing mine before I could storm off. "Have you seen that guy again?"

"His name is Thomas, and no." I sighed, my blistering frustration falling away at his soft touch. "I haven't." Which bugged me more than I'd like to admit. Especially to my ex-fiancé.

"You can't trust him."

"Oh, like I can trust you?"

His eyes flashed with warning. "I'm serious. You need to stay away from him. I'll explain why when I can."

"This is getting ridiculous, Miles." The heated wind knocked hair into my face as I turned to go.

"Yeah? Then why are you still here in the city and not at home with your dad? Huh?"

A hollow sounding laugh left me, and I shoved my hair out of my face. "*What?* Did you think I've been hanging around, waiting on you to grovel harder?"

"Fuck, your smart mouth makes me want to bend you over and fuck you senseless."

"Well, you've blown any chance of that happening again, haven't you?" Tears gathered, and I exhaled, trying to gain control of my whacked-out heart.

He saw them. "Hey, hey. I'm sorry. Are you okay?" Miles asked, crowding me against the brick wall.

"Just fine."

He smirked, and I wanted to punch him. "You know I love it when you lie to me." The humor dropped. "Really, though. Talk to me."

I wouldn't and couldn't do that. "I've got my period. I'm tired and grumpy."

His nose crinkled, but to his credit, he didn't shy away. He leaned in, arms caging and lips brushing dangerously close to mine. The scent of cherry gum smacked into all my senses, and my stomach roiled.

Did he chew that same gum before he'd slept with that other woman?

The smoothness of his bottom lip hit mine, and my eyes squeezed shut, my body dissolving into the hard bricks behind me as I let him pry my mouth open.

Stubborn claws tore at my psyche. The need for a different flavor took hold and made my hands push at his chest before I kissed him back. "Enough. I'll drop the ring off before I head home."

While he stood there stunned, I ducked out of his hold and stormed back down the street.

It was time to go home.

CHAPTER
Twenty

"So, this weird guy, Tommy, you're considering shacking up with him?"

I balked at the word shacking up, my feet pausing on the scuffed floor. "Firstly, his name is Thomas." Though he must have a nickname, surely. "And secondly, I'm not shacking up with him."

Hope snorted. "Sure you're not. What are you doing then? Because I know I'd want revenge on Miles's cheating ass too. There's no shame in your hating game, sister."

I huffed out an incredulous laugh. "God, stop it. Really, it's not like that."

"Hayden! Get that out of your nose right now." A pause, then, "Because otherwise it'll get stuck in your brain, and they'll need to cut your head open to get it out." Hope sighed, and I bit my lips, more laughter bubbling in my throat. "Great, now he's crying."

"Of course, he is. You scared the shit out of him."

"Dad said it to you when you were four, and you turned out just fine." She stopped and laughed. "I guess."

I tore off a chunk of my peanut butter sandwich, chewing. "Shut up."

"Anyway, what's this guy want with you if he doesn't want between your legs? If he knows about Miles, then he knows there could be a bit of a wait time."

I choked, belting my chest as I wheezed, "Jesus fucking Christ, Hope." Scrambling for the fridge, I broke my own rule and drained the last of the milk from the carton, trying to push the bread down. "Okay, I'm alive."

"Dramatic much?"

"I can't even with you."

"You love me, and I gotta go. Hayden's still crying about his brain."

Smirking, I tossed the milk carton into the recycling. "He's probably going to have nightmares, you know."

"Nah," she said. "I've said worse, and he's slept fine. Keep me posted on the weird dude and Miles. As much as I wanna kick him in the ass, I love hearing a good grovel just as much as the next girl." She sighed. "Your life, Jem. Seriously. Wanna trade for a day?"

Laughing again, I hung up.

As soon as I walked away from my phone, it started ringing again.

With laughter still coating my voice, I answered with, "Oh, I forgot to tell you, I already kneed him in the balls."

Silence.

"Hello?" I looked at the screen, realizing it was an unknown number and not my sister calling me back to say she'd forgotten something as she sometimes did.

Shit.

"Jemima." A quiet question layered around my name.

"Sorry, I thought you were my sister."

Thomas coughed a little. "Who did you knee in the, ah …?"

"Balls," I supplied, feeling the counter bite into my back as I leaned into it too heavily. "And Miles, of course."

"Of course," he echoed. "And when was this?"

"When he told me he'd cheated on me, then said I'd have to wait for him to be able to explain everything." I peeked at my chipped nail polish. "Which makes total sense."

Silence arrived again, and I was about to ask him why he'd called, especially after he'd said not to call him. Though I suppose that was before we'd kissed and had tea.

He spoke first. "As much as I'd love to listen to such gory tales of your ex, I need you to meet me somewhere."

"Sounds ominous," I joked.

It went right over his head. "It's a park."

"I was joking."

"Oh."

He told me where and what time, then promptly ended the call.

Feeling a sense of whiplash, I stared at my phone for a solid minute. Then I finished my sandwich and fixed my hair.

Lou Lou wrapped her arms around my legs as though she hadn't seen me in years instead of a few weeks. I squeezed her back, loving the fresh scent of cinnamon on her hair, then watched her run to a seesaw where another boy sat waiting. His mother sat on the other side of the park, reading a book.

I took a seat beside Thomas on the small bench, and he eyed the tiny gap I left between us.

"What do you do in the summer? With work and Lou Lou?"

His eyes were on my legs as I crossed them, his hands fidgeting in his lap a moment before he stilled them and turned his stare to his daughter. "I manage just fine. She knows when I'm busy, I'm busy."

"Well, if you need any help, I'm happy to take her a few days a week." I tucked some hair behind my ear. "I'm heading to my dad's for a little while, but Glenning isn't that far from here."

"I know."

Feeling kind of stupid, I shook my head. "Okay."

I was about to ask him which part of the city he lived in, realizing he'd never said over tea. Come to think of it, he'd mainly just talked about Lou Lou and listened to me prattle on about growing up in Glenning.

He spoke before I had the chance. "I have an assistant, but thank you for the offer."

Something about his tone had me surveying him again. Closer this time. He was stiff, stiffer than usual, and his demeanor cold. "What's wrong?"

He didn't answer, barely even seemed to breathe.

I prompted again. "Thomas?"

"I don't like it, okay?" he finally snapped but did so in a quiet, controlled way compared to most. His chest rose and fell faster and faster the longer he stared at me, his eyes wild and glowing.

"What?" I asked as softly as possible.

"That you were with him."

"Oh." I frowned. "Hang on ... how did you know?"

"That's irrelevant." He made a disgusted sound. "I hate it. After what he did to you. Not when he's—"

His mouth shut when I laid my hand over his. "We haven't been together, *together*." My cheeks reddened. "Not like that. Not since I found out about the other woman."

"Other woman," Thomas repeated with a slip of an irritated smile.

There was no way to stop my heart from wincing at the reminder, and Thomas noticed, his hand folding over mine, fingers like velvet as they stroked. "Sorry."

"It's okay."

I waved at Lou Lou when she looked over, and she smiled as she turned to run into a tunnel.

"I needed to see you because"—he paused, groaning—"I don't know how to say it …"

"You were upset?" I offered.

His phone chirped, and he pulled it out, inspecting it with a sigh. "I'm afraid it'll have to wait. I need to go." Putting his phone away, he turned to me, erasing the gap between our bodies. "But first, I have to do this again." He leaned in, lips capturing mine as his hands gently grasped my face.

I slid even closer, losing sight of our surroundings and only seeing him, smelling him, tasting him, and feeling him. He kept it chaste, even as my tongue pushed at the seam of his smooth lips, even as he made a quiet groaning sound when he inhaled, my top lip pressing between both of his.

One of the kids on the playground squealed, then laughter followed.

He tore away and practically fell from the bench with how quick he moved. Righting himself, he mumbled, "Just … be careful, Little Dove."

I was slow to take in his actions, his words, and my next breath as he traipsed over the grass and collected Lou Lou, who waved at me as he marched her to his car.

I stood as he helped her in but otherwise couldn't move. I didn't know whether to smile from the vibrations his mouth had left in its wake or wonder what the hell I'd done that had him running away like a boy who'd just stolen a kiss on the playground at school.

We'd done it before, after all.

A mixture of both settled while I watched his car speed off down the busy side street.

CHAPTER
Twenty-One

A BLACKBIRD CAWED HIGH ABOVE THE STREET, HIDDEN by the glow of the fading sun.

My duffel weighed a ton, so I left it for last and took my other two overnight bags down to my car. I unlocked it and shoved them into the trunk, my stomach flipping as I spun around and saw Thomas standing outside the drugstore next to the same door that led to my apartment.

His plain white shirt billowed in the breeze, then pressed against his lean chest as he straightened the leg he'd bent, his boot joining the other one on the asphalt.

Smiling away the shock that'd frozen my heart, I shut the trunk and walked over to him.

"You're going home now?"

"Yeah, just have another bag to grab, then I'm off."

His tongue poked the side of his cheek, his perfect combed back hair shifting as he ran a hand over it. Idly, I wondered how deep my fingers would sink if they were to touch it, to burrow down. How long it'd take for my nails to scrape his scalp.

Jesus, I needed a glass of water or something.

For as much as I'd floated along the unpredictable river that was Thomas Verrone, I'd never actually fantasized about him that hard. Until now.

"I'm sorry I ran off yesterday." The words carried no

sincerity, but I allowed them to mollify the kernel of worry that sat deep.

"That's okay." I slipped my hands into my jean short pockets, shrugging. "I guess you had places to be?"

"Unexpected work." His eyes finally met mine. "That, and you simply unnerve me, Little Dove."

I swallowed my shaky breath, my chest rattling as I basked in the honest words aided by the serious set to his sharp jaw and hard eyes.

"The feeling's mutual," I said, not sure if he'd even heard the soft words as the noise of the city street drowned out most things, including my stampeding heartbeat. "But I, um …" I hesitated, worried that he'd take what I was about to say the wrong way but knowing I had to let him know. If he didn't already. "Well, it's been a crazy month. I need some time, patience, but I'd like to maybe …" I stopped talking when a woman stepped outside the drugstore, huge glasses on and familiar red hair.

Thomas unstuck his eyes from me and looked over.

Amelia glanced at us, then dug around in her purse for something.

When Thomas still didn't look at me, I followed his gaze to where she'd stopped, talking on the phone a little farther down the street.

Thomas smirked at her, making her bristle.

"You know her?" I asked.

"Oh, she wishes I didn't." Thomas took a step forward, his hand settling over my hip. "Listen, I was supposed to arrange this with you yesterday." My thoughts gathered and dissipated, too distracted by his touch. It was the first time he'd held me, even if it was a loose hold, and he did so to bend down and whisper, "Meet me tonight, eight o'clock. There's a small bridge in Glenning that runs over the creek."

"I know the one." My eyes shot to his.

Seeing the questions in them, he rushed to say, "Not for that. I heard what you said, even if I already knew." A sigh left him. "But still, we have much to talk about."

His scent rolled into my nostrils as he leaned in, his lips gliding over my cheek. I listened to the sound of his drawn-out inhale, felt the way shivers wracked down my spine, and watched as he stepped away and walked by the drugstore where Amelia had been standing moments ago.

The time on the dash read 7:15.

Thomas's words had nestled deep inside my brain, unwilling to budge, not after he'd said we had much to talk about. Reasons as to why we had to meet in such a place, at that time, flitted through my mind, then left without a trace as I cast them all aside as ridiculous.

I didn't understand, and the only way I could was to meet him there.

I realized then, as I made sure I kept watch on the time, that I must've trusted him. At least enough to meet him where the water's shallow but loud, and darkness falls heavy.

As I gazed back out the window to the house where I'd spent months making memories, making dreams, and making excuses, that gnawing, acidic taste of my heart's pain returned, filling my mouth and my eyes.

It was time to say goodbye.

Miles's truck was in the drive, and I leaped from my car, quickly sliding the envelope that contained my false happily ever after into the green mailbox before the sorrow had my hands latching onto it, desperate for hope, for any longer.

Back in the car, my hand poised over the keys in the ignition, the tsunami of grief for what-if, for what could've been, rocked me. After all our time together—the good and the bad and the beautiful—this was how I was going to leave it?

No.

That wasn't me. I might have been foolish in blindly trusting a man who always seemed so far out of my reach, but I wasn't a coward. I unclipped my seat belt, wrenched open the door, and plucked the envelope out of the mailbox.

The porch light flickered on as I raised my hand to knock. Noticing the door was ajar, my hand fell to my side as I took a step forward.

"… may be so, but I'm your fucking wife. Don't I get a say?" a woman shouted, her voice, her pain, barreling down the hall to escape the cracked open door and lock my feet in place.

"I'm tired, Milo. Tired of the lies, of feeling like I'm losing you every week you spend with that child. You're getting nowhere anyway. Please, just go back to HQ and end this."

Milo?

Tears of desperation coated every word she hollered, but I definitely wasn't hearing things.

Torn, I looked back at my car, at the street, only just seeing the black SUV parked a few houses down.

"No, fuck that. You knew. You *knew* what this would involve."

My mind screamed at me to go, to leave. It'd connected the most important dots, but my heart was still unable to comprehend such insanity.

So I pushed the door open and walked inside.

Miles, or Milo, growled, "You fucking pushed me into this as much as Anthony, Shell. And don't you dare say you didn't." I'd never heard him sound so angry, so upset, but that didn't stop my feet from carrying me down the hall to the living room. It was what he said next that did that. "I told him we should leave her alone. We didn't need to go this far, and you disagreed. And now that we have, that I have, you're compromising everything by being here."

The envelope slipped from my hand, fluttering to the tiled floor. The floor we'd never got around to buying rugs for. The dining table mocked me from where it sat next to the window that faced the backyard, waiting to one day be expanded for more visitors.

And as they saw me standing there, right outside the living room, the audacity to look shocked by my presence, it was apparent I was the visitor here.

Amelia, or Shell, cursed and glared with wet eyes before storming right past me, the front door slamming in her wake.

"Jem," Miles rasped, his expression one of utter terror.

"I came by to …" I stopped, blinking down at the ground to where the envelope sat and made a gesture to it. "Yeah."

Then I turned and raced out the door. Miles's feet slapped against the tiles as he came after me.

With my keys already in the ignition, I peeled out without even checking for cars and battled the urge to throw up the whole way back to my apartment.

CHAPTER
Twenty-Two

H AULING MY DUFFEL DOWNSTAIRS, I THREW IT INTO the trunk as tears clouded my vision.

Milo.

Lies.

That child.

Everything became clear yet was still so fucking unclear at the same time.

Why? Why would he lie to me, and why would she and this other Anthony person encourage him to?

Headlights illuminated my trunk as I rearranged my bags, then shut it.

A door slammed as whoever it was that'd pulled up behind me got out, and I took that as my cue to get the hell gone.

Before I could close the door, I was hauled out of my car, a scream stuck in my throat.

"We need to talk. Now."

"Miles, let go." He slammed my door shut, and I struggled as he maneuvered me to the sidewalk. "I swear to God, I'll knee you in the junk again."

He chuckled, but the sound was dry and unfamiliar. "You can try, Jem. But I'm prepared this time."

"Seriously, let me go before I scream for someone to call the cops."

He lowered his lips to my ear. "I'm a federal agent, so that'll do you no good and only waste our fucking time." I stopped struggling and stared up at him in disbelief.

Remorse filled his eyes. "I'll explain, but we need out of sight. Unlock the door, please."

When I just stood there, not entirely sure I shouldn't elbow him in the ribs and make a run for it, he whispered, "I'll never hurt you," he paused, "not physically. But I need to keep you safe, and I can't do that if you don't at least hear me out." His cheeks puffed as he blew out a breath. "I can get in a lot of shit for telling you this stuff, so please believe me when I say I'm only trying to help you." He swallowed. "Because despite what you might think after everything, after whatever you heard, I do love you."

I unlocked the door, and he followed me upstairs and inside my closed up, lonely apartment.

Needing to sit down, I waited on my couch as he flitted about my apartment, plucking things out of cupboards, a fake potted fern on the windowsill, and then disappeared into my room.

Joining me in the living area, he opened the window, and I saw a blur of black sail through the air, the window locking before I could hear where they landed.

"Bugs," he said, then took a seat on the Ikea coffee table in front of me. It groaned beneath his weight, and he cursed, shoving it back and taking a seat on the ground instead.

"Bugs," I said the word over and over before finally acknowledging the obvious truth. "You planted them in my apartment?" The pieces kept clicking together, like a puzzle that suddenly warped in your mind's eye, and your fingers couldn't collect the pieces fast enough.

Miles waited, apprehension stamped all over his face.

My voice hitched over the words. "You're undercover."

A nod was his answer.

"You're married," a broken whisper.

Another nod.

I knew it then, that my initial wonder over this worldly, rugged, older man was for a reason. "It didn't make sense," I admitted with a self-deprecating laugh. "Your sudden and intense interest in me."

He dragged his hands down his face. "I wasn't, at least, not at first." As his hands dropped to his lap, his eyes glistened, and then he smiled. "But you grew on me pretty quick, Jem-Jem."

"Don't," I croaked. "Don't call me that. Your job, god, was anything real?"

"You and me, we were real, and yes, I did do some side landscaping jobs when I could. And you know I worked at the school."

Time slipped by as we stared at each other, as I tried to come to terms with this new reality.

"Why?" It was all I could eventually settle on, and really, all that mattered at that point.

Miles, or Milo, didn't hesitate. It was as if he'd been waiting. Just itching to tell me. "Thomas Verrone has been a pain in our asses for some time now. We couldn't catch a break. And then you, someone he was showing a great deal of interest in, applied for a teaching position at his daughter's prep school."

My heart sank. "You …"

He nodded once more. "I'm sorry, Jem."

I wouldn't have gotten that position. It was all setup. Invisible strings being pulled behind the scenes. "How?"

"One of our guys made it happen with a few fake endorsements." His head ducked. "And, well, a donation."

He let that sit there, and I let it bruise, but then I raised my shoulders and swallowed down the tears when I remembered the name for all of this. "Thomas," I said. "You're after him?"

"Have been for a while, but the bastard is too clever." Miles licked his lips. "We were never supposed to put you in this kind of danger." He croaked out a laugh. "Quite the opposite, in fact. Not long before you applied for the job, we found out he was watching you."

I knitted my brows. "Watching me?"

"He'd been doing some digging. Your family's farm, where you attended college, where your sister lived … and probably much more. You were a sitting duck, applying for jobs at the time and apartment hunting, so we made the decision to step in. To try to keep you safe as we watched and waited to see what he'd do while we continued with the investigation."

"You wanted to catch him? By using me?"

"No. But in a sense, if he were to try something, and you were under our watch, then we'd be able to act fast. We could keep you safer than if you'd been on your own, and maybe get closer to him. Two birds, one stone."

Fear skittered over and down my shoulders, and I clenched my hands together to quell any shaking from starting. "Keep me safe? What would he have done?"

Miles searched my gaze, hesitating.

"I can handle it. It's what you're here to tell me, isn't it?" My voice cracked from both trepidation and frustration. "So, tell me exactly why I'm in danger, and why you're doing all this."

"He's a murderer, Jem."

Bile gurgled up my throat in an instant. Images of Thomas's lips on mine, of his hands touching my face, of his scent, his rare smile, invaded and made my head pound. "What …? He …?"

Miles cursed and came to sit beside me, but the touch of his skin on my hand only further intensified the turbulence inside my stomach. "There are whispers of the things he does but never any proof. They call him The Sculptor."

My eyes shut, ears ringing. "Why?"

"Jem, you don't need to know that. You know enough to know he's danger—"

"*Why?*" I yelled, surprising him and myself.

"Okay." Miles raised his hands. "Okay." He drew in a breath, then nodded, as if confirming with himself that I could handle it. "He's … his victims, if they live, are scarred or disfigured. He's known to torture some of them, Jem."

Hearing him use my name in the same sentence he used to describe those horrors had me reaching my limit.

I raced, barely making it in time to the kitchen sink, heaving and retching and spitting, but nothing exited my stomach.

"I suppose it's stupid to ask if you're okay." Miles stopped beside me and laid a hand on my back. "I'm sorry, so fucking sorry for bringing you into this shit."

Tears spilled, my chest heaved, and I turned on the tap, splashing water into my mouth and onto my face. "You're sorry." I rounded on him. "Jesus, you asked me to be your wife, and you already fucking had one!"

Miles stood frozen, and if I could have seen out of the haze burning my eyes, I'd see the one burning his own. "I wasn't supposed to fall for you. But after that first time, here in this apartment with your fucking Care Bear watching …" He sniffed, chuckling. "It became real. It became all that mattered, believe me, and it screwed everything up."

I believed him. Even though he'd ripped my world out from beneath me with his lies, I heard his truth.

"I get that this is a lot to take in, but we need to talk about what happens now, Jem."

"I never asked for this," I mumbled, ignoring him.

"I know. Fuck, I know."

I'd always thought these things existed only on TV. In books. Inside nightmares. Never even once did I think the realities that people swore were real would invade my cozy, safe little life.

"What do I do?" I wheezed, raking shaky hands through my hair. "What the fuck do I do now? He ..." I stopped.

Thomas.

The bridge over the creek.

He thought I was meeting him. A glance at the old clock, the one my dad insisted on hanging in my kitchen, told me it was five past eight.

A killer was waiting for me.

"He what, Jem?" Miles tugged my wrists, taking my hands away from my hair, and I noticed dark strands had woven between my fingers. "Talk to me."

I couldn't. A boulder made of every emotion imaginable had wedged in my throat, and it was all I could do to breathe. I looked around my kitchen, at my apartment, not knowing what to do.

Home.

I had to go home. Where there were guns and miles of land. Where Thomas Verrone was supposedly waiting for me.

I couldn't think about that. He wasn't Hercules. He couldn't stop a moving car, and I couldn't stay here.

"Lou Lou." Her name left my lips without my brain even sending the signal, my heart squeezing painfully tight. "Oh, god. He has a daughter."

Miles's brows pinched, and he ran a finger over his chin. "She seems okay, and school records don't state any concerns for her well-being." He muttered what sounded like, "Clever bastard," again. "But ... she's not his."

"What?"

"We don't have proof exactly, but I think she's the daughter of one of his victims."

Jesus-someone-stop-this-crazy-train-Christ.

I stormed past him, intent on getting out of here, and yanked my keys from the door. I needed anywhere that wasn't stagnant, that didn't further increase the panic biting at my insides.

"Jem!" Miles called and grabbed my hand out in the stairwell. "Shit, wait. Where are you even going?"

"Home," I said over a rising sob. "I need to go home."

He cursed again, climbing down the steps until he was on the one below me. "I've got you, Jem." His eyes begged mine to trust him, but I couldn't. I couldn't trust anyone in this world I'd blindly walked into. "Come home, and I'll speak to my superior. Worst-case scenario, we'll get you set up in protective—"

"Oh, my god." A bout of laughter gurgled. "Oh, my fucking god," I cried and wiped beneath my eyes. "This is insane." The words were drawn out, my hands still shaking, keys rattling, as I dug my palms into my eyes.

Miles tried to pull me against his chest, but I pushed him away, almost sending him down the last four steps. "I'm going, and don't you dare try to stop me, *Milo*."

With that, I ran out into the night and climbed into my car. Adrenaline spiked through my veins and fueled my drive home.

Miles's truck followed me, but once I'd turned onto the long rock and dirt paved drive that led up the hill to my childhood home, he turned back.

CHAPTER
Twenty-Three

DAD FOUND ME IN THE BARN THE NEXT MORNING, cursing as I reloaded the barrel of the rifle.

"What's this about?"

"Life," I said, closing the casing and staring at my dad's sun weathered face.

"You look like you're nine years old again, running home after seeing a snake in the back field."

The memory had my shoulders rising with a huff. If only it were as simple as one deadly snake.

You could outrun a snake, shoot it, or lob off its head with a shovel. But the kind of snake that'd infiltrated my life, filled it with poison, and caused everything to turn inside out—a kernel of fear inside said there'd be no stopping him.

Didn't hurt to try, though.

I stared back at the holes marring the haphazardly hung paper. Paper that was worn from years of sitting on a dusty barn shelf. "I'm okay. Just trying to expel some stuff, I guess."

I couldn't tell him. Not when I was certain I wasn't even supposed to know. Retired cop or not, I didn't think that mattered when it came to federal investigations.

"Here," Dad said, taking me by the shoulders. "Square your feet more, that's it."

I breathed in, pictured Thomas's face—those eyes—and the

tremors that shot through my hand steadied as I took aim at the bales of hay where the paper bull's-eye hung.

I exhaled slowly.

You simply unnerve me, Little Dove.

I squeezed the trigger.

And missed by three inches.

The bullet shot through the wood at the back of the barn, and Dad clucked his tongue. "You never did master the art very quick." He moved behind me, hand on my lower back. "Cradle it like it's a fucking baby, Jemmie."

Trying to outsmart the burning in my eyes, I shifted my hold and steadied my breathing. My heart slowed to a steady pound in my ears.

Scared and battered, but *still beating*.

"That's it." With his hand still on my lower back, he said gently, "Inhale, good. Finger ready, two-thirds of the way out. Easy."

I took aim, exhaling as he said to.

I've got you, Jem-Jem. I swear.

Gently, I squeezed.

Bull's-eye.

Hay rained over the barn, the paper shredded and fluttering to the ground.

"Fuck yeah." Dad laughed. "But you're cleaning that up, Jemmie."

The sound of tires crunching over dirt had me running out of the kitchen to the porch.

I slipped on my flip-flops as Miles pulled up in his truck and jumped out.

Correction, *Milo*.

The screen door squeaked as Dad opened it to investigate behind me. "Shit's sake. Want me to shoot him? Or have you been practicing for this particular moment?"

Holding back a snort, I gently nudged him back inside. "It'll be fine. I'll just send him away."

He grumbled, rubbing his hands on a rag. "You'd better." He shut the door.

"Jem," Milo said, eyes red rimmed and wearing the same clothes as the night before.

I walked down the steps, making him follow me to his truck, out of earshot.

"What are you doing here?"

He frowned at my hissed tone, then whispered back, "I'm here to take you some place safe."

"I don't need your protection, *Milo*." My tone changed, dragging out his real name, but I found no joy from it when he flinched. "You're the one who got me into this mess. Leave me be. Despite what your wife said, I'm not a child."

A wrinkle deepened his brow, his rough voice hinting at his frustration. "I know you're not, but what I told you was no fucking joke. You think we'd upend someone's life this way for no good reason?"

I crossed my arms. "Were you going to leave your wife before you set a date for our wedding?"

"Jem, come on."

I ran the toe of my flip flop through the dirt. "Just answer the question."

"I told you, after that first night, it all became real, but Shelley…"

"Shelley," I echoed, as if saying her name would make this more real and less of a nightmare.

"It's hard. We've been together since high school—"

"Wait, so you never even had that pregnancy scare in high school."

He shook his head. "That happened to a friend." My eyes tingled as he continued, "Shell's been my best friend for most of my life, and I knew, I knew that I couldn't keep you both, and I told her that. She's …" He groaned, a hand slicing through his hair. "Complicated, and willing to put up with more than most other women are, so she doesn't give in easily, if ever."

"You have that right," I said. "So it was her you slept with." I didn't want to know, but I had to. "You slept with her more than once, didn't you? You would have, she's your wife."

He said nothing, and that said it all.

Inhaling a burning breath, I turned the tears off. "This is so messed up. You know that, right?"

"I'm going to fix it. It'll be just you and me, I swear. But first—"

I laughed, dry and shallow, shaking my head as I muttered, "Such an asshole."

"Jem, please listen. We're not the monsters here." He threw a quick glance at the house behind me, then lowered his voice. "I've spoken with my superior, and he's agreed we need to get you into protective custody. Until then, you're coming back to the house with me."

"The house you paid for or taxpayers?"

He cursed. "Does it matter?"

"Considering I lived there for months, yeah, it kind of does. No wonder you wouldn't let me pay the mortgage." I laughed bitterly. "Oh, wait, should I thank you for not just taking my money anyway?"

"Curb the sass, Jem, and get in the fucking truck." When I made no effort to move and merely raised my brows, he came forward. "Fine. I'll fucking take you myself."

My fists slammed into his granite back as he tossed me over his shoulder as if I weighed nothing. I screamed, kicking and punching as he threw open the back door and pulled a pair of handcuffs from his pocket.

Then I screamed louder.

The sound of a gunshot sliced through the air, pelting the dirt near Milo's sneakers, and rendered everything silent. Even the wildlife.

"Fucking hell." Milo almost dropped me as he released me, eyes huge as Dad marched over with a loaded shotgun.

I stumbled back toward the house. "I don't know what kind of hellhole you crawled out of, son, but I never trusted your slimy ass." Dad fired again when Milo made to walk around the truck, then froze, arms rising into the air. "You touch her again, and I'll blow your hands clean off."

"I'm going," Milo said, his chest heaving as he backed toward the truck door. "But Jem, please. For just a second, forget about everything else and think about this. You know I'm not lying to you." He climbed in and shut the door, motioning with his hand for me to call him.

"The hell is he talking about?" Dad asked, gun still aimed at the truck as Milo threw a three-point turn in front of the garage.

I inhaled through my nose and set one truth free. "He's just a cheating scumbag."

Dad shot at the truck, knocking out the right taillight. Milo swerved for a second before righting the truck and speeding off down the hill to the road. "Well, hopefully that'll get the asshole a ticket before he gets it fixed."

Dad's laughter trailed behind him as he squeezed my shoulder and went back inside.

Two days passed before my phone pinged with a text from Milo, saying there was an envelope waiting for me at the grocer just outside the city limits. The one the few residents of Glenning, and the surrounding rural towns, used when they didn't want to venture into the concrete jungle.

I ignored it, shoved my phone aside, and tried to continue reading. When that failed, I cleaned the house, wiping dust from places my dad either didn't see or chose to ignore and then vacuuming.

By late afternoon, my hair was sweat soaked, and I needed a shower.

Afterward, I slipped on a peach-colored cotton dress that I hadn't worn since high school and tossed my hair into a ponytail. A glance in the mirror displayed thinner arms and legs, the bones of my cheeks stark, and my eyes big against the harsher planes of my face.

I hadn't been eating well, but that was hard to do when my stomach had been in a constant knot for the past two months.

In the mirror, my phone haunted me as my eyes snagged on it.

I was safe, I kept repeating to myself. I was home, and it was hard to imagine such ugly things would reach me here.

My eyes shut against the memory of blue and red flashing lights. The cop car that'd pulled up in front of our house. My dad's colleague and friend, Bill, delivering the news about my mother, who'd died just a couple of miles from our driveway.

That child.

Curbing a frustrated scream, I grabbed my phone, purse, and keys, then told Dad I was heading into town.

Even though it was due to close soon, the little brown shop was bustling, waves of heat still crawling over the gravel lot.

I parked between a truck and a Beetle and climbed out, wiping sweat from my brow.

The sun was setting, orange and purple painting the sky, and still, there was no reprieve.

Inside, Honey, the woman who owned the shop with her husband, smiled from ear to ear when she saw me, then glanced at the register, plucking a white package from beside it.

"You tell your daddy he still owes Earl a case of beer." She eyed me, waiting until I smiled before releasing her hold on the envelope. Its light weight poked holes into my hand, and I knew. It would give me the details about what happened next.

Just as well.

I grabbed some gum and slapped a five down on the counter. "Will do, Hon. Thanks."

Before I could leave, she called out, "That man who dropped it off, he yours?"

Needles lunged for my chest, but I chased them away with a carefree smile. "No."

I waved goodbye as she tsked, and said, "Damn shame."

What a shame, indeed, to realize he never really was mine. To realize that the life I'd been living for the past year, none of it, was meant to be mine.

Hunger arrived as I was about to turn out onto the road that'd take me back home, and I turned the opposite way, hitting the drive-through before it left me again.

Chewing on my second cheeseburger and staring out the dust-grimed windshield to the highway beyond, I thought about texting Milo back. To let him know that I'd gotten his precious envelope.

That I wasn't a child.

Chucking the crumpled wrapper onto the passenger seat where said envelope lay, I decided against it and turned the ignition over.

I was sure either he or one of his cronies would check in with Honey.

The thought of leaving my life, as false and fucked up as it'd been lately, made my hands clench tight around the steering wheel in defiance.

How long would it be for? What would they tell my dad? Would he be safe if I left? What about Hope, Jace, and the boys?

If they'd gone this long without gathering enough intel on Thomas, who's to say they ever would? *I'd be holed up forever*, I concluded as I thought of Thomas.

Conniving, careful, calculating Thomas.

Then again, holed up forever was better than dead.

Who knew, perhaps some time away from all this would do me some good. It could help me figure out how to start fresh.

As soon as the thought hit, the bridge where I was supposed to meet Thomas loomed ahead. My headlights glowed a dull orange until I flicked on the high beams, then I screamed.

A familiar black car was parked across it, blocking entry to the road beyond. I slammed on the brakes, the tires skidding, then immediately put the car into reverse, attempting to back up and turn around, when I screamed again.

Another car had pulled up behind me, right before the bridge. I didn't even remember seeing someone following me.

There was no way out.

The screaming of my heart drowned out the screams that left my mouth as I fumbled, reaching across the passenger seat for the glove compartment where I'd stored a handgun just three days ago.

Once in my hand, I turned and aimed at the person opening

the door. The tall figure, swathed in darkness, knocked it from my hands in one quick sweep, then hauled me from the vehicle as if I hadn't just eaten my body weight in cheeseburgers and fries.

There was no time for begging, only doing. And so I wriggled, my legs kicking as he wrapped his arms around my midsection and lifted me from the ground.

The sight of Thomas leaning against his car, wearing his usual suit and blank expression, sent a fresh wave of strength careening through me, and I used it to drop my head down, then quickly slammed it back into my kidnapper's face.

He cursed, grunting as he dropped me, and I tripped around Thomas' car, leaping over the rocks by the creek before running into the forest.

Quiet.

Nothing but deathly quiet. Nothing but me and the sound of my feet snapping over twigs and scuffing over rocks, and my labored breathing as I pushed myself harder, farther into the unfamiliar terrain.

Then another sound.

His voice, echoing through the trees as though he had all the time in the world. As though he was walking languidly, lazily strolling behind me, uncaring of the fact I could get away. "You may as well stop, Jemima. We both know it's useless."

I would've scoffed if I didn't have better things to do. Like trying to stay alive.

I felt him getting closer.

Impossible, I thought.

Too busy tossing a glance into the gloom behind me, I tripped over a fallen, hollowed out tree trunk.

This wouldn't be how it ended.

My ankle panged in protest, and I forced myself onto my

hands and knees. The sound of leaves and twigs crunching filtered into my panicked brain, and my stomach heaved.

Before I could stand, a hand wrapped around my elbow, wrenching me from the damp, mildew-scented earth. In a blur of frantic movement, I acted on instinct, raising my knee to his crotch as I spun, then stumbled away when his hand fell loose.

Again, I ran.

I ran, ignoring the pain in my ankle, the fear that had me wanting to bang my head against one of the ancient trees to wake up from this nightmare, and I ran from the pain in my heart.

I ignored it all and smiled when I saw the headlights of a lone passing car through the curtain of trees and foliage.

I could make it. I could run home or at least run along the road until someone passed.

Air escaped me in a rush, and a shriek left me as a sharp bite penetrated my skin.

"Fuck," I whimpered, reaching around to pluck what looked like a dart from the back of my arm. With my heart trembling, even as it slowed, I staggered back into a tree trunk, warmth spreading from the stinging prick, steadily oozing into every limb of my body.

Losing control of my legs, I fell to my ass. Hard. Yet I couldn't feel it.

I couldn't feel a thing as I stared up at the sky, searching for the moon, for one last source of light.

I found it, clung to it as my breathing slowed and my vision frayed.

"I told you it was useless."

The moon disappeared, his calm words following me into the dark.

CHAPTER
Twenty-four

I STARTLED AWAKE, A LOUD INHALE SCRAPING MY LUNGS AS I blinked into darkness.

My head felt like it weighed a ton as I tried to sit up, but I couldn't move.

And it wasn't only because of whatever drug swam through my body.

Blood ceased to flow, my lurching stomach dragging my heart into its roiling depths as I discovered why.

My wrists and ankles were bound to a chair that seemed like one I'd sat in at the dentist.

The scent of Lysol and bleach coated the air I struggled to breathe as I drew in heaving gasps. Panic sliced sharp and deep, and I shut my eyes, trying to calm my frantic heart.

Opening them, I tried to raise my head again, getting a quick look at the fastenings around my wrist, but nothing else. My head fell, my body too weak to do anything but lay there and give in.

An overhead light flickered on, a dull orange that assaulted my retinas and caused my heart rate to soar even higher. Which almost scared me more than the man who'd turned it on.

"Good, you were starting to worry me. You shouldn't have been out for that long."

Waxy film covered my mind and the events that'd transpired,

that led to me lying here, unable to move, while a monster stood over me with furrowed brows.

"Worry?" I asked, the word husky. I swallowed, trying to rid the cotton-like residue coating my dry mouth.

Thomas nodded, reaching behind him to pull a stool over. The screech and drag of its wheels hinted the floor was hard. Wood or concrete. A puff of air escaped the cushioned seat as he lowered onto it and scooted close. "You shouldn't have been out any longer than an hour or two. The sedative was mild." He looked over his shoulder, into the shadows, pondering something. "Perhaps you have a lower tolerance, being that you've never been under much toxic influence in your life."

I ignored the obvious, that he'd dissected personal facets of my life, that his poison ran deeper than I could've anticipated, and focused on what mattered. "Are you going to kill me?" Was it better to know or to wonder? I clearly needed to know. "Is that why you were watching me, looking into me?"

"I figured they'd found out about that." Thomas twisted his lips in thought, then sighed. "You only have yourself to blame for being here, really."

"It's my fault?" I laughed out, the sound aggravating my sore throat.

Another nod. "Among other things, you took an interest in me. Others usually know what I am without knowing a thing and leave me well enough alone. Not you, though." His eyes gleamed, blue drowning out the white. "You don't know what that does to a man like me. A tiny smile, a tiny touch, one tiny kiss, a slew of questions, and it was only a matter of time before we ended up where we are now."

I'd known. I'd known since I'd first spoken to him that he was different, and I tried to tell him as much, but my lips pressed together in stubborn self-preservation.

God, it was a wonder I wasn't screaming. His words, my surroundings that were still hazy in the corners all struggled to map together. In the shadows, I briefly made out what looked to be an old fireplace and boxes stacked in a corner against the wall.

Thomas kept prattling on, either ignoring my turmoil or relishing in it. "Now, let's play a little game, shall we?"

The latter.

He reached behind him for something, and silver glinted beneath the weak light of the lamp that swayed above our heads. Tools. Weapons, maybe. I didn't need to see them all to know they weren't Halloween decorations.

"No, n-no." I shut my eyes, my thighs clenching together as the urge to pee barreled out of nowhere. "Thomas, please. Let me go. I'll—"

"Hush, Little Dove. You're in perfectly capable hands here." A ruffling met my ears, my eyes opening against the fear that longed to keep them shut. To shut everything off and disappear.

He flipped through what looked like pieces of paper on a clipboard. "Back to the matter at hand. The game is called true or false." He untucked a pencil from the top of the clipboard. "Quite basic. Let's begin."

"Begin?" I slur-shouted. "I never did *anything*. I didn't even know you were such a-a monster."

The pencil made a scratching noise. "That answers that question then. Next."

My hands clenched, sweat clammy and sticking to the inside of my palms. "Untie me, please."

"Not until we're done."

"Done?" I tried not to screech and failed.

With clinical detachment, he surveyed my body, then brought his eyes back to the clipboard. "Don't be so dramatic.

You're fine. I've had Murry fetch you some water and fruit to help you recover from your run in the woods."

Fruit? "What the fuck is going on?"

He sighed, the clipboard coming to rest on his knee. "I'm a patient man, Little Dove. But that patience only extends so far, especially after the past twenty-four hours." He leaned forward, his voice whisper soft but drenched in warning, "Start asking the questions that I know are blazing trails of fear through your beautiful brain, or things could start getting more difficult for you."

I didn't know how that was possible, but one look from the glowing menace in his eyes to the wall filled with glittering instruments had me swallowing and nodding. "Fine."

There was little else I could do anyway.

He waited.

Shit.

"I was told you're ..." I sniffed, licking my dry lips as he raised a brow, waiting. "That you've murdered people."

The pencil scratched the paper again as he surmised, "I'm guessing that was a recent discovery on your part."

"Yes," I said.

"True." Another scratch, which I guessed was him crossing out things on a list.

The way he freely admitted it had ice frosting my lungs.

I had to get out of there.

"I need to pee," I whined, my thighs bunching for emphasis. "Badly."

His nose scrunched with annoyance. "Your timing couldn't be worse, honestly."

After staring at me for a minute that seemed to eat at any reserves I had, he got up and undid my restraints.

Sitting up, I made to rub my wrist, where the scratchy

material had irritated, but his hand latched over it. The touch, gentle but firm, made my legs quake more than the residue of whatever he'd drugged me with, but I was somehow still thankful I didn't fall flat on my face as he steadied me.

Footsteps sounded on the stairs, and a man appeared, his back to us as he set a tray down. My mouth opened to scream at him, but some part of me quickly realized he worked for Thomas, and it'd be a waste of much-needed energy.

My tongue grew heavy and my head swam when I saw the water and neatly sliced pieces of fruit. I'd need all the energy I could get.

The man left, and Thomas walked me to the small workbench. I tried to ignore the faded smears and dents that decorated its once white surface while I gulped down the water from a small plastic cup.

"Easy, or you might get sick."

Surveying the room for windows, I found none and tried to wrench out of his hold.

Thomas tutted and tugged me toward a short hall that led to a tiny bathroom. There was an open shower, an old toilet, and the smallest sink I'd ever seen. No windows in there either, I noticed, as he released me and shut the door with a quiet snick.

I went for the cupboard beneath the sink. Locked, of course.

The urge to pee overrode desperation, and I used the toilet, thankful there was at least toilet paper. How humane of him.

After, I scrubbed my hands with soap, rinsing them as my eyes searched for anything that could help me up those stairs. There was nothing but a toilet brush, toilet paper, shower gel, soap, and a plug.

My eyes swung back to the toilet brush, and a knock

sounded on the door.

"Feel better?" Thomas asked as he opened it half a minute later.

I didn't wait. I leaped at him, knocking him off balance as he grabbed me and stumbled back to the floor.

Which was definitely concrete.

I winced, my elbow smacking into it as I held the plastic brush to his neck, trying to cut off his air supply.

He flipped me over in a heartbeat, the brush flying across the room with a clatter, and his eyes blazing as he laughed.

He fucking laughed.

Shocked by the rusty, musical sound, all I did was lay there, blinking up at him as my elbow panged. "Resourceful, Little Dove." Then came the anger. "But unfortunately, it'll cost you."

Still too dazed, I didn't even fight him, which made me simmer with self-loathing as he picked me up and laid me back on the chair.

His touch was gentle, but his skin vibrated with warning, a warning that said he wouldn't tolerate another attempt at freedom as he redid my restraints.

"We'll try again tomorrow." The light blinked out as he ascended the stairs above me. "Until then, Little Dove."

Alone in the dark, I was forced to get friendly with all the things I could ignore better during the light. So many things. So many obvious, taunting things.

It all circled back to Miles.

Milo.

What was his real last name?

A pinch of regret slid over my skin, seeping into weary

bones when I remembered the last time I saw him and how horribly it had all played out. As it sunk in with dirt-crusted claws that it could have been the last time he ever saw me.

I hated him, but some part of me hadn't stopped missing him, either. And it was in the confines of my captive's dungeon, or wherever the hell I was, that I let that knowledge spill down my cheeks.

Milo was a good man with good intentions. But good men were clearly still capable of breaking hearts and ruining lives. Would I ever get the chance to see him again? To say I was sorry, and that maybe one day, I could forgive him?

The memory of his wife dampened such fanciful notions.

Maybe Hope was right to make fun of me, I thought as I struggled to keep my eyes open as sleep tempted to take me away. Growing into a teenager, she'd dance out of my room, a roll to her hips and eyes as she said, "Fairy tales are for suckers, Jem. Time to get real."

"Get real," I whispered, the hoarse, wet sound echoing in the dark. "Well, this is about as real as it gets."

And so it wasn't being captured by a monster that broke the final piece of me.

It wasn't the fear, the worry, or the helplessness.

Inside my heart, among the bruised and battered tissue, there was a piece that still flickered bright with belief. That flicker then snuffed itself out, curled into the dark broken mess, and finally admitted defeat.

Fairy tales, those perfect happy endings, were indeed for suckers.

Suckers who could very well wind up dead.

The light clicked on. "Good morning, Dove."

I'd slept for what felt like days but had probably just been hours.

Movement upstairs had woken me a while ago. The floor creaking kept my eyes open even as I longed to return to my escape. A soft material slithered over me as I'd moved, checking to see if I was still restrained. A blanket. A knitted blanket had been draped over me at some point while I'd slept.

I wasn't sure whether to be thankful or perturbed by the fact someone had been here while I was asleep.

Then again, I was restrained in someone's basement or torture chamber. Having someone watch me sleep should've been the least of my worries.

Thomas, in one of his signature suits, his back facing me, tinkered with things that made a clanging sound over at one of his workbenches. "Sleep well?"

"Like a baby," I said, then tensed at my own audacity to spew such a bold lie.

Thomas didn't say anything.

My legs felt stiff, my mouth tasted foul, and my head was pounding. "Can … can I have a drink?"

Thomas turned, leaning back into the bench and crossing one foot over the other.

Slippers. He was wearing slippers.

"Are you ready to try our game again?"

"If it will grant me another trip to the bathroom, food, and water, then yes."

He grabbed his clipboard but opted to stay standing this time. For which I was grateful. I didn't want him that close again. "Whenever you're ready, Little Dove."

I'd had what felt like hours to mull over everything, so I was more than ready. In fact, I think I'd want to ask them even if he wouldn't give me what I wanted in return.

I started with, "Is it true what they call you?"

"And what would that be?"

"The Sculptor."

I was unable to make out his full expression when the light only shined on my little corner of the room, but nevertheless, I knew by his silence he was contemplating the question.

"Yes," he finally said.

Holy shit. "W-why?"

"Whys aren't on the list," he clipped.

"Bullshit," I blurted without thinking.

Thomas tutted. "Unnecessary. Next."

Thrown, I tried to pull my next question to the surface, then changed my mind and went for a different one. "Did you know they were investigating you?"

The pencil skittered over the paper on his clipboard. "I eventually figured it out."

He said it so casually as though he didn't even care. "That doesn't worry you?"

His eyes lifted, meeting mine. "Dove, it's not the first time, and it won't be the last. Next."

"Do you always kill your victims? How many have you killed?"

Another tutting sound. "That's two, but I'll let you bend the rules." He hummed. "I don't keep count. I used to. But after a while, it simply becomes boorish and tacky. And no, I don't always kill them. Murry, my assistant, is testament to that."

"The guy who brought me food?"

"Yes."

"You"—I cleared my throat—"what, hurt him?"

Thomas bobbed his head a little. "Quite a bit, yes. You'll see a glimpse for yourself soon enough."

BLOODSTAINED Beauty

Rage mingled with fear, burning hot through my veins. "You're a monster."

Thomas, writing something, paused, his shoulders lowering a fraction. "That's not a question. Next."

I didn't want to play anymore, but … my sweet girl with her golden curls and dimpled smile. "Lou Lou."

Thomas looked at me again, waiting.

"She's not yours?"

"That lousy fed of yours really did try to protect you, didn't he?" He scoffed, tossed his clipboard to the bench where it thwacked the wooden surface, then he grabbed his stool.

Taking a seat, he rubbed his hands together. "She's mine in every way that counts."

His words had tears pricking my eyes. Where were her parents? Wouldn't they miss her?

"Did you take her?"

"I did." The sound of his palms gliding against one another somehow soothed my increasing heart rate. "Lou was the daughter of a drug addict. This woman, Lou Lou's mother, was an important client's mistress for a time, but a decade ago, he fired her."

"Your client fired her?"

He nodded. "I cannot tell you specifics like names, so don't ask. But this woman, she did okay for a while and enjoyed her freedom with the money he gave her when they parted ways. But attracted to those with corruption in their veins, she soon met another man. A bottom of the barrel drug runner, apparently, who used her and her money, knocked her up, then got himself shot near the border a year after Lou was born."

My heart sank. "So she went back to your client?"

Thomas nodded again. "When Lou was two years old, she attempted to. She wouldn't stop, even as he turned her away time after time. She was older and wasn't as nice to look at anymore. Not after the drugs and harsher lifestyle had left their mark. And my client's new wife had zero tolerance for mistresses." He shrugged. "So he phoned me, and I took care of the problem."

Shivers bit into my skin. "Here?" When he said nothing, I tried again. "At her house?"

"Yes." Silence dropped like a heavy curtain, his expression giving nothing away. Then he continued, "I used to do many jobs like that, but since Lou arrived, I try to keep them to a minimum. It's a risk, being out in the open too often. I'm not behind bars for a few reasons, but it's mainly because I'm careful, and I do some of my work here." His eyes fell on me.

He did his work here, in the very chair I was stuck to.

"But how have the cops not found this place?"

"I'm a dentist by trade." When my brows rose, he smirked. "On paper, anyway. So, even if they got a warrant, they'd have a hard time finding concrete proof."

Bile coasted up my throat, and I dragged in a long breath through my nose, then exhaled slowly. "Lou Lou … keep going."

Knowing I probably needed the distraction, he did, "He was one of my first clients, and I tend to do favors for those who are loyal if the price is right. Even if the mark doesn't always deserve it. Lou's real name is Katie." A hint of a smile softened his words. "She waltzed out, more like waddled really, of the disgusting bedroom in the trailer where they lived, thumb in her mouth, huge innocent eyes, and just stared at me."

Tears pressed, and I tried to furiously blink them back.

Thomas seemed stolen by the memory, his voice soaked in nostalgia and obvious affection. "There I was, covered in her mother's blood, her mother outside in a body bag waiting to be taken away under the cover of darkness, and she said, "Want some milk?" She was two, almost three, and didn't give one single shit about who I was or what I'd done." He shook his head. "She was offering *me* something after I'd just taken her entire world away."

Hearing Thomas curse felt like a nail was softly running over my skin. Soothing, daring, and tantalizing.

"Then you took her?"

He sounded pained as he said, "No, I left her. For three whole days. Until the urge to go back and see if she'd been taken by authorities got the better of me. She was curled up asleep by the door, her curls tangled, and surrounded by food packaging." A husky tone carried his next words. "Then I took her home, told Murry I needed to see if she had any living relatives, and waited."

"No one," I guessed instantly. "She had no one else."

Thomas stood, heading for the water pitcher and cup. "I could've let her go into the system, but I was selfish. I knew I could give her a better, if somewhat unconventional, life."

He set the cup down on the bench closest to my head, then started undoing the cuffs around my wrists. I watched his eyes and the rigidness to his jaw as he swam adrift in a current of feelings I knew he wasn't well acquainted with before Lou Lou.

At that moment, I was too shocked, too thirsty, and too invested in Lou Lou's story to even think about fleeing.

Thomas helped me up, the chair moving with me, which was actually great, seeing as I had no energy to hold myself in a sitting position. Then he passed me the cup.

"Does she know?" I asked, taking small sips and letting the cool liquid pool on my tongue.

"She knows her mother is dead but not by my hands. And clearly, she doesn't remember her father."

After he undid my ankle restraints, I handed back the cup, flexing my fingers and my toes. "Does she think you're her real dad?"

"Yes. It's safer that way. She can attend school and live a normal life without questions arising. She won't ever need to lie about too much."

I wanted to ask what she did need to lie about, but my stomach growled, and Thomas pressed something high on the stairs behind me. A button, I noticed as I looked up.

The door opened a second later, and footsteps descended. That guy, Murry, placed another tray down, his voice deep and jovial as he said, "I'll be back with some cookies in a few."

Cookies? My confusion grew infinitely. But the smell of chicken and bread lured and almost had me launching off the chair. I knew I'd likely face plant, so I looked at Thomas.

Murry was gone before Thomas could walk over to collect the sandwich.

I chewed in silence, struggling with Thomas's warning about taking it slow as my taste buds came alive, and my hunger tried to snatch the food from my mouth and force it to my stomach.

"Does she know I'm here?" I asked, brushing my hands over the plate. Crumbs landed and scattered over the cream porcelain.

"Lou?" At my nod, he said, "Yes, she does. She thinks you're sleeping off a cold, that you have no insurance or help available from your family and need our help. She's excited to see you."

A hollow laugh left me after I'd swallowed the last bite of buttery chicken and bread.

Thomas reached over to the cup of water he'd refilled, and with strength I didn't know I had, I slammed the plate down on top of his head, then leaped from the chair.

Hearing him curse and groan behind me, I stumbled but quickly righted myself, latching onto the wooden railing and not looking back as I hauled myself up the stairs and into blinding light.

CHAPTER
Twenty-five

A KITCHEN GREETED ME.

A large kitchen with old oak cupboards, an island, and filled with the aroma of freshly baked cookies.

I paused long enough for my sight to adjust, and then raced across the white and black checkered floor to the screen door on the other side.

"Miss Clayton?"

Fuck.

I stopped, the door within reach and my heart slamming into my ribcage with the abrupt movement. Ignoring my shaky breath, the trembling of my limbs as adrenaline demanded I move, I mustered a smile. "Hey, Lou Lou."

Lou Lou shifted on her bare little feet and tugged at her white dress with red roses. "Where are you going? Are you feeling better?"

The sound of feet coming up the stairs had me backing up to the door.

But Lou Lou … her eyes, her dad, *this place.* Could I really just leave her there?

The door opened behind me, and a scream lodged in my throat as a man entered wearing a suit and an apron with printed words that read, *world's dodgiest chef,* stared down at me.

He had what looked to be a permanent smile etched into

his face. Twin scars met and ran from beneath his lips, curving around his mouth and cutting through his cheeks before stopping at the corners of each eye. My own eyes watched as his hand, which was missing an index finger, moved behind him.

Holy mother of hell.

My heart, which had been dancing like a trapped bird, stopped moving as the lock clicked on the door, and the panel beside it beeped. All traces of adrenaline fled with the sounds, and I tore my eyes away from the disfigured face. "I-I ..." I had no idea what to say.

"Murry," Lou Lou chirped. "This is my teacher."

Murry, with a hand at my back, gently directed me back through the kitchen toward the door I'd just burst through. I looked up at him, ignoring the scars, and pleaded with my eyes and a whisper, "No, please."

"Wanna come color with me, Miss Clayton?" Lou Lou asked. When all I did was blink at her, she looked at the open door. "Oh, is Daddy working?"

"He is," Murry said, stopping, then gave me a look that said, "What did you do?"

Thomas appeared in the dark at the top of the stairs, a finger pressed to his lips as he met Murry's and my gazes.

"Hey, Lou. Would you mind getting me the old cookbook with the French flag on the cover from the library?"

Lou Lou groaned. "But I'm hungry, and it's too far away."

Murry raised a brow. "You'll get your cookies after, I promise."

With that, she bounded out of the room, and Thomas moved out of the shadows, a look of pure annoyance on his face as he stared at me with a hand pressed to his bleeding head.

"What did you do?" Murry voiced, his tone curt.

My mouth hung open.

"She hit me over the head with a plate," Thomas answered for me. "And why didn't you close the door?"

"I was coming back with cookies." Murry groaned, his dark eyes filled with dismay. "From the cream set?"

Thomas winced, pulling his hand away and frowning at the blood. He rubbed it between his fingers, and my stomach heaved at the action. "Afraid so."

"And the status of the plate?"

My eyes zigzagged from Murry to Thomas.

"Don't worry about my head or anything, will you?" He rolled his eyes when Murry continued to wait for confirmation. "Dead."

Murry cursed up a violent storm beside me, and I slowly backed away, my ass connecting sharply with the countertop.

"They were vintage," he said, bending and tugging out a tray of cookies from one of two ovens. He tossed them to the stovetop with a clatter.

"Never mind the plates. I might need a stitch or two."

Murry sighed, then walked over to inspect Thomas's head. "Downstairs."

Dazed as hell by them just leaving me there, I watched as they walked into the dark.

The large door shut and locked behind them, and I noticed another panel beside it, high up on the wall. Intercom and a keypad. I assumed the door could only be unlocked with a code.

Fueled by the fact the hardest obstacle had been hurdled, I turned for the window at the sink. Outside of it, all I saw was dead grass, wildflowers, and an old dam surrounded by weeds. I checked but found it locked, then caught sight of my reflection as a cloud moved over the sun.

My hair stood at every angle imaginable. My eyes were smudged with old mascara and exhaustion, and as I looked down at my dress, I found it crinkled and ripped in places.

I looked like a wild animal, but Lou Lou didn't care, returning and thumping a book onto the counter. "Are you better now?"

"Um." I walked closer, smoothing down my hair as much as I could. "Much better, yes."

Her eyes were bright, unfettered happiness shining back at me. "Want a cookie?"

I glanced over at the tray, and the memory of the man who'd made them, his face, and the anger he no doubt felt toward me for breaking one of his plates had me saying, "I think we should wait. They might be a bit hot."

"Okay, come on then." She came and took my hand.

"Where are we going?" I asked as she dragged me from the kitchen. *This was good*, I told myself. I'd be able to explore a little and maybe find out where I was.

"Back to your room, silly." She peeked up at me, her tiny nose scrunched. "You really must've been sick."

"My room?" We entered a sprawling dining room, complete with a never-ending dark oak table, matching chairs, old artwork, and giant crystal chandelier.

"Yeah, Daddy said you're staying with us for a little while until you're all better, 'cause your daddy is old, and you don't want him to get sick." We exited the dining room and moved into what looked like a foyer. Lou Lou lowered her voice at the base of a gigantic, winged staircase. "'Cause old people can get sick easier and maybe die."

I smiled, somehow, and glanced behind me at the large front double doors. Another security panel was on the wall beside them, and there were numerous locks on the doors. I'd bet that every single one of them was latched into place.

Sighing, I let Lou Lou lead me upstairs.

She stopped where the stairs reached the second floor, and my eyes traveled up the remaining stairs as we walked away from them, wondering where they led.

We continued down a wide hall with polished marble floors, Lou Lou filling me in on all the fishing, coloring, and cooking she'd already done over the first three weeks of summer break.

Weeks. It was hard to believe life could change that drastically in such a short space of time. But I knew it to be true. I'd already discovered the hard way that, in an instant, your entire world might cease to exist, and you were left to traverse a new foreign one where nothing was ever the same.

Vases of wildflowers decorated mid-century styled hall tables. Faded oriental rugs ran the length of each hall. The place was like a museum. An old, classic home that was either restored to much of its vintage origins or had been expertly kept.

"Here it is," Lou Lou said, pushing open a door at the end of the hall.

The door opened to reveal a queen-size white bed, matching white linen, and matching armoire. Hesitantly, I walked in and spied my bags at the foot of the bed, zipped shut and taunting.

He'd taken my bags.

Someone had been to my father's house.

Lou Lou's comment about my dad had the rising nerves settling. He wouldn't. I didn't know why, but I knew he wouldn't have hurt my dad.

An arched window with vines covering half the panes was the only source of light. A small window seat sat below, and I ran my palm over the gray fabric covering it, longing for the one I had at home.

"You can see the woods from here," Lou Lou said, jolting me out of my musings and stabbing a finger at the glass as she climbed onto the seat.

"So you can," I said, taking in the treetops and the flock of birds that shot into the sky above them.

What I wouldn't give to be among those birds, taking flight, leaving all of this behind.

"Will you read my new book to me? Daddy said you like to read a lot." Lou Lou tugged at her ponytail, a small giggle drifting past rosy little lips. "And I said I already knew that, which made him smile."

"Oh, yeah?" I sat beside her, my sore muscles grateful for the reprieve.

"Yup. Daddy's usually always right, so when I'm right first, it makes him smile."

Smiling again myself, I reached over and tweaked her nose. "Grab me that book of yours, and we'll read."

She jumped up. "Okay."

I stood after she'd left, knowing my phone wouldn't be in my bag but wanting to check anyway.

I sank back down when she returned to the doorway with her hands on her hips. "Don't leave."

"I won't," I lied.

Lou Lou frowned as if able to sniff it out. "Promise?"

Surrender loosened my limbs, and I nodded solemnly. "I promise."

With a smile, she left, and I shifted my gaze to the window, my forehead meeting the cool glass.

For as many questions as Thomas had answered, new ones sprouted in their wake.

What kind of monster kills and tortures people, yet gives a little girl a much-needed home?

A complicated one.

CHAPTER
Twenty-Six

Thomas

"HONESTLY, MURRY. HOW LONG DOES IT TAKE TO glue two bits of skin together?"

"About one hundred and fifty times longer than it does to sever them," he shot back. "Be grateful you don't need stitches."

"Grateful," I grumbled beneath my breath, tension coiling tight in every muscle as Murry kept dabbing at the back of my damn scalp. The urge to shove away his none too gentle touch held strong, but the need to make sure I didn't have a gaping head wound won out.

I suppose I was grateful.

She was here.

In my house.

And she'd tried to kill me twice.

I smiled, and Murry, ever the perceptive, sensed it. "That kitten has claws."

"Much sharper than I thought," I surmised, inspecting the plate that was in pieces on the floor. My head pounded, but the volcanic blood coursing through my veins when I thought of her and that violent fear in her eyes distracted me.

"You want me to wake you tonight?"

"I'm not concussed."

"Done." Murry's hands disappeared, finally. "Let me look at your eyes, just to be sure."

"No." I stepped away and removed my jacket, which was covered in specks of blood.

Nothing new there. Except for it being mine instead of someone else's. "Any updates about the dad?"

After locking the first-aid cabinet, Murry walked into the bathroom, his voice rising over the sound of running water as he washed his hands. "He read the text sent from her phone about her road trip to Indiana to see an old high school friend. Judy received the phone this morning and is prepped in case he calls or texts her."

Judy worked for me and a few of my friends. She liked expensive things and loved the fact she only had to work simple jobs that sometimes only lasted ten minutes and didn't require her to open her legs to get paid handsomely.

"Is he worried?"

A pause preceded his return down the small hall. "Not overly. Delov said his guy tapped into a phone conversation that her dad made to the grocer and, apparently, to her ex, but he soon settled after that."

"The fed?" I asked, rage curling my fingers. My thumbs cracked my knuckles at the thought of the undeserving idiot. At the violence my hands longed to do to his smug face.

"He didn't answer the call, and I doubt her dad will try again now that he's not all that concerned. He apparently loathes the guy."

"Excellent. Make sure Judy returns the phone in a week." I took my jacket with me upstairs, Murry following a second later and marching straight to his cookies to inspect them. "And we need to replace the phones."

"I just did two weeks ago."

"Again. Order more, and have Sage and Beau do the same." I draped my jacket over the back of a stool. "They must've tapped in when I was discussing the Claytons with Beau. Even though it was last year, we can't afford to get sloppy." It had to be the calls as I'd done the rest of my digging in private, unfollowed, and over the span of the past several years. Never quite sure what to do with the family that took everything from me.

Murry's eyes shot to mine, and he nodded. "Makes more sense now, how she winded up playing house with him."

Humming, I took a cookie, chewing as I glanced around the kitchen, looking for any sign of my Dove.

"Do you think she's searching for another way out?" I asked as I opened the two-door fridge and yanked a bottle of water out.

"Doubtful with Miss Lou keeping her busy."

I drained half the drink bottle, the plastic crinkling. Giggling, faint but audible, sounded through the house, and my heart swelled.

"Besides," Murry said, eating a cookie as he placed several onto a plate. A disposable one this time. "There's no other way out. The only reason the kitchen door was unlocked was because I took the trash out." He put the disposable plates back inside a drawer. We kept them to feed visitors that needed to stay alive, and who most definitely couldn't be trusted with porcelain. "I'll be sure to lock it and take keys next time."

"Ensure you do." I had faith in my Little Dove, but I'd failed to remember she didn't do well locked in a cage. "Let's hope she knocks it off soon." I set the bottle down on the counter.

Murry snorted, halting my journey out of the kitchen to the sound that was tugging me toward the stairs. "You're overly optimistic about this situation."

"Your point?" My tone was cold.

Murry was used to it by now and continued as he placed the rest of the cookies inside a weird looking glass jar. "I'm not trying to upset you. I'm just being honest when I say I think it'd be wise to remember what you are." His eyes rose, three fingers falling to the countertop as he leveled me with the full effect of what I'd done to him. "Remember that not everyone, in fact, hardly anyone, will be accepting of that."

Backtracking, I took the cookies from the counter and tried to leave his words behind.

I was unsuccessful. They haunted my every step, plagued my mind with terrible what-ifs, and threatened to darken the spark that resided in my chest.

The one she'd placed there.

She couldn't extinguish it. It wasn't in her nature, claws or not. But I knew all too well that she could leave, sooner rather than later, and that might be the last I ever saw of her.

My thoughts fled at the sight of the two girls curled up together on the window seat, Lou Lou smiling and pointing at the page of a book they were reading.

I didn't want to disturb them.

I wanted to join them.

And though I knew Jemima wouldn't like it, I still tapped on the open door.

She looked over, and the smile that'd transformed the beauty of her face into perfection wilted as she ducked her head.

It hurt worse than having a plate slammed over my head. "I have a delivery for you."

"Cookies!" Lou rushed me, almost sending them to the rug covered floor with her excitement.

"One minute. Have you washed your hands?"

Lou scowled but didn't even try to lie. She left the room to use the bathroom down the hall. "Do it twice," I called.

She groaned.

"Twice?" my Dove spoke.

Moving into the room, I set the plate down on the white armoire, then took a seat on the bed. "She's got a hamster. Too many germs."

"Clinkers," Jemima said. "She brought him in for show and tell once."

"That one is dead," I said before thinking, then rushed to add, "but I replaced it before she noticed. And he is actually a she, but Lou hasn't figured that out either."

Jemima smiled. Then, as if reminded she shouldn't, she turned her attention out the window.

Sitting in the silence, I listened for the patter of little feet, but heard none.

"Is your head okay?" Her voice was strained as though she didn't want to ask but something had compelled her to.

"Nothing Murry couldn't fix with a little glue."

She looked back at me. The sunlight highlighted the tangles in her usually glossy hair, the smudges beneath her eyes, and put her turbulent emotions on full display.

And still, she was the most beautiful thing my eyes ever had the pleasure of viewing.

"If you're not going to hurt me, why am I here?"

"Because I wanted you to be here." I struggled to keep her gaze as I admitted, "I needed you to know more and to see you before your fed took you away."

Her brows puckered, pink lips parting. Questions arose in her dark eyes. Questions she visibly casted aside with a shake of her head, then asked, "When can I leave?"

The sound of Lou's feet thundering down the hall made me shut my mouth, hide my disappointment, and rise from the bed.

"Whenever you like. My only request is that you come find me before you do."

Her eyes shot up to mine, confusion darkening them.

"Lou." Catching her as she tried to barrel past me to the cookies, I tilted her chin and ran my palm over the silken curls of her hair. "Make sure you share and don't pester. Miss Clayton needs lots of rest and food after being unwell."

"Of course, Daddy."

With one last look at Jemima, who was biting her nail as she stared at me, I forced myself from the room. It was the last thing I wanted to do, but too much at once was never good when someone was acclimating to a new environment.

CHAPTER
Twenty-Seven

COME FIND ME BEFORE YOU DO.

It was a trick. A carefully veiled trick.

He knew I would struggle to willingly seek him out after all that'd happened. He also knew that I was more confused than ever before.

And that was how I spent the next day holed up in my room, showered, changed, fed, and somewhat rested.

Lou had joined me whenever she could but was called away every few hours to help Murry, practice piano with her dad, or do regular things like take a bath, eat lunch, and get ready for bed.

Such normal things in such bizarre company.

It was as though Thomas didn't want her presence overwhelming me too much but couldn't exactly stop her from seeing me. I was glad for it. To see her and to have time alone. Even if both only further complicated everything I was feeling.

Lou brought puzzles, coloring books, and even Clinkers to my room.

But by eight thirty, any proof that she was still this side up of dreamland vanished, the house turning eerily quiet as nightfall descended.

He came to me then.

Clad in his suit and with his hair swept back in its usual

perfection without a strand out of place, he strolled in, shut the door, and sat on the bed.

Watching from my preferred perch by the window, I tracked his every move as he leaned forward, his hands clasping together between his knees, and his eyes lowered to his slippers. His jacket was undone, gaping open to reveal what looked like a small notebook tucked inside one of the inner pockets.

Was that some fucked-up ledger? I snorted at the thought and returned my attention to the moonlit trees.

"How are you feeling?" he asked.

The silence that'd arrived with his presence was one so violent that the ticking of the old grandfather clock in the hall could be heard through the thick wood of the bedroom door. "Fine."

"Little Dove," he started.

"Don't call me that."

Silence again. Then a few ticks later, "But that's what you are."

My gaze swung to him, sharp and accusing.

He didn't even flinch, but his eyes lifted, and the honest shine to them almost blinded me as much as his next words. "That's what you are to me."

"I don't want to be," I said, not knowing if it was exactly true but wanting it to be. Desperately.

He did flinch then. "You've tasted my lips, and I yours. You can lie with your words, but what will it cost your heart?"

"My heart has nothing to do with this fucked-up bullshit," I seethed.

His lip curled. "But doesn't it? How else have you ended up precisely here?"

He was right, and I wasn't in the mood to argue.

After untold minutes had passed, I dragged my finger over the cool glass of the window and asked something that'd been eating at me. "How did you end up like this?"

When he didn't answer, I glanced over at him, trying again. "How can you do the things that you do and not feel ashamed for it?"

"Shame is personal, Little Dove. I feel shame just like any other person would, depending on what I've done. But I won't lie to you. I don't lose any sleep over what I do. It's just"—his hands spread—"what I do."

"You must like it then," I stated.

He scrubbed his chin. "Yes, I do. I'm good at it, and it's good money."

Sickened, I shook my head.

When he eventually spoke, his words were soft, decadent, and matter of fact. "There is art in blood, Little Dove. And I'm somewhat of a connoisseur. If I look closely, I can find it in every fine detail of ending one's life." He exhaled roughly. "I'm not expecting you to understand. I'm merely trying to explain myself, and …" He paused. "I'm doing a terrible job of it."

"I'll say," I muttered.

"That's probably because there is no defending it. I'd like to say that I've only killed and harmed those who deserve it, but I'm no judge or jury."

"Merely the executioner," I said.

He agreed. "Right. Most of my victims, if you'd like to call them that, wind up being that for a reason, though. It's not simply for sport."

"What happened to you?" I whispered, hating that I sounded concerned for him. "What made you decide that you'd just wake up one day and kill someone?"

"I don't always kill them."

I scoffed. "Because letting them live like Murry is much better?"

He sucked his teeth for a moment, and I wanted to slap myself for admiring the way his cheekbones erupted even more with the action. "Murry has his own story to tell. When or if he's ready, I'm sure he'll tell you."

Intrigue mixed with disgust, and at that point, I didn't know if I was more disgusted with him or myself. For a variety of different reasons, on my part.

"If you won't tell me how, then at least tell me when you became this person."

Thomas sighed. "After my parents died."

I slumped back against the wall and waited for more, but it didn't come. Then what Milo had said came forward again. "You were digging for information on me and my family. Why?"

He watched me for a pulsating moment, his expression blank. "Did you ever find out what happened the night your mother died?"

My eyes narrowed, heart tightening. "Why are you asking me that?"

"Humor me."

With a sigh, I lifted my feet to the window seat and stretched the fabric of my nightgown over my bent knees. "My dad said it was an accident, so I never pressed for more details."

A lone finger rubbed at his brow. "It looked like an accident, yes."

My hands met, and my arms clenched tight around my legs. "What?"

"I know of your love for stories, Dove. Allow me to tell you one before I leave."

It wasn't exactly stated like a question, but still, I nodded even as apprehension coiled around my muscles.

"A couple driving home hit your mother's car."

"I know that much."

"A married couple." Thomas stood and paced the length of the rug. "They'd been arguing, you see. The husband had been having an affair for well over a year. Nobody knew, except for the misbehaving pair, until one day, a little boy saw them in the woods behind his house, and he was so spooked, his mother almost had to beat what he'd seen out of him."

"Thomas," I cut in, my throat drying.

He lifted a finger and continued pacing. "The boy was young, and he didn't know there would be consequences for telling the truth. But he wouldn't realize until years later that the events that'd transpired after the affair came to light were not his fault."

My chest caved, the oxygen in the room becoming too thin.

"The boy's mother was enraged. Threatened to leave his father if he didn't end it. So he did. For a time, anyway. A few months later, she discovered them herself, and that was the final straw. By that stage, the boy's father had decided he wanted out. He wanted this other woman even if it meant he lost half his fortune to his wife. The wife, once she realized she couldn't win, did everything she could to keep him, but it was in vain."

Thomas slowed his strides, his tone becoming less factual, more nostalgic. "The father took the wife out for dinner one night, and the boy will never forget how happy his mother looked. Radiant in her shimmering blue dress and red painted lips. Her eyes aglow with hope."

I didn't think I could hear anymore. "Stop, please."

"Almost done." Thomas went on, "Little did she know, the dinner was a means to get her to sign the divorce papers. He tricked her into signing them, knowing she wouldn't, by folding and slipping the last page of the papers with the check for dinner." Thomas laughed, hollow and dry. I didn't like it. I liked his rust-stained, melodic laugh. His real laugh. "The boy's father was a fool, gloating over what he'd done to his distraught soon-to-be ex-wife on the drive home. So distraught was she, that when she saw his mistress's car parked near the entrance to our property, waiting in the dark with the headlights off for my father to produce the good news, she grabbed the wheel at the last second, and ended them all."

Thomas stopped, his eyes flat and lacking any warmth as he said, "My parents killed your mother, and your mother killed my parents."

CHAPTER

Twenty-Eight

I TOOK IN THE WINDOW, THE WOODS, THE WALLS OF THE room and their beautiful crown molding, and the furniture.

The boy in the woods.

The castle.

My mind and heart wouldn't stop skipping. "How old are you?" I asked, needing yet more confirmation when it wasn't needed at all.

"Twenty-nine."

He watched with patient eyes as I tried to count backward. "I'm almost twenty-four …"

"I'm not lying to you, little girl."

My brain stopped computing, my mouth hanging open as I remembered. I remembered him calling me little girl.

Go back, little girl.

"So you were going to kill me and my … my family."

"I had plans to, yes, though maybe not all of you." The words were said without a hint of remorse. "And then I met you, and evidently, you went and ruined those plans."

"But your parents' death wasn't our fault," I whispered.

"No." He tilted a shoulder. "But it was your mother's."

"And your father's," I shot back.

When he blinked, my body swayed.

"Knowing your fragile state, I wasn't going to tell you this just yet, but it kills me. It outright disgusts me that you've been spoon-fed lies upon lies."

"M-my dad …" My words broke, and I shut my eyes, re-opening them to find Thomas kneeling in front of me.

"He knew," he said gently. "He was married to his job at the time, and wanting to keep things normal, wanting to keep her, he turned a blind eye."

Memories of my mother before she'd died infiltrated, but … "Not once did she seem unhappy," I said aloud.

Thomas reached for my hand, and too shocked, I let him take it, his thumbs gliding over my skin. His touch was comfort-ing and warm, and I wanted all of him wrapped around me to rid the cold swimming through my bloodstream.

I knocked the want away, about to do the same with his hands, when he spoke. "She was probably very happy. And how were you to think anything was amiss if that was the case?"

He was right, but tears still collected on my lashes, wait-ing to fall. Reaching up, he brushed a thumb over one set, and licked the wetness from it. "You're beautiful even when you cry, but I still don't like it."

"I …" A ragged inhale shook my chest. "Why? I don't un-derstand … *why*."

With his brows meeting, Thomas stared at me hard for a long moment as my chin and lips shook, then I was in his arms and he was on his ass on the floor. Strong, gentle hands coasted up and down my back as my body convulsed with the force of everything I could no longer contain.

"Hush, Little Dove." I could've imagined it, but I swore ev-ery time he repeated those words, his lips brushed over my hair. "Hush, now."

At that moment, it didn't matter that he was a monster, or that I felt more lost than I had after being told my mother was never coming home.

All that mattered was that his cinnamon and mint scent clouded the cracks in my heart, and his touch steadied my breathing, and his words made me feel safe. As though he'd hold me together, if only I'd let him.

I had no one and nothing else, and so that was what I did.

In a sea of feathered quilts and silken blankets, I dreamed the next day away with eyes wide open, blinking at the wall.

For the first time since I'd arrived at this … castle, I'd slept soundly. Thomas had held me until my eyes decided they were done staying open, then he tucked me in and sat on the end of the bed, silent and still, until I drifted away.

He was gone when I'd awoken, which was no surprise. What was a surprise was that I wasn't disgusted with myself for allowing him to touch me. For allowing him to comfort me. What I felt was gratitude and that familiar warmth stirring beneath the tangled ropes of fear that'd now loosened and were no longer knots.

Not knowing how to place what I was feeling against what I knew, and what Thomas had told me about our parents, I decided to let it stew.

Growing up, my mother used to say, "Mull it over," whenever we didn't understand something or couldn't decide what to do.

Funny how she never knew that her actions would one day lead us all here.

Did she mull it over?

She would've, I concluded, when the sun's rays changed from golden bronze to dusky orange outside the window. She would have, and still, she'd made up her mind. I chose not to believe she'd leave us. I was unable to match such a callous action with the woman I knew. The woman who was rose-scented soap, cookie dough, wide smiles, and gardening hats.

She might've made plans to leave her husband, or maybe in the end, she wouldn't have, who knew, but either way, she'd never have abandoned us. That much I did know.

And my dad ...

The sun had fallen behind the trees before I decided that when I saw him again, because I now knew I would, I wouldn't say a word. There was no point in dredging up old wounds and reopening them. He'd loved her. He'd ignored her, putting work and other commitments first, but he'd still loved and lost her. He'd already suffered enough.

His resentment toward men who he deemed were failing their women, even in the slightest way, now made a little more sense.

I did plan to tell Hope, knowing she'd never forgive me if I didn't.

Sitting up, I stretched my stiff limbs and decided it was time to go, and that meant I had to find Thomas.

After showering and dressing in a clean pair of jeans and a pink T-shirt, I ran a brush over the damp strands of my hair. With the company of the ticking clock at my back, I padded down the otherwise silent hall, finding a few toys abandoned in archways and alcoves. Barbies and stuffed animals, mainly.

Curiosity got the better of me when that little girl inside me reared her head, screaming at me to explore. Opening a few doors upstairs, I discovered a sitting room awash in the last glow of daylight, resplendent with an old chaise and matching armchairs and heavy drapes.

The next room was locked, and I knew, if not for it being

locked but from its position at the top of the stairs, that it belonged to Thomas.

Before I could open the next door, Lou Lou's voice traveled up the stairs. "Miss Clayton, come see what I did!"

Such exuberance was almost envious, and I painted on a smile, the steps cool beneath my bare feet as I meandered down them. "You didn't visit me today."

Lou Lou swung her leg behind her, leaning on the end of the railing. "Daddy said you were extra tired and sleeping." Her eyes narrowed. "Isn't that boring? Sleeping and lying around all the time?"

Taking her hand, I squeezed gently. "It so is. Come on, show me what you did."

She dragged me to a small room that was bathed in warm pinks and violet purples. Toys were carefully situated in woven baskets, and there was a long kid-size table dressed in sheets of blank art paper. Orange tin cans were filled with paint brushes, crayons, pencils, and markers. The room itself wasn't overdone, but a space any child would appreciate losing hours at a time playing in.

He cared for her, that was obvious from the start, but it wasn't until the moment he'd explained how she came to be here, in a lair filled with would-be horrors, that I saw just how much he loved her.

Lou Lou gazed up at me, her finger pointing at a stick figure drawing on the white marker-colored paper. Her eyes oozed innocence and anticipation as she waited for me to take in her creation and give her feedback.

"Who are they?" I asked, absorbing the tall figure, the tiny one in the middle, and the one wearing a triangle dress on the other side.

Despite knowing already, I waited as she explained, "That's

you, me, and Daddy. That day we played on the playground." Her voice lowered to a loud hissed whisper, her amber eyes skirting the room as her lips twitched. "We never *ever* got in trouble."

Unable to stop it, even if I wanted to, a smile hitched my lips, and I ran my palm over her braid. "I love it. Who did your hair?"

"Murry," she said with an unmistakable huff of annoyance. "Daddy usually does it, but he was busy this morning."

"You don't like it when Murry does your hair?"

Her eyes bounced around the room quickly. "Not really," she whispered. "It's always too tight."

I imagined the sight of either man doing her hair and found that the visual came easily.

A small laugh lifted my chest. "Why don't you just ask him not to do it so tight?"

Her shoulders slumped. "I guess I could, but Murry, his face …" She chewed her lip, and I waited a beat, then nodded for her to go on. "He was in a real bad car accident, and I don't want to hurt his feelings."

It made sense that they'd fabricate that kind of story, but I had to wonder how it'd all play out when she grew up and learned the truth about her father.

Bending low, I whispered, "You won't hurt his feelings. Not if you tell him why and ask nicely."

She turned, tiny hands lifting to my own hair. "Your hair is growing longer now."

I'd started my first year of teaching with it sitting on my shoulders, and now, it sat below my shoulder blades. "So it is."

Lou Lou ran her fingers through it. "I like it. You still look like Snow White, but even prettier."

A surge of pure affection flooded my heart. "Is Snow White your favorite?"

"Belle used to be, but now I like Snow White more."

I grinned. "Belle's my favorite. We share a love for books." *And beasts,* something inside me whispered.

Hearing a throat clearing behind me, I jolted, and Lou Lou giggled. "It's just Murry."

Straightening, I pasted on a smile as I turned to see Murry wiping his hands with a towel in the doorway.

He didn't return it, and I guessed he was still not over me ruining one of his beloved plates. "Time for your bath, Miss Lou."

"Where's Daddy?" she asked.

"Busy in the library." Murry made a hurry it up gesture, and Lou Lou groaned.

"Can Miss Clayton help me instead?"

"Uh," I hesitated as Murry's brows rose. "I don't know—"

Murry grinned then, and I tried not to flinch, to react at all, as the scarred tissue struggled to move with his smile. "If she'd like to, sure. I'll even let you show her where everything is."

Without so much as a backward glance, he strode away, and my mouth opened and closed in uncertainty.

"Ready?" Lou Lou stuffed crayons back into the tin.

"Ah, yeah."

Hand in hand, we left the playroom, our hands swinging thanks to Lou Lou's enthusiasm as we coasted down the hall. She sniffed the air, a sound of unbridled delight leaving her before she said, "Lasagna. I love lasagna!"

Inhaling the mouthwatering scent, I could see why she was overjoyed.

I followed her back upstairs and down the other end of the hall to where a smaller bathroom sat. A mirrored version of the one on the side of the house that I used, but different thanks to the size, little girl products, and toys.

Lou Lou washed herself under my instruction, and I helped

her out before wrapping her in a purple towel. As she tugged on the nightgown Murry must've laid out, I made sure to empty the toys out of the tub before draining it. Back downstairs, we followed the smell of lasagna to the kitchen, where Murry was setting down platefuls of it at the island.

Lou Lou climbed onto a stool, dragging her plate toward her, then looked over at me. She patted the stool next to her but looking at Murry's back as he washed something at the sink, I ignored my hunger.

I had to go home, and there was no point making normal with a family that was anything but.

"You eat. I've got some things I need to do."

Lou Lou frowned, rosy lips pouting. "Like what? Aren't you hungry?"

"I'll eat later." With a wave, I started walking backward.

"Will you tuck me in tonight?"

Shit.

I didn't pause too long, knowing Lou Lou, for as much as she didn't know, was still perceptive. She wouldn't understand that my hesitation had nothing to do with her and everything to do with her father.

"Come get me when you've brushed your teeth."

Lou Lou found me at eight o'clock, interrupting the staring match I was having with the woods beyond the window.

Like a foreboding shadow, Thomas appeared in the doorway behind her.

He had his jacket off and was folding the sleeves of his white dress shirt over his tan, smooth arms. Veins bulged and dropped with every roll of the material.

He cleared his throat, and my eyes burned at being caught, darting up to meet his amused ones. "Lou wants to say good night."

"Nuh-uh," Lou Lou said, hands on her hips and outrage puckering her lips. "Miss Clayton said she'd tuck me in."

Thomas looked to be sucking his teeth for a second, then sighed. "Say good night Lou, or there'll be no bedtime story."

Lou Lou looked like she was about to cry, and I was finally able to unstick my tongue from the roof of my mouth, where it had been since I got busted ogling Thomas' arms.

"It's fine." I stood from my perch. "I told her I would earlier."

Thomas's brows furrowed. "You don't need to cater to her every whim. I might be rich, but she's accustomed to not getting her own way every now and then."

His dry words made me want to laugh. I swallowed the urge, walking across the rug covered floor to take Lou Lou's hand in mine. "I want to." I met his eyes as he shifted for us to skirt by him in the doorway. "And I don't break promises."

Eyes thinning with consideration and something else I was too scared to name, Thomas nodded once. My arm brushed his as he refused to move out of the way completely, and I felt his gaze hot on my back until we'd entered Lou Lou's room near the other end of the hall.

It was two doors down from the room I guessed belonged to Thomas and tastefully decorated in pinks and purples. The walls were white and pink candy striped, the rug a yellow sunflower, and artwork was taped over every surface as though no one had the heart to throw out anything Lou Lou had created over the years.

Her bed was a twin and surrounded in silken purple drapes that were tied back to white posts. I helped her shift unwanted pillows aside and collect toys she had to have with her while she slept as she listed her reasons why.

"Mister Hodge Podge gets lonely, and I like a good night's sleep." Her nose wrinkled with annoyance as she poked him and got comfortable beneath the feathered duvet. "I got sick of listening to his whining."

I snorted out a laugh, unable to contain it, and she tilted her head up at me and stared for a long moment. "How long are you here for, Miss Clayton?"

The question both freed and trapped me. Because it reminded me I could leave. Apparently, I wasn't some prisoner meant for torture or death. And it trapped me because looking at her—acknowledging the way my heart plummeted at the thought of returning to what was left of my life outside of the castle's walls—I knew I wasn't ready for reality.

Changing the subject, I smoothed my hands over the cover of the book she'd selected, *Snow White*, and said, "Do you know my first name?"

"No," she said through a yawn.

I opened the book to the first page, noticing the inscription, and paused.

For my very own little dwarf. May you grow into the kind of princess who can always rescue herself.

My eyes tingled, and I ran my finger over the perfectly scrawled words.

Of course, he had beautiful handwriting, I thought before Lou Lou snapped me out of it. "What is your name?"

It was time to acknowledge just how much had changed. Including my job. There wasn't much point in holding on to titles made to separate when I might not return to Lilyglade.

And when a part of my heart belonged in Lou Lou's tiny hands.

"Jemima," I said, then cleared my throat. "You can call me

Jem. Or Jemma. Or just Jemima."

Lou Lou smiled, displaying a missing front tooth that had been there when I'd last seen her. "I like Jemma."

"Jemma it is." I turned to the first page of the book. "When did you lose your tooth?"

She looked as though her eyes would close at any second. "Oh, after dinner when I ate an apple."

I tried not to cringe. "Did it hurt?"

She shook her head. "Not one bit." Rolling over a little, she lifted her pillow, displaying a tiny gold bag. "It's in here," she whispered. "Ready for the tooth fairy."

The image of Murry playing tooth fairy made me smile until the smarter half of my brain smacked the image away because I knew who really did it.

Part monster. Part fairy.

My smile stayed in place as I read, and Lou Lou fell asleep before the climax even hit. I read on anyway, taking comfort in the familiar tale. Perhaps, if I wasn't ready to leave, not tonight anyway, I'd search for a book of my own to get lost in.

Quietly, I shut the beautiful hardback and returned it to where it'd sat on her cubed white shelves. After turning off the lamp, I padded to the door but wasn't sure whether to leave it open or close it. I opted to leave it ajar.

Lou Lou stirred at the small squeak the hinges made, her sleep-coated voice tumbling into my ears and infiltrating my chest as she mumbled, "You should call me Lou." Her lips smacked together a few times as her eyes drifted closed. "Like Daddy and Murry."

I whispered, trying to hide the emotion clogging my throat, "Okay. Good night, Lou."

After watching her sleep a moment, I went in search of a man and a library.

CHAPTER
Twenty-Nine

Thomas

"**L**AST LOCATION?"

"Along a string of apartment buildings down by the docks."

Still in the city then, I took note. "There's something there if this is the second time you've tracked him to the area."

"There's nothing here but run-down apartments and the rank stench of rotting fish in old warehouses."

"It's one of those two then."

"Rotting fish?" Sage joked.

I didn't bite, and instead, I penned the last word I'd been looking for. "They must be meeting there somewhere."

"Tom, look, I can be out here every night for weeks, you know I'm good for it, but what if I don't find anything?"

Light footfalls approached the library, but I didn't remove my eyes from the page of my journal. "You will," I said.

"If you say so." Sage sighed, and I hung up.

Locking my phone without looking, I set it down on the side table next to the armchair I was sitting in. "Looking for something, Little Dove?"

"You, actually." My head rose, eyes studying the way her hands folded over her midsection. With her pink lips parted, her gaze roamed the room. "And a book."

"Luckily for you, you've stumbled across a two for one."

She smiled, and my pen scratched a line of black ink across the sentence I'd just labored over.

Unable to find words, I gestured for her to look around and watched as she ran her fingers over the spines of old history books. She walked the perimeter of the room then stopped at a shelf by the fireplace, her gentle fingers tugging and inspecting some of my mother's favorite books. Bodice rippers, mainly. But I wasn't one to judge.

Jemima's shoulder leaned into the shelf as she read the blurbs for three books, her lashes fluttering, and I knew when she'd found one that piqued her interest due to the way her eyes flared the slightest bit.

I tamped down the urge to ask a million questions, settling with the knowledge that if she was looking for something to read and putting Lou to bed, she was growing more comfortable here.

My hand had rubbed at my chest after overhearing my Dove tell Lou to call her by her first name, but I didn't dare to hope that meant what I wished it did.

That she'd stay. That she'd look beyond the blood and the scars to see what lies beneath.

It was a part of me, yes. In fact, it worried me to think what I'd do without the particular outlet that I'd come to depend on. But it did not define me. We all had our passions when it came to careers. Mine was merely a little more … unique than some others.

"She fell asleep before I could finish the story." Her sweet voice, combined with her attention falling on me, made the pen slip from my fingertips. Inwardly, I scowled at myself for acting like such a buffoon.

Such things just couldn't seem to be helped around her.

"Yes, she never lasts long after eight," I informed.

Jemima crossed the rug and came to sit in the twin wingback chair across from mine. As she eyed my phone for a second, her bottom lip vanished between her teeth. "How did you come up with the name Lou Lou?"

"It was my aunt's. When I was young, she lived with us when she was undergoing treatment for breast cancer."

Little Dove's lashes lowered, her palm skimming the cover of the paperback on her lap. "I take it she didn't survive."

"No," I confirmed. "But she was … different."

Dark lashes rose as her eyes lifted. "What was she like?"

Her interest snaked thorny branches into my gut, hooking and trying to drag me closer. "She was vibrant and bold yet soft. She was older than my mother by seven years, but they were best friends, no matter how different their lives had turned out. My mother married an Italian mobster, a hard businessman, while my aunt remained single and alone most of her life, backpacking and adventuring any chance she could."

At my pause, Jemima asked, "So she came here for help?"

I nodded. "Even my father, despite being cold-blooded most days, wasn't immune to the Lou Lou effect."

A sad smile tugged at Jemima's lips, weighing down her brows. "I see."

I tilted my head back against the plush leather, waiting.

She did the same as she continued, "Your aunt brought life and love into this house."

"She did."

"And your Lou does the same."

Feeling as if I'd been drugged, I stared at every perfect curve of her face. From her forehead to her cheekbones, to her chin, she had the face of an angel and the heart of a queen.

Depriving me of her eyes, she scratched at a scuff mark on the leather chair. "How did you get her enrolled in school? Being that she's not really yours."

So very inquisitive. "Fabricated birth records. Her father's name was wiped from her and her mother's lives, which wasn't hard being that he wasn't around long, and mine added."

Her eyes narrowed. "How?"

A scratchy laugh preceded my words. "*How*, she asks. Little Dove, this world rotates via currency. And the right price will get you just about anything you need if you know where to look."

She twisted her lips, and I wanted to smooth them back out. With my own. "And you know where to look, how?"

"My father was an influential man who had ties to the mafia, slave rings, and many other unsavory types."

"Unsavory," she said in a mocking tone. "Because what you do is absolutely respectable."

"Careful, Little Dove," I whispered, my dick rising as her tongue snuck out to lick her upper lip.

"Or what?" she whispered back. But despite the overconfident words, apprehension still lingered.

I merely smiled, and she looked more perturbed by that than anything I could've said.

"So"—she cleared her throat and straightened in the chair—"you said to come find you before I could leave."

I purposely dropped my gaze to the book in her lap. "You're leaving tonight?"

"No, but that's what you said I needed to do."

Contemplating my next move, I grabbed my journal and pen, setting them down on the side table before standing.

Her innocent eyes followed every move, and although I'd told her I'd let her go, I tamped down the guilt by reminding myself that I never agreed to how or when.

"Are you ready to strike a bargain, Little Dove?" I held my hand out to her.

She studied it, then looked up at me. "A bargain?"

"That's what I said. You can leave, but first, I must ask for something in return for my … hospitality."

An angelic laugh flowed past her lips and transformed her beauty into something ethereal. She wagged a finger at me. "I should've known there'd be a cost."

"I never said there wouldn't be."

Her smile slipping, she set her book down, then finally, placed her soft hand in mine. "Fine." I reveled in the touch, clasping her warm flesh within mine, and wondered what it might feel like to slide my tongue over every inch of her creamy skin. "What is it you want in return?"

I knew she was humoring me, and she knew it too. Though if she pretended this was what she had to do in order to walk away, then she'd be able to do it without any guilt.

Noticing the heat in my eyes, in my touch, and the way it pulled our bodies flush against each other, she croaked out, "No sex and no blood."

Her head fell back at the affronted look on my face, another laugh delighting my ears and sending mixed signals to the organ in my chest.

Using her distracted state, I wrapped my arm around her, my hand coasting over and up to gently grip the back of her neck, while my other hand waited for her chin to drop, then grasped her face.

"We've done this before," I said, feeling her heart pound against my chest and the beautiful, frantic beat of her pulse below my fingers.

"Not like this," she rasped, her eyes moving to my mouth

as she lifted to her toes. "And afterward, I can leave... anytime I want?" Her words floated over my lips, the sweet warmth of her breath searing.

"I'd rather you stayed, but I'm a man of my word."

Hesitant hands landed on my waist, the touch snapping the last frayed thread of my control.

And so I kissed her.

I kissed her with purposeful gentleness until her breathing became heavy and her lips parted mine. Velvet stroked at my tongue, and I groaned, sucking hers into my mouth and walking us backward.

Her hands tugged at my shirt, and mine at her hair, wanting more, needing more.

The wood of a bookshelf bit into my back as she wrapped her hands around my neck, and I lifted her from the ground. Legs became a noose around my waist, and the push of her breasts against my thundering heart rendered me blind, incapable of doing anything other than feeling.

Her little moans as I nipped gently at her lips had me straining against my slacks. The guttural sound I made as she rocked over me had her hands gripping my face, tilting it for more access, then sliding into my hair.

Then my phone chirped with an email notification, and the spell was broken.

Jemima nearly fell to the floor with how fast she broke away from my mouth.

"Shit," she breathed as I held her steady. She looked up at me, her skin delectably pink, lips mouthwateringly red, and her hair in tantalizing tangles, then swallowed and backed up toward the door.

Think, think, think, you insufferable moron.

But the swollen head inside my pants was overriding any

function I had left of the one on my shoulders. I ran a shaky palm through my mussed hair as she mumbled a rushed good night in the doorway.

She was long gone by the time I muttered, "Until next time, Little Dove."

CHAPTER
Thirty

CHILDLIKE WONDER FOR THE LOOMING STRUCTURE returned as I dragged my fingers over the rails and walls, drowning out any remnants of trepidation.

Thoughts of my mother, of Thomas's mother, haunted me as I wandered deeper into the gigantic house the next day. Not to escape, but to explore.

No matter how hard I tried, my thoughts would always shift back. My fingers would always try to climb to my lips. And my heart would always try to block out rational thinking.

Inside a parlor, I trailed my fingers over the glass, staring at the couple behind it. It had to be one of the only photos of them in this home as I hadn't come across any others.

He was every inch his father, and for that, I couldn't entirely blame my mother for being tempted to risk it all.

Except for his eyes.

The rare shade of blue belonged to the blond-haired woman with a tight, red-lipped smile. She was beautiful in a classic way. The kind who won pageants and had men looking more than once.

My finger drifted, tracing the place where her husband's hand held her waist, and although I tried, I couldn't find the room to hate her for what she'd done. For her hand in stealing something irreplaceable from me and my family. There was only a resounding pang of sorrow for what could have been.

It was a tragedy caused by love.

And I was no stranger to the risks and perils that accompanied losing your heart.

"Beatrice and Antonio Verrone." Murry's voice startled me, and my hand fell away as I turned to find him in the doorway.

"They were beautiful."

A hint of a smile nudged his lips, his arms crossed over his chest as he looked from me to the floor-to-ceiling window behind me.

Behind the window sat a courtyard of sorts, and in the center of it, surrounded by rose bushes and sandstone benches, was a pool.

Entranced, I stepped closer, then stopped, standing breathlessly still at the sight of Thomas doing a flip turn before swimming half the length of the pool underwater. Even as my cheeks started to flush, heat spreading through my body, I couldn't drag my gaze away. I now knew how he maintained that lean swimmer's physique as I watched him swim lap after lap, his movements fluid, arms slicing through the water.

Murry cleared his throat, and I stepped back, ducking my head and tucking some hair behind my ear. "You know, for someone who was hell-bent on getting out of here a few days ago, you're looking pretty comfortable now."

I was, and that was a problem. One I was trying to solve. That was hard to do when Thomas seemed to hold me prisoner through his presence alone.

"And what about you?" I asked, strolling out the door. "Why are you still here after what he did to you?"

Earlier, I'd discovered the third floor contained an attic, or storage room, and a cracked open door revealed what I guessed to be Murry's room. I'd peeked inside to find a room that was the size of three bedrooms, handsomely decorated in reds and grays with the turret providing a circular living area.

Murry decided to follow. "I don't know if you're ready to hear that particular story."

Tossing a smirk over my shoulder as we neared the stairs, I said, "It would take a lot to shock me at this point."

Murry considered that, then joined me as I continued down the hall. "I wasn't a good man before I came here," he said, then scoffed. "In fact, I'm not completely sure I'll ever be."

"Oh?" I didn't believe that. Not wholly. "What about the way you run this place, and the way you take care of him and Lou?"

"I get paid very handsomely for all I do, trust me."

I knew that wasn't why he treated Lou like a loving uncle would, and by my silence, he knew I saw through his words.

"I used to smuggle women across the border."

I stopped walking. "To help them flee?"

He rubbed the back of his neck, eyes flitting around. "Not exactly."

"You abducted them," I said, the words cutting into my tongue as guilt creased his features. All except for his scars.

"Yes. The sex slave industry, which I guess you've heard about to some extent, is big in some parts."

Walking again, to keep from sliding an accusing glance at him, I asked, "And how did that lead you here?"

"By stealing the wrong girl," he said dryly. "She was a senator's daughter and had been out partying for her eighteenth birthday in Mexico with her boyfriend and some friends. Me and the guy I worked with at the time stalked particular hotspots where more privileged beauty would appear, and we took her and three other girls."

"Did you"—I shook my head, trying to understand—"did

they escape?"

"No," he said. "Years later, the daughter was found half dead in some sixty-year-old millionaire's bedroom. He'd purchased her. And the others …" The way his eyes glassed over said it all.

Dead.

I blinked at him. "How did you do it?"

He knew I didn't mean in the literal sense. "When you grow up with nothing, and your next meal isn't guaranteed, it … hardens you. You need to become as hard as the life you've been living to survive. As a kid, I started dabbling in the drug trade, just trying to make ends meet. And as I got older, I wanted more. More than the run-down trailer I lived in, more than the constant scent of mildew on my clothes. I wanted more than a cheap, watered-down existence. So slowly, I started asking around, and eventually, I got an in."

"Was it worth it?"

"Never," he said with vehemence. "I did it for ten years, but money means nothing when you can't taste the food you can afford to buy or see the nice new apartment you were able to lease. I was either working, or I was blowing what remaining money I'd earned on booze and drugs. Anything to block out what I'd sentenced hundreds of girls to."

The word *hundreds* wrapped around my heart like a noose, and I wanted to reach over and gouge his eyes out, but when I looked, *really looked*, I saw the wetness in them, saw the way his strong chin trembled, and relaxed my hands.

"One night, I was walking back to my apartment, drunk as fuck and strung out after coming down from some average high, and there he was." A smile lingered in his voice. "Sitting on my apartment steps, a gun in hand, and no expression on his face."

"He shot you?"

"No," he said. "But I was beyond giving a shit if he did. To be honest, relief was the only thing I felt beneath the numbness. I went to him willingly, which I think shocked him more than any other client he'd had, not that he'd ever shown it."

"But you know him now." I stopped at a tall oblong window that faced another dam, this one decorated with shoulder-high weeds.

Murry made a sound of agreement, stopping next to me and leaning heavily against the wall. "Anyway, I woke up in his chair, courtesy of the half dead girl remembering my appearance and that my colleague at the time had said my name, and it soon began." He smirked as I waited for more. "No need for those details." A visible shiver assaulted him as he straightened from the wall.

"Wait," I said before he could walk away. "So the senator wanted you dead?"

He nodded. "But he wanted answers first. The whereabouts of my colleagues, my employer, anything he could get."

"And clearly, Thomas didn't kill you."

"Clearly," he said with a lift to his lips, then sighed. "I'd answered anything he'd asked instantly, and I think the fact I didn't beg for my life, but instead, begged for it to be over, made him stop."

"Then he offered you a job."

"It was that or death," he said, leaving me to work out the foggy details. "Which was what waited for me if he'd set me free anyway."

"But don't you have any family? In Mexico? Anywhere?"

His hands dipped into his suit pockets as he walked backward. "None more important than this one. They assume I'm dead and never helped in making sure I survived growing up. So"—he shrugged—"blood ties don't exactly mean a lot to me."

Pondering that, I leaned back against the window, staring at the floor.

"Oh, and Jemima?" I looked up as Murry threw a quick glance behind him, then said quietly, "I always thought he was asexual, so take that into account before you eventually race out of here."

That drew a burst of laughter from me, but then I frowned. "Wait, seriously?"

"We don't tell lies here."

"Huh," I said aloud, my heart sticking to the bottom of my throat. "Hey, Murry?"

His head appeared around the corner of the end of the long hallway. "Hmm?"

"I am sorry … about your plate."

His deep laughter made my next breath scathe as he left me with all he'd said.

Letting it sink in, I mulled over what kind of life Murry must have had before. How bad it must have been for him to sentence his soul and many women to a lifetime of hell.

In the study, an old record player snagged at my peripheral. Traipsing over to it, I spotted a shelf of records, and after only a momentary pause, I started shifting through them.

"Boo!"

Jumping, I sputtered out a laugh as I turned and saw Lou, her hair damp and her smile warm. "You scared me, little Lou."

Her smile grew, her bare feet shifting over the floor.

"Have you been swimming?"

Lou Lou nodded. "Daddy teaches me twice a week, but I finished a while ago. I had to take a shower, then I've spent forever trying to find you."

I grinned at this newfound knowledge. "Well, you've found me."

She sidled up to me, inspecting the records. "Daddy says those belonged to Grandma and Grandpa."

"Are you not allowed to touch them?"

She peered at the record player, which looked to be in perfect condition, and without a speck of dust atop it, then hummed. "I'm not, but"—she grinned up at me—"did he say you can't?"

"Nope." Normally, I'd abide by parents' wishes but not this time. "He did not. How about you close your eyes, and wherever your finger lands, that's the one we'll play."

Lou bounced on the soles of her feet, her lip tugged into her mouth as her hand blindly slapped at the air. We laughed as I directed her hand closer, and she plucked out the first record her finger touched. My heart sank and soared at the same time when I saw it was Fleetwood Mac's *Rumors*.

The memory of my mom, hips swaying and gentle voice humming to that same album as she cleaned the house or gardened infiltrated with razor-sharp talons.

I pulled the record free as Lou opened the plastic casing on top of the player.

Wanting to see if it worked, and because I wanted to rid an array of heartbreaking stories from my head, even if only for a little while, I carefully placed the record down, then set the needle to track number four.

A scratchy noise filled the room, and I tweaked the tonearm a little until the strains of "Don't Stop" began.

"Ooh," Lou sang, clapping her hands. "I like it!"

Tears smarted, and to keep them at bay, I took Lou's hands. "Come on."

In the middle of the room, surrounded by ghosts of ancestors gone by and haunted by their stories, I swung my arms and moved my feet with Lou, and I smiled it all away.

Her laughter was almost as loud as the song and even more magical. It had the ability to dry tears and chase away ghosts. Her little soul was a gift to a dark, enigmatic man and to anyone else who was fortunate enough to know her.

And it didn't matter that I was dancing like I was at a children's disco. For a fleeting minute, nothing mattered except being.

"Daddy!" Lou dropped my hands, and I froze at seeing Thomas in the doorway, his hair and his white shirt damp as though he'd hurriedly tugged it on.

I swallowed, expecting to see anger at having touched his things, at filling his house of horrors with laughter and music, but then I swallowed for a different reason. He was smiling, his teeth imprinting his bottom lip as he tried to contain it.

"Come dance, come dance!"

Still looking at me, he let Lou pull him into the room, and a second later, I felt his hand in mine. Smiling, I ducked my head, and we began to dance once again. Thomas was just as goofy as we were, made worse by his stiff and restrained movements. But for Lou Lou, he was trying, and for my heart, that was a dangerous thing.

Because it dawned like a late to rise sun that if Thomas Verrone loved someone, there wasn't anything he wouldn't do for them.

The song skipped to another, and I felt Lou's hand slip from mine, but too caught up in the hand that'd replaced it, and the slow tune of "Songbird," I didn't look to see where she'd gone.

"Little Dove." Thomas pulled me close and whispered his lips over my cheek. "What am I to do with you?"

I was embarrassingly close to saying something I shouldn't, so I shut my eyes. "You're a fantastic dancer, Monster."

He chuckled. "I'm well aware that's a lie, Dove."

"Fine, a whole bunch of six and seven-year-olds dance better than you."

His head fell back, a loud laugh bellowing into the room, cording his neck and drowning out the music.

Marveling at the sight, I blinked a few times as his head lowered, and then he pressed his forehead to mine.

"And how about now?" he asked as his hands brought mine flush between us. One moved away to hold my back, and he rocked us side to side.

"Passable," I admitted, my voice unrecognizably soft.

He heard me, his lashes fanning over his cheeks as his eyes dropped to my mouth. His scent was something I'd become accustomed to long ago, yet try as I might to ignore it, it still made my stomach clench and my mouth water. "You're still here," he said, more of a plea than an accusation.

"So I am," I said.

A heaviness sat upon my chest as he lifted his eyes to mine, gentle wonder swimming among ice layered depths. "Why?"

It was a whisper, and I answered in kind. "Honestly?"

He blinked, the smooth skin of his forehead rubbing mine as he jerked his head in a nod.

"I don't know." As true as it might've been, what was more alarming was that I was growing less concerned with not having a reason.

For the remainder of the song, our bodies swayed to the music, but our gazes never strayed.

Before the music came to an end, his forefinger and thumb found my chin and he closed the tiny distance between our mouths. His warm lips scorched a trail to my heart, setting aflame every nerve ending in my body, and all he had to do was rest them on mine.

For that was all he did, and I stopped counting the seconds

after twenty, riding on the sensations of breathing him, tasting him, and feeling him—of feeling everything.

It was the most intimate experience I'd had in my entire life, and it wasn't until he pressed his lips to my forehead and left the room that I remembered I'd had it with a murderer.

CHAPTER
Thirty-One

Miles

THE COFFEE CUP POPPED OPEN, DARK BROWN LIQUID raining down the yellow painted wall.

"Calm the fuck down, Carlson."

I slapped my hands down on the table, growling, "Calm? You said to wait it out until I saw you. You"—I stabbed my finger at him, an errant laugh slipping free—"said you'd have a fucking plan."

But he'd arrived with nothing and no one.

"Well, where is it?" I spun in a circle, my hands spread wide. "What the fuck is going on, Pete?"

The apartment, the one the team leased to reconvene and stay on track, was fucking closing in on me.

I'd been there for days, waiting.

As if I didn't have the ability to get a team together and storm that sick fuck's property if I wanted to.

If only they'd give me a warrant, which Pete said they couldn't or wouldn't do.

"We did, but it's …" He loosened the collar of his shirt, blowing out a breath. "It was unethical, and they wouldn't sign off on it."

"Unethical?" I scoffed. "They do know we're dealing with

Thomas Verrone, right? Tell Anthony I want a meeting. Now." Straightening, I crossed my arms over my chest and waited.

Pete's pale round face tinged pink.

"What?" I asked.

"We don't know anything for sure. We have no proof she's been taken. No evidence of foul play."

My hands speared into my hair, and I did my best not to think about what my girl was going through. "And you fucking believe he hasn't? She's there!"

He cursed. "Calm down, Carlson. Jesus Christ, you're worse than working with Jamison." His nostrils flared as he huffed. "What's got you so damn wired?"

"I want her safe."

Pete sighed and scooted the chair back, the old wood scraping beneath his weight, and stood. "Listen, you don't need to tell me, but where's Shelley?"

More people than I'd like to admit knew about our situation. Not that it was her fault. I'd only said those words out of anger and frustration.

I knew I was the one to blame.

I could've said no. We could've picked someone else to step in. I could've given up this case and moved on months ago. I could've kept more of a distance between her and my damn heart.

But I didn't do any of those things.

And now, the woman I was going to give up *everything* for was in the hands of a monster, and no one seemed to give enough of a shit about it.

I knew their aim. They were waiting. They were used to this and so was I. But what I wasn't used to was this feeling cinching my chest tighter as each day passed.

Finally, I admitted, "Shell took a leave of absence and went home."

Home, where we grew up and got married, was three hours north of this mess. And I didn't blame her for finally giving up.

Shelley was strong. She knew the job and what it sometimes entailed intimately because she worked in the same branch, but everyone had their limits. She'd reached hers far later than I thought she would.

It made me smile for a brief second.

"Shit, Carlson. That's rough." Pete patted his pockets for his keys, tugging them free. "Sorry man, but I need to head back. I'll be in touch."

Nodding, I looked over at the wall of intel I'd gathered, not seeing it, not seeing anything besides the rage that'd kept me going for the past week.

A map of his house, coordinates, and supposed sightings of him around the city mixed with photographs of him in his obnoxious suit, his daughter, and some of his connections.

My eyes zoomed back to Lou Lou.

Unethical, yes.

But sometimes the only way to lure a lion from his den was to steal his cub.

CHAPTER
Thirty-Two

"**Y**OUR, AH, MONSTER REQUESTS YOUR PRESENCE AT dinner," Murry said at the door with a hefty dose of smugness in his tone.

With a leaping stomach, I folded my sweater and tucked it inside my bag, then scanned the room for other items. It was the tenth time I'd done it, but it made me feel better if I at least got prepared for the moment.

The moment when I'd walk out of here and never look back.

It was that last part that sealed the valves to my heart, blocking my next attempt at oxygen. And the reason I hadn't left my room all afternoon.

Murry escorted me to the room at the top of the stairs in silence, and after rapping on the large doors, he opened them and left me there.

Steeling myself, I squared my shoulders and walked inside.

The door shutting behind me echoed right through my fingertips as I inhaled the smell of rice and spiced chicken, and let my eyes adjust to the bright space.

Heavy black curtains draped arched windows, two on either side of the room, and a set of French doors that opened to a small balcony. They were peeled back and tied with satin bows, allowing the last vestiges of daylight to leak in and cast the large king-size bed in orange and gray shadows.

Removing my eyes from the monstrosity that was dressed in black and gray linens, I walked over the oriental styled rugs to where Thomas sat at a small dining table, writing in that little brown book of his.

He shut it as I approached, then rose to pull out my chair.

"Hi," I said, finding my voice as I took a seat.

"Good evening. Wine?" His rich, dark voice combined with the mouthwatering scent of butter chicken as he lifted the lids on our meals had me almost salivating.

I shook my head, and he poured himself half a glass, filling mine with water from a crystal decanter.

Steam billowed into the air, trailing to the opened doors where the summer breeze drifted in to kiss my bare legs and feet. "Your room is beautiful."

He stopped fussing with the cutlery and took a seat. "Thank you."

I had to know. "Was it your parents'?"

"It was," he said without a hint of emotion.

"That doesn't bother you." Not a question.

"Not in the slightest." His eyes met mine after a beat. "Dove, it's just a room."

"Of course," I said, forgetting for a moment, as I was often doing nowadays, with whom I was speaking with.

The food was too good to pass up to stomach roiling thoughts, so when he gestured for me to eat, I gladly did.

After I'd demolished half my plate, I glanced out the doors to stop myself from watching him eat. It was fascinating—the way his jaw worked and his Adam's apple bobbed—in a way such normal things shouldn't be.

"I'd almost forgotten it was summer." Thomas eyed my dress, and I laughed. "You know what I mean."

He waved his fork. "I suppose. Though I never said you

needed to stay indoors. Or stay period."

That was true.

I ate another mouthful even though I was getting full to avoid answering that.

"We never finished our round of questions," he said after a few minutes had passed.

"Ask whatever you like," I said, taking a sip of water.

"No." He set his utensils down, picking up his glass of wine to take a sip. "I want you to ask me." At my raised brow, he swirled his wine. "You and I both know you still have questions."

"I've already asked you what I want to know, and you refused to answer me."

His lips twisted. "I wouldn't say I refused …" When I laughed, he huffed, "Fine."

I pushed my plate away, waiting.

He took another sip of wine, and then did the same, most of his food gone.

"I first killed someone when I was seventeen. My uncle."

I tried to stop my eyes from growing, but judging by the slight lift to his lips, I was unsuccessful.

Thomas set his glass down. Rising from the table, he took measured strides toward the bed, his finger rubbing at his brow. "My father left Italy for good after meeting my mother here in college. My uncle Matias was his half-brother, the son of one of my grandfather's side pieces, but he was all he had when my father left, so he tried to groom him to run the family business."

My eyes absorbed his blank expression. His ancestry explained the tan skin and the chiseled, god-like angles of his face.

"My grandfather was too unwell to fly here for my parents' funeral, and he died not long after the accident. So my uncle Matt came to arrange everything and stayed a few months. I never remembered much of him growing up, being that he never visited the States often. The few memories I had were from when I was young, and we'd visited my father's family for a Christmas or two. And in those memories, he'd barely said two words to me."

With rapt attention, I watched as his feet ate the length of the room with long strides.

"My grandfather was dead and my grandmother too old to take care of me or travel, so I was left in Matias's care. But instead of caring, he spent his time here emptying our bank accounts, transferring half of my father's fortune overseas, and arranging a contact for my school should they need to check in, and then he left."

A dry, humorous sound raised his shoulders. "He came back a year later. Surprised I was still attending school and not in the system or dead, he gave me a pat on the shoulder as if I'd made him proud. But I knew why he'd returned, and though it destroyed me, I couldn't stop him."

He groaned. "The rage I felt brewing inside as he fed me lie after lie about being here for work, all the while he drank my father's whiskey and smoked his favorite cigars, the ones I'd kept dust-free and locked in his study as if he'd never even left … it became too much."

"He took more money."

Thomas nodded. "And before he left again, as he tossed a few thousand at my feet, muttering something about putting the house on the market when he returned, I vowed to myself there wouldn't be a next time. I took that few thousand and my rage and marched downstairs to the basement. There, I found the safe my father had hidden and tucked the money inside with the rest. You see, I couldn't even access money from my father's bank account. Not until I was eighteen."

"But …" *There would've been nothing left.*

"Exactly." His eyes gleamed with a malice I'd never seen before. "So when he came back a few years later with plans to sell the house, the very home my father had paid for through blood and savage deeds, I swore it'd be the last thing he ever made plans to do."

He shook his head, a smile forming. "It was easy, really. He followed me downstairs, dollar signs in his eyes and missing one of his ears, which I later found out was due to owing the family money. Money he was stealing from me to pay them back."

My hand fluttered to my lips as my eyes watered.

"Lured by the promise of a locked safe that I'd said I was having trouble opening, I knocked him out with a brick, tied him to a beam, and fled upstairs."

A dark, nostalgic laugh drifted as he ran a hand over his hair. "I was shaking so hard I thought I'd chip my teeth. Once I finally calmed down, I realized he would likely escape and probably kill me or starve to death. Once that sunk in, this weird calm washed over me."

"How?" I asked, my voice a croak. "How did you kill him?"

"A hunting knife." He took a seat on his bed, kicking off his leather shoes, then tugging off his socks. "I could've done it while he was restrained and made it easier for myself, but I was too angry. Some part of me needed the challenge. Some part of me had changed. I untied him while he was still unconscious, unlocked the door, and waited at the top of the stairs."

Lost in the sight of his bare feet, his next words knocked me from my trance.

"As soon as he appeared, I tripped him before he could even see me." Another dry laugh. "I missed, stabbing him in the nose, but the second time …" His eyes met mine, unflinching honesty in them. "I made sure I didn't miss the second time. Or the sixteenth."

"Holy shit." My tongue felt thick but not for the reasons it should. "Thomas ... you were so young."

He tilted a shoulder.

"What happened then?"

"I'd found my father's drums of acid years ago," he said. "I used them and the ..." He saw my grimace and paused. "Anyway, my father's cousin, who now runs the business, came looking for him a few months later. But instead of killing me, he grinned and hired me."

I shook my head. "You were seventeen ... How did you survive after your parents died until then?"

"Money, same as anyone else who has it." A smirk curved his lips. "It's quite easy"—his eyes lowered to the rug—"until it runs out."

"So you worked for him here? What about school?"

Thomas eyed my bare feet, eyes skating up my legs, then swallowed and directed his gaze out the window. "I finished. Just. I might've been on my own, but after a short time, I preferred it that way. Going to school and being around that many people, people with ordinary lives and mundane problems, it drove me crazy."

"What about your mother's family?"

His jaw twitched at my distraught tone. "Aunt Lou Lou was gone, and so were my mother's parents."

My eyes threatened to well. "Did you go to Italy? After they hired you?"

"No," he said. "I traveled or took care of anyone they sent here. It was good for a time, but I got sick of being told what to do. That happens when you have no authority in your life for so long."

I smiled then, finding it hard to imagine him taking orders from anyone. Not unless it suited him. "How'd you get out of working for your family?"

"I haven't; it doesn't work like that. But I told them I was going into business on my own, and if they wanted my services, they needed to pay more money. I was almost twenty-five by then and didn't know enough about their dealings to be too much of a concern." He huffed. "Or so they thought. Regardless, those ties can't be cut without bloodshed. I'm still in touch with Loren, my father's cousin, for when he needs something here and vice versa."

This man ... all he'd been through. "Jesus, Thomas."

He frowned at my blasphemy, and I stood, my legs liquid as I forced them closer to him, forced them to bend and take a seat.

Numb, I hardly felt the feathered duvet sink beneath me. "Before you finished school, you what, survived on money in that safe?"

Thomas undid his jacket, standing to drape it over an armchair by his bed, then took his seat near me on the bed again, a lot closer than he'd been before. "I made it last. Tuition was paid in full, curtesy of my uncle. When I got sick of walking, I taught myself to drive my mother's car and would use it to get to the nearest bus stop, where I caught a ride into the city. But my perfect attendance started slipping after the eleventh grade. Once food and money became scarce, and my uniforms grew too tight."

The image of that tall, lanky boy in the woods came forward. "When I saw you in the woods ..."

A tender smile lit his eyes. "I was hunting." At my frown, he laughed. "Don't look so forlorn. People do it all the time. And the activity that stemmed from childhood boredom paid off."

"In what ways?"

He rubbed the bridge of his nose. "I don't know if you want to hear—"

"Tell me."

He sighed. "When I started running out of money, about four months before my uncle reappeared for the last time, I'd learned to do more than hunt. I skinned and gutted rabbits and deer, caught fish in the creek, and made do with old canned goods I'd found in the basement."

My stomach heaved, my hand lifting to it.

Thomas grabbed my hand, fingers gently circling my wrist. "You could say my ability to shed blood was born from fun but also from the need to survive. Neither reason has changed."

Understanding dawned. It wasn't enough, but it was enough to empathize and see how he'd gone down the path he had. "So that's why."

He let go of my wrist, flopping back down onto the bed. The action was so childlike, so unlike him, that I had to stop myself from saying his name to reassure me it was him.

"Dove, if everyone had an excuse for the person they'd become, a reason to blame their subpar existence or terrible situations on, the world would be even more of a miserable place." He sucked his lips, then gazed up at me. "Look at you. You were taken by a supposed monster, had your heart broken by your supposed fiancé, found out what really happened to your supposed perfect mother, yet just today, I saw you smile and laugh. I saw you thriving despite what's happened to you." He let those words sink in. "Why do you think that is?"

Knowing what he wanted me to say, I licked my lips, captured by his rich voice and haunting blue stare. The beauty of this man was stained in blood, but it was still there, drawing me closer with its relentless tugging.

He answered for me with a knowing smile. "Because you chose to."

I managed to get my brain up to speed. "I get what you're

saying, but it's not always that simple."

He shrugged. "Perhaps. But ultimately, is it not?"

I laughed. "Now you're just confusing me."

He laughed too, the sound a buttery whiskey. "Should I have just gone with, I like it because having that part of me desensitized enables me to ensure I never have to eat out of date canned goods again?"

"I like both," I said.

Our smiles fading, we stared a moment. Thomas appeared to be lost in the past, and me, lost in the present.

Flopping back down onto the bed, I blinked up at the crown molding and the chandelier on the ceiling. "For five whole years, no one knew you lived alone?"

"Money makes people shut up, and I spent enough to ensure I was left alone."

"Unbelievable." I shifted, leaning on an elbow to face him. "All those years tucked away in this castle. Like some long-lost dark prince."

He snorted. "Hardly, Little Dove."

"You missed out on so many experiences," I said. Even if he went to high school, his life was so far removed from his peers.

"Like what?"

"Well, did you go to parties? Prom?" I paused before asking my next question. "Ever have a girlfriend?"

"Even before my parents died, I wasn't one to socialize much and only had a handful of friends who put up with my eccentric ways. My only saving grace was that I was on the swim team, and that curbed most bullying about my frequent trips to the library."

He looked over at me when he noticed I was still waiting. "I've had a few girlfriends, yes. Swim team, remember?" He raised a thick brow. "But they never lasted long. Not once we got to the stage of wanting sleepovers or proper dates."

"So how did you, you know …?" Heat crept into my cheeks.

"The last girlfriend I had, senior year, was the second girl I had sex with. We had sex about three times. Locker room twice, back of her car once. Before her, there was one girl. We got rid of our virginities and basically went our separate ways."

"What about after her?" I all but squeaked, my stomach warming and making me feel sixteen again at the way he so freely said *sex*.

He shook his head. "When you live on the fringes of society, normality only touches you as much as you let it." He met my shocked gaze with a cold one. "And as I said, I got sick of letting it."

Unable to fathom how a man who looked like him, who could kiss in a way that burned and touch so reverently it froze the blood in your veins, hadn't had sex in years, I blurted, "But why?"

"I'd become accustomed to being alone." A sigh lifted his chest. "And being that I never leave this place unless I must, the opportunity rarely presents itself, and when it has in the past, it was usually in the form of a potential STD." At my still shocked expression, he hurried to add, "Don't worry, I still masturbate, and no, it's not to gory images."

"Oh-kay," I laughed out.

Scooting closer, he twirled a strand of my hair around his finger. "I'll bet I even discover what you like in a matter of minutes."

"Whoa." I was still reeling from the fact that this man—this beautiful, shadowed Adonis—was way less experienced than me in the bedroom. "Thomas, I didn't realize that was what you'd want to do"—I waved a hand, then let it fall to the bed—"when you invited me in here."

"Dove, no." Eyes gentling, he said, "I just wanted to spend time with you, but now …"

"But now?" I repeated on a whisper.

His lips curled, and my toes reacted in kind. "Now that I can see what you want, that I can taste it in the air we're breathing, you're not leaving this room until you've let me inside you."

His uncanny ability to read me had never frustrated and turned me on more. "Thomas," I started.

"Hush." His finger pressed to my lips as he leaned over me. "Let's not waste time with false objections when we could be using it"—his finger dragged down my chin, dipped to the column of my throat, and stopped, rotating over the skin above my cleavage—"doing much better things."

My hunger for him peppered my taste buds, flavored the thickening saliva on my tongue, and burned deep, crusting the cracks of my heart. But I couldn't let it take control just yet. "Why do you want me, Thomas? Why are you trusting me?"

He answered instantly, voice deep and firm with conviction. "Because I knew …" His breath heated my lips, his eyes swimming into mine. "I knew from the first moment your eyes met mine that you were meant for me. I struggled with it, with wanting you, and then I surrendered. Though I didn't know for sure, I had hope that you would be the one to see me."

My hands reached for his face, thumbs rubbing over the day-old bristle on his jaw as I pulled his mouth to mine. "I see you, and you know what?"

"What?" The word drifted between my parted lips.

"I'm not scared." My thighs and lips opened farther, making room for him to fall between them.

Heaven floated in my veins; a mixture of tingling heat and cool rapture as his tongue stroked mine, and his hand skimmed my bare thigh. My dress rose higher thanks to the friction of his rubbing hips. I took his hand and guided it between my legs, allowing him to feel the evidence for himself through the cotton of my panties.

His groan was a lit match tossed onto an already burning flame, and it sent my blood boiling with desperation.

His fingers were hesitant at first but taking encouragement from the heavy breaths escaping our kiss, the ones I couldn't control, he pressed and teased.

Tearing my lips from his, I gasped out, "Move it aside, touch me."

His nostrils flared as he studied me with molten eyes, then he was gone, the sound of his shirt hitting the floor had my head lifting in time to see his tan torso lower back on the bed.

My head fell back as his thumbs hooked into my panties, and his lips followed their descent, licking slowly, ardently, as if he were starved for the taste of my skin.

"Every inch of you," he breathed once my panties had hit the floor. "I want my lips to traverse every inch of your skin."

The thought was tempting, and shivers wracked me as I took in his enraptured stare, which was roaming up my legs, his eyes homing in on the space between my thighs.

"Another time, maybe," I said, gesturing for him to come to me.

He ignored me, and my eyes squeezed shut as his fingers and tongue moved up my legs so slow I was close to panting by the time he spread me open. The feel of his appreciative gaze and the sound of his increased breathing washed away any embarrassment I might've felt for being on display for so long.

"You're shining for me, and so fucking pink I can hardly breathe."

"So don't. Come here and kiss me instead."

Again, he ignored me, and his breath washing over my

thighs was the only warning I had before his mouth was right there.

He licked up and down, getting to know what I liked, as he'd warned, within minutes.

Less than two minutes later, if I was being honest, my thighs shook and my hands gripped his hair as he circled and circled, and then I saw bright sparks.

He watched my body shake, I could feel it, but it didn't bother me. It only made it harder to refocus on my surroundings.

"Incredible," he breathed, then said, "Again," right before his mouth lowered, his tongue firmer and his hands joining too as he began with renewed determination.

Laughing and squirming, I clamped my legs around his head. "No, stop."

Prying my thighs apart, he rested his chin on my lower stomach. "Why?"

His tone conveyed genuine confusion. Knowing he hadn't had sex in a long time, since he'd entered adulthood, really, I fumbled for the right words to describe it. "Have you ever been able to masturbate twice in a row?"

"Yes."

"Oh."

He smirked. "But I understand your point. Sensitive."

I scooted up the bed, and he scowled, reaching for my ankle. I shifted out of reach, then sat up, and lifted my dress over my head. My bra was next, landing somewhere behind me on the floor.

Thomas crawled over the bed, eyes on my chest before rising to my face. "May I?"

"You just put your mouth between my legs," I said with a raised brow. "Usually you touch breasts first."

He paused, reaching for me. "I didn't think that mattered."

He was right. "I guess it doesn't."

"Do you prefer to have your breasts touched beforehand?"

Blinking, I tried not to flush as I admitted, "I like it, sure. But …"

"But?"

Getting to my knees, I pushed him to the bed, my hands reaching for his zipper, then tugging at his pants and briefs. "But I like having your attention between my legs more."

Placing his arms behind his head, he watched me pull his pants down his thick, hair dusted thighs, then assisted me by kicking them off.

Drawing in a deep breath, I removed my gaze from the lean muscles of his arms, the concentration marring his brow, and dragged them over his packed stomach to take in his length. He was long, thick, and perfect, and I couldn't stop myself from wrapping my hand around him.

Thomas hissed, and I looked up at his tortured expression. "Are you okay?"

"More than okay, but …"

"But?" I smirked as he peeled one eye open.

"I'm afraid that if you keep touching me, this will be over soon."

My hand fell away, but not before I dropped my mouth to the tip. I swiped my tongue over the engorged head, tasting the salt of his own excitement. "Holy Mary mother of …"

Laughing, I moved up his body, straddled him, and took his lips. "No need for blasphemy."

Then I was on my back, his tongue sweeping furiously into my mouth as his hand gripped my thigh, lifting my leg to wrap around his back. He broke away, his forehead resting heavily on mine as he rocked into me, every one of my nerve endings sparking for more.

"In," I demanded.

He didn't need to be told twice, and I waited, ready to help if he needed it, but he aligned himself and pushed forward within seconds, the tight fit making both of us groan.

It dawned on me then, as I felt him swell, fully seated inside me, that this was the first time I'd ever let a man inside me without a condom. It didn't frighten me, at least, not until I remembered … "Shit, wait."

Thomas stopped, the muscles straining in his shoulders and neck the only indication it was costing him. "What's wrong?"

"I've never, well, done it like this."

It took him a moment, then it registered, and he smiled. The white of his teeth drew my eyes, and my fingers. I ran them around his lips. "You have the most beautiful smile I've ever seen."

He huffed, shifting inside me, then groaned. "As much as I love hearing compliments from you for a change, I want to know what the problem is."

"I was on the pill," I said, "until you took me."

Thomas didn't say anything for an unbearably quiet moment.

"Thom—"

His mouth fell on mine, his body too, as he started thrusting, slowly finding a rhythm that matched the mating of our tongues. He tore his lips away a second, breathing out raggedly, "I love hearing you say Tom."

Like a drug, his mouth and his cock pulled me under, but I broke away after a minute. "Wait, you didn't—"

"If you want condoms, I'll get some. But for now, let me have you like this." His hands reached between our lips, a finger dragging over my bottom lip. He pressed his mouth to mine, then whispered, "With nothing between us but skin."

He didn't last longer than another minute, which I thought was a feat, all things considered. But if I thought he was done, I was wrong. I was half asleep when the sheets shifted over my skin, the cool night air making me reach blindly for them, but I found a head of hair instead.

"Lift your perfect ass, Little Dove."

I obeyed instantly, exhaustion evaporating.

He tucked a pillow beneath my stomach, then made me lift again as he tucked another on top of that one.

Getting curious about what it was he planned to do, I opened my mouth to ask him, then promptly snapped it closed, my eyes almost rolling shut as his fingers spread me open, and one slid down my center, playing with some of the cum he'd left behind.

"It does strange things to me," he said, voice layered with lust and sleep. "Seeing me inside your body. Leaking out of you."

Wicked delight pebbled my arms, and I whimpered.

After a few minutes, he carefully eased a thick digit inside. "I want you like this next."

I think I mumbled something, I wasn't sure. I wasn't sure of anything other than knowing it was going to be a long night.

CHAPTER

Thomas

BROWN EYES WELCOMED ME BACK INTO THE LAND OF real.

And all at once, I decided I hated sleep. If she was here, sleep was a barrier I didn't need. Though, as much as I'd tried to make the most of having her with me in my bed, my Dove passed out in the space between two and three in the morning.

I might've had some questionable morals, but there were plenty of lines I refused to cross. Having intercourse with a sleeping woman was just one of them.

"I want to stay, but we can't stay locked away here forever."

Her voice was clear as though she'd been awake much longer than me, stewing on her thoughts.

I shifted closer, my hand gripping her hip. Our legs were intertwined, the touch of her skin, and the fact she was here when I thought she'd escape to her room at first light made my dick excruciatingly hard, and my chest squeeze.

"Tom?" she questioned with a tiny smile, and I realized I'd just been staring at her. Admiring the way the morning light dripped over her delicate features and lit up the bronze specks in her dark eyes.

I yawned and turned my head to smother it with my pillow. Turning back, I mumbled, "If you're worried about your fed, don't be. He'll give in like the rest of them have."

The conversation woke me up, thanks to the annoyance that stemmed from the subject matter.

Little Dove rose onto an elbow, her hair falling into her face. My fingers gently nudged it back.

"Miles," she stopped, correcting herself, "Milo … I don't know. He's gone to a lot of effort. He won't give in easily, if at all."

I dropped my hand, but she took it in hers. "He will if he knows what's good for him."

Jemima's eyes bulged, which made me chuckle. "Never fear, Dove. If you want him alive, even if it kills me, I'll respect your wishes." Though I longed to pluck off every one of his fingers, then remove his hands, for simply touching her.

"You're a sweet monster."

I brought her hand to my lips. "Above all else. What I feel for you rises above all else."

Her eyes glistened.

A series of bangs thundered on the door. "Tom, wake up."

Jemima sat up, the gray sheet pressed to her chest. "It's okay," I said. "He won't come in."

Another bang on the door. "I know you're, ah, occupied, but you have a visitor. One you've been waiting for."

I sat up in a flash, calling, "Give me ten." Looking over at Jemima, I asked, "Want to shower with me?"

A nervous laugh tinkled through the room as she kicked her legs over the side of the bed, collecting her dress and bra. "Maybe another time."

"You know I will hold you to that."

She dropped the sheet, and my heart slid into my throat as her rosy nipples pebbled and she stretched her arms over her head. Little tease. "Come here."

She snapped her bra on, then tugged her dress over her head. "No, I've got morning breath."

I smacked my lips together with a cringe. "Good point."

Her laughter followed her out of the room, and I stared down at my hard dick, sighing.

Beau and Sage were sitting at my kitchen counter as I shrugged my jacket on and entered the room.

"...can't just borrow someone's hacksaw," Beau was saying, his tattooed hands wrapped around a coffee mug.

"Why the hell not?" Sage asked, turning the page in today's paper.

Beau shot him an incredulous look, of which Sage ignored. "That's a personal thing, man. There's memories attached to it."

I nodded at Murry in thanks as I took the cup of coffee he held out to me, ignoring the knowing smirk on his face.

"Tom, can I borrow your hacksaw?"

"No," I said, then looked at Beau. "He's downstairs?"

He nodded, glancing over at the door. "I stuffed a gag in for you. He's a noisy son of a bitch."

"Appreciated." I turned to Murry. "Lou?"

"She's upstairs doing Jemima's hair."

Both men's eyes landed on me at hearing that, Beau's nose still showing slight signs of bruising from where my Dove had nailed him. "How'd you get him?"

"We came by to check in and saw the beat-up old truck farther down the road."

"Nothing like a run through the woods in the morning," Sage murmured, taking a sip of coffee.

"Caught him near the creek where he slipped on a rock." Beau drummed his fingers on the countertop. "He wouldn't say shit."

"Which will make it all the more enjoyable." Sage licked a finger, turning another page.

After taking lengthy gulps of my coffee, I set the mug down and moved to the basement door. "Anything else I should know?"

Beau tilted a shoulder. Sage shook his head.

"Make sure Lou stays away from the kitchen." Murry knew the drill, and although the basement was soundproof, I didn't like to risk it.

My steps were slow. A warning that I was coming, and I wasn't in a hurry.

The room was bathed in darkness, but it was my domain, my safe place, so every detail was imprinted in my mind. The darkness didn't bother or hinder me.

But it apparently bothered my visitor.

Muffled complaints tainted the air, along with the harsh stench of sweat. Fear did strange things to people.

Some passed out.

Some urinated on themselves.

Some had bowel movements they couldn't control.

Some sweated profusely.

Some shook until their teeth rattled.

The list goes on, and judging by the fellow lying on my chair, he was scared, but he had some control. Which told me plenty. He knew about me, so he knew the risks of the job he'd been working.

Still standing in the dark, I let him work himself up some more, then decided it was time.

The light flickered on over our heads, the room aglow in a

dull, swaying yellow.

The whites of my visitor's eyes exploded, and muscles strained in his neck as he heaved unsteady breaths around the gag stuffed into his mouth. His hair was a bushy black and gray, his blue eyes bloodshot and lined with wrinkles, and his bottom lip busted. No doubt thanks to one of my friends upstairs.

I snapped some gloves on and pulled up a stool to sit beside him.

He didn't make a sound, yet thrashed against his bonds. "I'm sure you know why you're here."

The idiot had the nerve to shake his head.

"Let me repeat that," I said, leaning back and nabbing a needle from the prepped tray behind me. "I'm sure you know why you're here."

His beefy hand was red, and I gripped it tightly. With the tiniest bit of pressure, I pierced the skin beneath his thumbnail, then pushed. He squealed, nodding his head as his eyes watered.

Slowly, I pulled the needle out. "Oh, ready to talk already?"

He nodded emphatically.

To make sure, I repeated the process on every finger, his muffled shouts and thrashing body white noise as I calmly removed the needle from his pinky finger and tossed it into the jar of antiseptic.

I tugged the gag free and laid it down beside him on the chair, then waited as his red face took me in, water still leaking from his bloodshot eyes. "You sick fuc—"

"Anyone who's ever been in your position has said it all before. I know what I am, so please don't bore me and waste our time." I scooted closer, my voice menacing as I seethed, "Now, tell me who you are and why you're here."

He considered me a moment, a moment that was about to cost him severely, but then finally, he admitted, "I was hired to follow you."

I waited. Because surely, he knew that wasn't going to cut it.

"To get any information I could on you, and to …"

"To what?" I asked carefully even as my blood raged for vengeance.

"Your daughter. I was asked to find proof she wasn't yours, but I couldn't, and then I was told to … to just t-take her."

Without even looking, I grabbed the shears from the tray. Never mind that he was talking, or that there was more to be said, my heart couldn't cope with the idea of someone taking my sunlight.

"W-wait," he stammered. "The fuck? I told you!"

He thrashed as I stuffed the gag back into his mouth.

"I know," I said and wrapped the metal around the tip of his thumb. "But before, I was curious. Now, well, as I'm sure you can understand"—my hand squeezed the handles, and his screams, even muffled, drowned out the sound of the metal slicing through nail and skin—"I'm enraged."

I stopped right above the bone. Bones were troublesome things, and I didn't like to waste time. I'd rather pluck someone's teeth out than hack through bones.

That was a chore I saved for special visitors.

He continued to writhe and scream, and I stared as the blood ran rivulets down his hand, over the restraints, and left droplets on the chair.

I became nothing but collected rage at the thought of people conspiring against me in that way. It was one thing to attempt taking me down, but another entirely to involve my heart.

When he'd quieted some, I removed the gag, and asked, "Who asked you to take my daughter?"

Whoever it was, he mustn't have feared them much. He gave the information easily. "He was an agent, Milo or some, fuck me," he groaned, spit dribbling down his chin, his blood coated hand clenching, as he hissed through his teeth, "s-something like that."

I sighed, knowing I'd have to somehow break it to my Dove that the fed had to die after all.

"You're not a cop?"

He shook his head. "No, shit. No. But I work small jobs for undercover guys. I wasn't even going to take this one, but he offered me ten grand and paid half up front. Plus, m-my accommodation and airfare."

My teeth threatened to turn to dust, grinding as I gritted, "You offered to take a child for ten grand?"

He swallowed. "I wouldn't have hurt her, I swear. I just needed the—"

The gag shut him up, and I grabbed my favorite knife.

I pressed the intercom, and Beau picked up with a whistle. "Done already?"

"I lost my temper."

Beau laughed.

"Just get down here or send Murry if he's free. This one weighs a ton."

Beau trudged down the stairs a moment later, and I handed him the box of gloves.

We loaded the body onto a tarp, wrapped it up, then set it in the far corner.

"Think you and Sage could get it out of here?"

"Pigs?" he asked, smearing some blood between his fingers. The plastic glove crinkled as he opened and closed the digits.

"Half and half. The drums have been refilled."

He watched as I rolled up the soiled chair cover and tossed it into the fire I'd lit before he'd walked downstairs.

Then I went to the sink in the bathroom and plugged it, dumping a heap of bleach into it, followed by the shears, knife, and needles.

"He say why he was strolling through the woods like an amateur?" Beau asked as I rummaged through the cleaning supplies in the cabinet beside him.

"If he were that much of an amateur, why didn't you or Sage find him until now?"

Beau sighed. "Admittedly, I didn't bother looking that much." When I glared, he shrugged. "I thought it was just another fed, and Sage felt the same."

"*Just* another fed?"

"Come on, man. He was after the fed's girl. He lost, and the asshole can't let go. Hiring someone to find her wasn't going to do shit." Another shrug. "So, we didn't think the risk was all that high."

"He was after Lou."

"Fuck."

"Hmm." I sprayed the chair, then wiped it clean as Beau choked on his guilt.

"Tom," he started.

"Don't worry about it." I looked at him then, and snarled, "But know I don't give a fuck who you are, where you came from, or what you can do; you're no friend of mine if you can't even do me the courtesy of telling me you're not going to hunt someone properly."

I'd met Sage via Beau and some other contacts too. Beau I met formally four years ago when we'd both been hunting the same mark. We'd recognized each other from having attended the same school. He was a few years older than me, which often boggled my mind.

The night we ran into each other, years after our families had wronged us, instead of competing or killing each other, we split the money from the job and remained in touch.

Beau's jaw clenched, his tongue skating over his teeth behind shut lips. After a tense moment, his blue eyes hard on mine, they softened. "Yeah, I get it. Won't happen again."

We discussed what time he and Sage would remove the trash from my house, then he left me to my thoughts while I cleaned the floor.

After some time staring at the chair, I swallowed down the residual anger and fear that'd compelled me to end a stranger's life, and quickly cleaned up in the tiny bathroom.

Towel in hand, and wearing only my suit pants and briefs, I switched off the light and made my way upstairs. I entered the code, then pushed the heavy door open.

Sunlight assaulted my eyes and noticing a speck of blood inside my wrist as I shifted my hand to shield them, I quickly wiped at it with the damp towel as the door shut behind me.

I heard her, *felt her*, before I allowed my eyes to savor the sight of her in a pair of denim shorts and baby yellow T-shirt with frilled cap sleeves.

The pale hue to my Dove's skin and the fluttering of her skittish pulse in her neck had me pausing with the towel around my hand.

"Great," I muttered as she turned and made haste out of the room. "Just as she's acclimating, I had to go and kill someone."

CHAPTER
Thirty-four

THOMAS CAME TO MY ROOM NOT LONG AFTER I'D SEEN him walk out of that basement with blood smeared on the towel in his hands, but I didn't answer the door.

He stood there a few minutes, then I heard his soft footfalls fading down the hall as he chose to let me be.

I'd been thankful, and then I'd been angry that I'd been thankful he'd left me alone.

My head swam in a million different directions, but the strongest current kept taking me back to the night before. When he'd shared intimate parts of himself, and then refused to keep his hands off me long into the night.

Matching that man with the one downstairs was hard, but it wasn't as hard as it should've been. Which was troubling, to say the least.

After Lou had braided my hair into some twisted looking rope, I'd walked downstairs to get breakfast and coffee, and I knew, after seeing those two men in the kitchen, who observed me with clear intrigue, what kind of visitor Thomas might've had.

I didn't even bother asking where he was. I'd merely smiled and nodded a quiet hello, forgot about any food, and took my coffee upstairs to find Lou.

I shouldn't have gone back in search of food.

Thomas knocking on my door that afternoon reminded me that I hadn't been back downstairs since I saw him, and I still hadn't eaten.

The door was open, and he strode in, his gaze on me as he said, "Lou, go draw me a picture with a really big sun on it?"

Lou Lou looked from Thomas to me, and I smiled in encouragement. "And maybe some rain."

"A sun-shower?" she asked.

I squeezed her hips, setting her on the floor. "Yes, I love sun-showers."

"Me too!" She raced out of the room.

Alone, Thomas shut the door and came to sit beside me on the bed. His hand reached up, and his eyes seemed to ask permission, to which I just kept still. With his thumb smoothing over my cheek and his warm palm pressed against my skin, I could almost forget what he'd done that morning.

Almost. "Is your visitor still here?"

Thomas removed his hand, as if knowing his answer might force me to push it away, and he'd rather do it himself than have me reject his touch. "No."

Silence descended, and I shifted on the bed, tucking my knee beneath my chin as I studied him. "Why do you wear suits all the time?"

Seeming a little shocked, his lips parted, and his eyes skated down his clothing. "I'm a businessman. It would do me no good to appear otherwise."

"Your friends," I started to say, then thought better of it.

"What about them?"

I pulled the memory forward of the shoulder-length blond hair on one, his jeans and T-shirt, and tattoos. Then the almost shaved head of the other, and his cargo shorts and wifebeater. "Do they work in the same line of work as you?"

Thomas scrunched his nose. "Some might say yes, but there are differences."

"Including your wardrobes."

He sighed. "You don't like my suits?"

I laughed, partly because we were discussing suits when I assumed he'd just killed someone hours before, and partly because he looked downright perplexed I was questioning his clothing choices. "No, it's not that I don't like them. I guess I was just wondering."

"I want to be taken seriously and"—he paused, weighing how much he wanted to admit what he was about to say—"I guess, after wearing them for so long, I forget what else I like."

The day in the woods swam in, and our date at the coffee shop, as I murmured, "Jeans and a black polo shirt."

He met my stare with wonder filling his eyes. "Can I kiss you?"

It hurt, the word *no* threatened to reduce my mouth to cinders, and so I just shook my head.

It was his eyes that gave away any sting my reluctance caused as they turned from hopeful to downcast. Then he stood, adjusting the sleeves of his jacket before checking his pocket watch.

"Your visitor is dead, isn't he?"

"Yes," he said with his back to me.

His hand wrapped around the doorknob, and I asked one more question. "Who was he?"

"Someone your precious fed sent. To retrieve something precious from me."

I sucked in air so sharply, he pinned me with one last look over his shoulder. "It was kill or risk everything, Dove. There was too much at stake to let what I feel for you tamper with my better judgment."

"Girl, you're testing the limits of that man's feelings."

I looked up from where I'd been studying the back of a paperback in the library. "I'm sure he's fine."

Murry's incredulous laughter and my own lies made me cringe.

I slid the book back onto the shelf and plucked out a different one. "Did he send you to check on me?"

He scoffed. "No, he'd sooner chase you down himself than be made to look a fool asking where your feelings lie."

I smiled, opening the paperback and flicking through the time-worn pages.

"So where do they lie?"

I snapped the book shut, placing it on the small pile I'd gathered on the side table. "I'd rather not talk about it." I raised my eyes to his, offering a closed-lip smile. "No offense."

He lifted a shoulder, then straightened from the shelf he'd been leaning against. "No problem, but tell me this, are you afraid of him?"

"No," I said immediately.

"Disgusted with him?" A brow lifted.

That one I was incapable of answering as quick, and I sighed, taking a seat in the armchair beside my borrowed stack of books. "It's not that. I mean, I knew, and I thought I'd wrapped my head around it …"

Murry's voice softened with understanding. "Then it actually happened."

"Yeah."

He hummed, surveying the hall behind him quickly. When he looked back at me, he said with a lowered voice, "Lou Lou …

she caused fractures in his exterior. But you? You charged in and demolished every single one of his defenses." He tilted his head. "I don't know how, but you've changed him."

My words were all breath. "I don't know either."

A heavy pause made the echo of my heartbeat frighteningly loud.

"I guess there is no how." His eyes darted to the side table, then back at me. "There's just you."

With that, he left me to digest what he'd said, and my gaze followed where his had swung to the side table.

To where that small brown journal sat.

Everything warned me not to touch it, but with Murry's fleeting glance, and the way it was left out in the open … I didn't listen.

My fingers wrapped around the smooth leather, and I opened it.

I'll breathe for you
as you thaw
and hold you
as you melt
and wait for
the moment you ignite
and catch fire
in my arms.

Stop thinking the story is over
when you reach
the end
the end
is merely a guide
from written certainty
to the wonders of the unknown.

Pages upon pages of poetry stared back at me.
No dates and no time stamps.
Just words.

Shame has no place
where her heart leaves its trace.

To realize you were lonely
is to measure your past
against your present
and long for the future.

> Lie to me, Dove,
> then grip my skin tight.
> Lie to me, Dove,
> then whisper your sighs.
> Lie to me, Dove,
> then give me your cries.
> Lie to me, Dove,
> then cradle my thighs.
> Lie to me, Dove,
> then make it all right.
> Lie to me, Dove,
> then kiss me good night.

Oh, sweetheart
don't overthink it;
it's just your heart
and my heart
learning to beat
to the sound of
eternity.

You are an addiction
that shallows my lungs
with every inhale.

But not just words. Dark, haunted, and beautiful emotion.

I'd almost thought he wasn't writing about me until I saw the one on the last page.

Lie to me.

The last line had been written harshly, the tip of his pen indenting the page with his pain.

Pain that I'd caused.

With guilt tearing at my chest, I left my book selection behind and blinked back tears from blurring my vision as I left the library.

"Enter," Thomas clipped as soon as I knocked on the door.

He looked over when I did, and I shut the door behind me. "Is Lou asleep?"

"Yes."

His blunt answers reminded me of the first few interactions I'd had with him, and I told myself I deserved it, then raised my shoulders and feet, moving deeper into his room.

There was no sign I'd been in there. None. The remains of our dinner had been cleared and the bed made. The scent of our time together long faded from the cavernous space.

"What is it you need, Dove?" he asked, unclipping his cufflinks and tossing them onto a glass tray on the black dresser.

You, I tried to say, but the word wouldn't budge past my teeth.

Instead, I did my best to ignore his glacial stare and pulled the journal from behind my back. "You ... you wrote all these?"

Ice blue eyes flared as they caught sight of his words, his

heart, in my hands.

His tone was as crisp as his stare, when he finally said, "What did you think I did in my spare time? And with that journal?" When I hesitated, he laughed bitterly. "Don't answer that."

The small journal weighed down my shoulders and my heart as I said, "Thomas, I'm—"

"Back to Thomas now, are we?" He unbuttoned his shirt, his frustration making a few pop and sail to the floor, rolling and scattering. "Look." He sighed, walking closer but stopping a few feet away from me. "I never asked you to like or share my job with me. All I hoped was …" he trailed off, a hand rising and fingers pinching the bridge of his nose.

I took a step forward. "Was what?"

His hand slapped to his side, and his white shirt gaped open, that sculpted body doing its best to draw me closer, but I stayed put. "All I hoped was that you'd *like me*, that you'd may-be want to *share my life* with me."

Knowing I shouldn't, but that I didn't want to lie, I opened my mouth. "Those aren't the same thing?"

"No. I've already told you. I like what I do, as sick as that might make me appear, but it's not my life."

I glanced around the extravagance of the room, unable to stop my eyes from narrowing.

His laughter was dark and riddled with exhaustion. "Forget it."

I placed his journal down on the end of his bed. "I don't want to."

"You sure could've fooled me," he muttered, tearing his shirt off and reaching for the button above his fly.

"Tom," I tried again.

"Just go, Dove. It's been a long day, and quite frankly, I

don't care to have you torment me any further tonight."

His tone offered no room for argument, and really, I had nothing else to give him.

Except me.

So I backed up toward the door, watching his smooth back as his body heaved with heavy breaths. Then I left.

CHAPTER
Thirty-five

THOMAS WAS CALLED OUT TO A JOB THE NEXT MORNING. He left without a goodbye and had been gone for ten days.

Yet I refused to leave. Not out of fear of what waited beyond the castle's walls, but because anytime the thought even touched my mind, a searing pain would grip the organ in my chest, stalling my heartbeat and stealing my breath.

I bandaged my bruised feelings, my worries, and my longing by spending time with Lou. But after hours spent indoors and despite the size of their home, she grew bored as summer dragged on.

"Are you allowed outside?" I asked one morning as I helped Murry clean up after breakfast. He'd tried to stop me but gave in days ago when I didn't relent.

"Of course." Lou sucked jelly from her fingers, then released them with a loud pop. "Oh! You haven't met Jeffery, George, and Babette."

Murry cursed, a plate falling from his hands and into the sink.

"You okay?" I asked.

"Fine," he said, reaching for a dish towel and drying his hands. "Miss Lou, how about you go grab your hat, and we'll show Jemma together?"

"Okie dokie."

I waited until she'd left the room. "I'm sorry, I forgot that—"

"No," Murry cut in, hanging up the towel and then untying his apron. "That threat is gone, and most wouldn't dare enter this property. But … I'll come with you."

It wasn't until I saw the three huge pigs in a pen half an acre behind the house that it clicked.

The pancakes Murry made threatened to somersault out of my mouth, but I painted on a smile when Murry raised a brow, realizing his earlier hesitance wasn't so much about Lou Lou's safety.

It was about what they used the pigs for.

The pen was huge, and next to it sat a barn that had seen better days. Probably many years ago at that. The wooden doors were half opened, stuck in the dirt-crusted ground, and the white and cream paint was missing from most of the exterior.

Lou tossed the pigs a small bucket of scraps, laughing as they snorted and hobbled over to the fence.

Leaving them to eat, we strolled to the other side of the property, toward the woods that separated Verrone and Clayton land, Lou Lou racing through weeds that were almost taller than she was.

We stopped beside what I thought, when I'd looked out my bedroom window, was a dam, but was actually a neglected pool.

"Why is it," I asked, a hand over my eyes to shield them from the sun's glare, "that the inside of the house resembles the period it was built in, not a speck of dust or wear in sight, yet out here …?" I trailed off, knowing Murry would catch what I was saying.

Lou Lou skipped over to a patch of wildflowers.

"To scare people off."

Murry's words made sense, but it seemed a shame that a

place I once thought of with such reverence in my child-size heart looked as though it'd been abandoned.

We ate lunch together, and then Lou and I retired to the living room upstairs for a Disney movie marathon.

It was just after dinner, and Lou Lou had passed out with her head on my lap when Thomas's shadow spread over the arched entryway, followed by the man himself.

"Hey." I tried to tamp down the relief, the persistent burning and longing dancing through my bloodstream by stretching my arms, being careful not to wake Lou.

Thomas paused when he saw she was asleep, then frowned down at the food stuck to her cheeks. "She's six. She's allowed to go to bed dirty every once in a while."

"I can bathe her," he said, bending to brush some golden curls from her sticky face.

"You'll do no such thing. I'll run a washcloth over her face and hands when she's in bed if that'll make you happy."

He finally looked at me then, and dark pillows sat beneath his eyes, making the blue that much more vibrant. "Murry said you went to see the pigs."

"We did." I bit my lip. "You know, my dad always said to be wary of a man who owns pigs."

His eyes were on my mouth. "Your dad's a smart man."

"Babette is my favorite."

His brows furrowed as he studied me. If he was waiting for me to make another remark about his reason for having them, he'd be waiting a while.

When he realized that, he rose to his full towering height and went to leave.

"I missed you," I blurted.

All the oxygen in the room seemed to disappear as his body locked up.

Then, slowly, he pivoted and strode back, gripped my chin, and tilted my face to his. After staring his fill and finding my eyes reinforced my words, as well as the grip my hand had as it wrapped around his wrist, he pressed his mouth to mine.

After ten blissful seconds, where I felt my heart shrink and heal a fraction more, he took his lips away, and left me with whispered words, "I'm glad you're still here, Little Dove."

A little while later, after Lou was tucked in bed with her face and hands clean, much to her dismay as she smacked and whined at me, I went in search of my monster.

The door to his room was open, but he wasn't in there. Nor was he in the study or the library.

Searching downstairs, I heard voices funneling down the hall from the kitchen.

"It's not that pipe. Here, get out of the way," Thomas said.

I watched from the doorway as Murry crawled out from beneath the kitchen sink and grimaced, rising and using the countertop for support.

"What's wrong?" I asked.

"Something's blocking the pipe. I have a feeling it's built-up food, but I can't get the sucker undone."

Thomas, who'd changed into jeans, a T-shirt, and his slippers, slid the tool bag closer, already ducking beneath the sink.

Murry looked at his hands, disgusted, and stormed out of the kitchen.

I smothered a laugh and went to sit by Thomas on the black and white floor.

"Hi, Monster."

"Hi, Dove."

I smiled. "Where'd you go?"

"Do you really want to know that?"

"I do, actually. I'd also like to know why you didn't say goodbye to me."

He took his time answering, and I watched as his shirt lifted higher, exposing the patch of dark hair above his jeans that tempted my fingers to touch. "I had a job in Arizona, but it wasn't an easy find."

Nodding, I waited for him to tell me the rest.

"And I didn't say goodbye because I was behaving like a petulant child who couldn't seem to get his own way."

"You weren't that bad," I said, drawing out the words.

"Liar," he teased, and his slipper-covered foot nudged my bare one. "Can I ask you something?"

I nudged him back. "Of course."

"Your fed, do you miss him too?"

Oh.

"Um. Well, honestly"—his leg muscles looked tense as he waited—"since you kissed me that first time in the library, I've hardly thought about him."

"And you loved him?"

That had my hackles rising. "I did."

His silence told me he thought otherwise, but I ignored it and asked something I'd been curious about since he'd left. "The first time you kissed me, in my car …"

"He'd bugged your car."

"Right." I didn't know why I was disappointed when I'd suspected as much already.

"But Dove?"

"Hmm?" I stared down at my unpainted toenails.

"I wanted to, so I guess you could say I took advantage. But that second time I kissed you? It was just because I wanted to do it again."

A smile twitched my lips, and my feet swayed as I got lost among the memories, joining all the pieces that once seemed so puzzling together. "That's why you said not to call you, right?"

"Right." A clanking sounded before he said, "I'm curious. What about him lured you into his trap so easily?"

I wanted to argue that, no, it hadn't been that easy, but I'd be lying. I'd fucked up and trusted too soon. It was as simple and as complicated as that. "Do you really want to know that?"

At hearing his words repeated back to him, a low chuckle reached me. "I do, actually."

I smiled, but it was quick to fall as I thought of those first few weeks with Milo. "He was just, I don't know … larger than life. A dream."

Thomas snorted. The rare act lifted my lips. "You were enamored."

"Enamored?"

"Yes. Infatuated. Love-struck. Besotted. Enamored."

I frowned as that truth sank deep. "I should've known it was too good to be true."

"You're not that insecure."

"I'm not. It's just, we were worlds apart from the start. I didn't question it, just ran right to him. Open. Willing. Foolish."

Thomas was quiet for a moment, his body still. Then he murmured, "You might've been a job, but he didn't need to agree to it. He would've dissected everything about you before he even muttered a word of commitment." He made a groaning sound, then cursed, another rare act that I relished. "The guy wanted you. It was a win-win in his eyes."

Raising my knees, I leaned forward, peering around the cupboard door. "Want isn't the same as love though, is it?"

His arm moved, muscles flexing as he twisted something

back into place before carefully slinking out from under the sink. A pile of hair wrapped gunk hit the floor with a splat, followed by a wrench.

He closed the door and leaned back against it, looking at me. "It's not, but some might say it can lead to it."

Words formed and dried over my tongue as I watched him stand and take the gunk with him to the trash, then wash his hands.

Kicking the toolbox aside, he stood there a moment, and I could feel his eyes on top of my head, but I didn't look up. "Can I ask you something?"

In answer, he held out his hand, and I placed mine in it. His warm skin curled around mine as he effortlessly tugged me from the floor. With his hands framing my face, his eyes bouncing between my own, he waited.

"I know you said I can leave." His lashes lowered, then rose as I said, "I don't want to. Not yet, but I need to call my dad and my sister."

After staring at me for the longest time, he pressed his lips to my forehead, then stepped back, collected the wrench and toolbox, and set a phone on the countertop.

I tucked my lips between my teeth to contain my spreading smile and swiped at the tear about to roll down my cheek.

"I got your text. I'm glad the rain let up."

Puzzled, I was about to ask what he was talking about, then remembered.

My phone. Thomas probably had it.

"How's Cora?" he continued.

Cora? "Um, good," I said, pacing the rug in slow strides.

Seeing as I didn't know anyone named Cora, I ditched the subject. "So I know you won't want to hear this, but ..." A smile stretched my face and tinged my voice. "I kind of met someone."

Dad's silence made my heart pound and my feet stop moving. "Are you sure you're ready for that?" He puffed out a rough breath. "I'm not sure *I'm* ready for that."

Peering out the opened door of my bedroom to the bronze lit shadows beyond, I continued to smile. "I think I've been ready for him for a long time, but I just needed life to mess everything up first."

Dad laughed. "And this guy, he's a friend of Cora's?"

Walking to the window seat, I moved the curtains aside. The silver moon lined the treetops, and I could picture my dad in the two-story farmhouse on the other side of those trees, drinking his second cup of tea for the night on his recliner in front of the TV.

"No, he's from home, actually."

Dad yawned. "Well, I hope to God this one has more manners and respect, that's all I can say." He grumbled something about Milo beneath his breath, then sighed. "But you already know ..."

"You won't think any man is good enough." I laughed. "I know."

His smile was evident in his voice as he said, "You were always too sweet for the average Joe. When are you coming home?"

Knowing what I knew now, about Mom's affair, I wanted to run through the woods and squeeze him in a hug. But the need to respect his wishes overruled the urge, no matter how much it hurt.

"I'm not sure," I admitted. "But I'll call you once I figure it out."

"Make sure you do. And bring this new fella around. I need an excuse to polish my guns again."

Laughing, I said, "Love you, Daddy. Good night."

"Good night, Jemmie."

I hung up, then stared at the screen saver on Thomas's phone. It was a picture of Lou Lou from earlier this year. She was dressed up as a lion for book week, tiny ears sitting atop a headband on her head, and whiskers painted on her cheeks.

As I tried to remember my sister's number, I briefly wondered about what kind of things I'd find on the phone in my hand. Shaking my head, I gave it my best guess and pressed the phone to my ear again. He wouldn't keep anything incriminating anyway.

"Hello?" my sister's confused voice sounded.

"Hey, it's me."

She seemed to be checking the number. "Did you get a new phone?"

I'd called the house phone to speak to Dad, and so he wasn't able to see where I was calling from. I didn't think about that with Hope and inwardly kicked myself. "No, it's charging. I'm staying with a friend, and I'm using hers."

"You're staying with a friend."

"Uh-huh," I steered the conversation forward. "How are you? How are the boys?"

"Being little turds, but good. What friend are you staying with?"

Shit. "Cora, from school."

"I don't remember a Cora."

Double *shit.* "She started after you'd already graduated."

My eyes clenched shut until Hope said, "Okay, then. So what are you guys doing?"

"Uh, shopping and stuff. Mainly just hanging out."

She guffawed. "Cut the shit, Jemima. You hardly ever speak to your old friends, and you only shop when you need things or books. Where are you, and why lie?"

What to say, what to say, what to say.

I settled on being as honest as possible. "Remember that guy I was telling you about?"

"The weird one?"

I frowned. "He's not …" I exhaled a loud breath. "Okay, yeah. That one."

I waited for her to come to her own conclusions, knowing that would be the easiest way to deal with this. "You've been with him?"

"Yeah."

"And you didn't tell anyone because, *why?* You felt it was too soon? Or you were scared it'd all blow up again?"

"Kind of, but there's more." I licked my lips, dropping to the window seat. "Have you got time for a long-winded story?"

"Let me pour a glass of wine."

When she was ready, I told her everything. Everything besides Thomas taking me, and what he did for a living.

After she'd gotten over her shock, she asked, "Who was he investigating?"

"I don't know, he wouldn't say," I lied.

"Probably not allowed. Still, what a fucking dick."

Smiling, I agreed. Then I told her about what happened to Mom, how it'd involved Thomas's parents, and made her promise not to tell Dad about it.

"Yeah," she said after taking a moment to digest it all. "Better he doesn't know that we know. He's obviously kept it from us, thinking it was for our own good and for his."

I chewed my thumbnail. "Do you think she would've left us?"

Hope mulled that over for a minute. "I'd like to say she wouldn't, but when you love someone, you do some crazy shit." She snarked, "Like letting your husband pretend to be in a relationship with another person for a job, or lying to your family to hide away in a castle in the woods for weeks."

I laughed, relishing in how the reminder of what Milo had done no longer pinched.

"Seriously." She laughed. "Your life." Then her voice lowered. "So, is it like, just one giant fuck-fest?"

"He has a daughter, and no, we've … been getting to know each other."

"Oh, that's right." She hummed. "A bit strange, that you're with the son of the man Mom couldn't have. Kinda kinky." She swallowed some wine. "I like it."

"You're not upset?" I asked with a hint of disbelief.

"Over Mom?" She scoffed. "I was sad for years, but I'm done being sad. And you know what? I'm glad I didn't know back then. I would've been a lot worse of a teenager, that's for sure."

"So true."

"Hey," she jeered. "Anyway, you can't skimp on the details. Wait, just send a photo of him."

"No, you can meet him and see for yourself." Apprehension over the idea of Thomas and Hope being in the same room made me rush to say, "One day."

"You're such a bore. Not even a sneaky dick pic—"

"You're married," I hissed.

"What? I can still look." She snorted. "Not like Jace doesn't. Marriage doesn't make you blind, for Christ's sake."

I let her ramble on a while longer until the silence outside my room grew thicker, and my mind started drifting to the man in the bedroom at the top of the stairs. Then I said I'd call her in a few days and said goodbye.

Collecting a nightgown and a fresh pair of panties, I traipsed down the hall to the bathroom and showered before arriving at his door with his phone, a bare face, and my nipples beading against the black fabric clinging to my damp body.

CHAPTER
Thirty-Six

Thomas

"ELIMINATED?"

Sighing, I wrenched back the sheets and tossed pillows aside. "Yes."

"Eliminated how?"

"Brains splattered against the wall and enough evidence to suggest suicide, eliminated. Check the local news for your proof."

He coughed. "I see. I'll wire the rest of the money through now."

"Pleasure doing business with you." I hung up the phone and dumped it into my nightstand drawer.

The flighty pedophile had sent me on a wild goose chase through the desert, but unfortunately for him, he'd touched the wrong man's child. Now he was rotting in the hottest depths of hell.

After showering, I tugged on some briefs and climbed into bed. Not even a second later, a light knock sounded, and I called, "Come in."

I watched from where I was lying as she entered the room, shut the door, and set the phone down on the shelf by the window. "Thank you."

"Your family is okay?"

"Dad was fine," she said, walking with deliberate slowness toward the other side of the bed. "Hope knew something was up, so I gave her half the story."

My brow quirked, my eyes falling from hers to her breasts, her nipples hard against the fabric of her nightgown. "Half?"

"The half that wouldn't have her calling the cops." I shifted, my dick at full attention, as her knees hit the bed. "May I?"

"Never ask, Dove." I lifted the sheets, exposing my bare chest and thighs. "Always just do."

She tucked some hair behind her ear, a timid smile playing on her perfect lips as she spied my tented briefs.

"It's summer," I said with a shrug.

"And I've decided it's now my favorite season." Her lust-filled voice caressed the hardest parts of me, her nightgown drooping as she crawled across the bed, exposing the swaying globes of her breasts.

As soon as she was within reaching distance, I latched onto her upper arms and gently tugged her over me. My hands went to her thighs, smoothing up them to palm her ass, then pushed her panties down until they sat beneath her cheeks. "What was your favorite season before?"

"Spring," she murmured, her eyes darkening as she gazed down at me.

Grabbing the back of her head, I made our lips collide, then rolled her to her back and tore her panties down her legs.

"Open for me," I rasped. "Show me your wet flesh."

Her knees parted, falling to the bed, her feet rising as she brought her nightgown higher.

She let me stare, then let me murmur incoherent things to her intimate parts as I toyed with her, my fingers soon drenched in the glistening evidence of her want for me.

She was a squirming mess by the time my tongue met that swollen little bud, and she exploded, her legs trapping me as I lapped up everything her body felt for me.

"Tom," she said between pants.

I nipped her thigh, then soothed the sting with my lips and tongue, our eyes meeting over her soft stomach. "You're in here from now on." Rising, I kicked off my briefs, then motioned for her to come to me in the center of the bed. "Your things in this room, and you in this bed."

The breeze billowed the curtains, and an owl called high into the sky, but I couldn't think, feel, hear, or see anything but her as she lifted the satin barrier over her head, then straddled me.

"Every night, always," I said, taking a nipple into my mouth and sucking as I gazed up at her.

Her eyes were half open, the remnants of her orgasm making her body pliant and her voice husky. "We'll never sleep."

My tongue ran over her neck, over her chin. "We'll sleep when we're dead." I took her lips, hers meeting mine with a hunger that made my heart pound through every limb of my body.

Her hips rose, her hand reaching between us to squeeze gently before guiding a sinner into heaven.

CHAPTER
Thirty-Seven

"**A**NOTHER WORD FOR CRAZY?"

I took a sip from the floral teacup, pondering Thomas's question. "Mental."

He hummed. "Not right."

I turned the page of my book. "Batty."

He made a huffing noise.

I looked over at him, a smile teasing my lips. "Unhinged."

His eyes blazed. "Perfect."

Watching as he scrawled the word in his journal, then bit the end of his pen, I took another sip of tea and returned my attention to the book in my lap.

It'd been two weeks since I'd moved into Thomas's room. Two weeks of sleepless nights followed by lazy days spent with him and Lou. Some days, like today, spent with only him. We slept in late and without fail, every morning, he'd tighten his arms around me and whisper the same sleep coated words, "My Dove."

I'd never felt more cherished, more loved without any whisper of the word, and more at peace. As though life had tossed and turned me into this woman who was prepared to take on the task of loving a man most would run screaming from.

Yet it didn't feel like a task at all. It felt as natural as breathing.

Thomas was a paradox.

Benevolent tenderness oozed from his heart even as blood and violence tainted his soul.

Never would I have thought the combination could mix. Or that it'd make any sense.

But it did.

He did.

Thomas Verrone made perfect sense to me.

His phone broke the spell of my thoughts, and he fumbled blindly for it in his jeans pocket while trying to finish whatever it was he'd been writing that morning.

"What is it?" The widening of his eyes had my hand pausing as it carried the tea cup back to the side table.

"How the hell can someone steal a six-year-old from a party?"

With a crash I barely heard, the tea fell from my hands, splashing onto the rug and pooling around the shattered porcelain.

Thomas didn't seem to notice, and instead, he was pacing the room, his journal and pen discarded on the floor. "No, just get back here. Now."

He hung up and went to leave the room, and with my heart stuck on pause, I choked out, "Lou?"

Murry, wanting to give Thomas and me time alone, had taken her to Rosie's birthday party. Murry couldn't be seen in public, not with a price tag on his head, but he'd dropped her off and said he'd watch her walk in and wait out front.

"Taken," Thomas clipped, then disappeared down the hall.

Wanting to go after him, to reassure him she'd be okay, I tried to force my limbs to move.

Then a bang sounded downstairs, and I knew my presence wasn't what he needed right now. Right now, he needed a plan.

I stared out the window, silent tears tracing my cheeks until finally, Murry, driving Thomas's car, raced down the drive, and I raced downstairs.

"Did you see who took her?"

"He walked right in front of me, smiled, and I got out, ready to chase after him, but then he was gone. Put her in the back of some blue truck." He wiped a hand down his face, distraught. "I chased them but lost them once we hit the outskirts of the city."

Thomas cursed up a storm, his hand repeatedly diving into his hair, tugging as he paced the rug in the parlor. He looked like a caged animal, and if I wasn't so distracted by the description of the truck, I'd want to wrap my arms around him.

"Miles, I mean, Milo took her?"

They both spun around—Thomas's eyes filled with cold, hard rage, and Murry's remorse. It tugged at his scars and flattened his lips as he nodded.

The front doors boomed closed, and a second later, Beau appeared, his hair wet and his eyes hungry as they skated over the room. He rubbed his tattooed hands together. "Right, what's the game plan?"

"We don't have one," Murry said.

Beau frowned, hands dropping. "What?"

Before I could even open my mouth, Thomas was in front of me, pressing a gun beneath my chin. I swallowed, the cold metal biting into my skin, but it was the searing of his betrayed blues that hurt the worst. "What did you do?"

"W-what?" I tried to talk, but the pressure of the gun trapped my jaw shut.

"Tom, fuck. Put it away," Murry growled.

"Shut up." I heard the safety unlock, and Thomas's voice became so cold, his breath singed the skin of my lower face. "You've been waiting, haven't you? Biding your time."

His head cocked to the side. "Tell me, Dove. Was this your plan? Fool me into believing you were comfortable, that you *wanted* to be here, that you cared too much about us to betray us"—his nostrils flared, eyes narrowing to slits—"only to give him enough proof, and my kid, as leverage to end me?"

"T-Tom," I tried again to talk.

He pressed harder, and I winced as pain lanced through my jaw. "Because if I find out that's true, regardless of whatever you two might think you can do to me, I'll kill him …"

"Tom." Beau appeared behind him, tone filled with warning. "Come on, enough."

"I'll kill him," he continued, "over the course of a week, and I'll make sure this bullet, in this very gun, only enters your beautiful, traitorous brain after you've seen me remove every piece of skin from his body. Every. Fucking. Piece."

Beau pulled him back, and Thomas shrugged him off, eyes never leaving mine as I struggled to draw air into my lungs and gingerly shifted my jaw.

"They can't just snatch a child from a birthday party, Thomas. Fed or not, kidnapping doesn't fucking fly," Beau said.

Thomas rubbed at his brow, the gun hanging from his other hand. "In case it's not obvious, he's not playing good cop anymore." His chest rose sharply as he dragged his eyes from me. "Get her out of here. Murry, take her downstairs."

Murry rounded on Thomas. "Tom, think about this a minute."

"Too late for that. Thinking is something I should've done weeks ago."

Beau took my arm, his hold surprisingly gentle as he steered me out of the room and toward the front doors.

My wet eyes and pounding heart made it hard to see. Made it hard to shake my thoughts together. "Wait."

Beau stopped, talking low. "Don't even try it. You need to go unless you want to end up back in that basement. If you think he was joking—"

My hand swept through my hair. "No, I know. But Milo … he wants me."

Beau frowned and let go of my arm. "Explain."

My words were rushed, my hand stuck in my hair. "I was his pawn. I was his way in. And Thomas is right, I am the proof he needs. And I know you might not believe me, but that doesn't mean I conspired against him, or that I plan to tell anyone anything. Just …" I let out a shaky breath. "Take me to him. Please. I'll get Lou back."

Beau leaned forward. "And how the hell would you know where he's keeping her?"

"I know where he'd be. If this was his plan, he'd make it easy for me."

Beau sucked his teeth, staring at me a long moment. It was a stare that made me take an unbalanced step back as blame lurked in his eyes, further lighting my burning heart ablaze. I knew he didn't believe me, not entirely, but his shoulders sagged. "Fine. Lead the way."

"But …" I glanced back down the hall.

"Forget it. He's too much of anything right now to think clearly. Let's go."

My knees threatened to buckle as I stepped through the front doors.

I knew Thomas was scared, that he was hurt and angry, and deep down, I couldn't even blame him for accusing me of betraying him.

Deep down.

For on the surface, all I could feel was his ice layered threats, and the cool metal of his gun against my trembling skin. Skin he'd promised to cherish and to worship with penned words and warm whispers.

He wasn't my monster anymore; he was now the monster he needed to be to get his little girl back.

Even if that meant ruining me.

CHAPTER

Thirty-Eight

"**W**HEN YOU GET DONE WITH THIS ASSHAT, CALL. Your purse, phone, all of it, is in the back."

I blinked for what seemed like the first time since we'd left Glenning and turned around to snatch it from the back seat.

"Not gonna ask me how I got it?"

"Does it matter?"

Beau chuckled. "Okay. Well, I took it from your car. Which is parked in the barn." As I remembered the barns permanently half opened doors, he added, "There's a back entrance to that old thing. Thanks for the busted nose, by the way."

My eyes bulged at that. "That was you who grabbed me?"

His top lip curled. "Sure was."

"I won't apologize for the nose, then."

Beau breathed out a laugh and then turned up the radio.

"I know what you're thinking," Beau said after a song had finished playing over the silence, and then barely looked before driving into the rows of colorful traffic heading into the city.

My stare remained trained on the window. "I'm sure you think you do."

Again, he chuckled. "I like you and all. I think having you around has loosened Tom up some. But you need to realize you're not with a rational man."

"I know." *Boy, did I know.*

He veered toward the city exit. "So why do you sound like you might cry any minute?"

"I'm fine. Just worried about Lou."

"Uh-huh. Tom just threatened to kill you and blames you for all this, but you're fine."

I let my lashes flutter over fresh tears. I had to turn them off. "I will be. We just need to get her back."

Beau sighed. "Look, you and I both know your prick of a fed won't hurt her. It's you that you should be worried about."

"He won't hurt me either."

"Hasn't he already?"

I shot a glare at him, and his grinning face made my hands itch to smack something.

I diverted the subject. "And what do you do for a living, Beau?"

He tsked. "What a question." He paused before saying, "All you need to know is I do what I want."

"Does it involve killing people?"

Cursing, then laughing, he glanced at me. "Get straight to the point, why don't you?" At the unamused look on my face, he raked a hand through his dirty blond hair. "At times, sure."

I already knew that, but I was too lost inside the feelings tearing at my insides to care.

Beau turned the radio down once we got closer. "So what are you going to tell him?"

"Nothing."

He made a scoffing sound. "That's probably not going to work. You need a plan of action. You need to give him something to get the hell out."

He pulled over, and I unclipped my seat belt and jumped

out two houses down from the one I shared with the man I thought I'd marry. "You don't need to worry about me."

"Okay then, lady." Beau laughed around the words. "Send her out as soon as you can. I'll keep circling the block until I see her."

Milo's truck was parked in the drive, sunshine glinting off the chrome bumper. Beau turned around and drove away.

My legs were concrete as I forced them up the drive. My hand a boulder as I pounded on the door as hard as I could, and my eyes weighed down by more tears as Lou Lou opened the door. "Jemma!"

"Hey, little Lou." I wrapped my arms around her, inhaling her cinnamon scent, then whispered, "Beau is coming to pick you up, 'kay? Go stand at the end of the drive and wait there until you see him."

"Okay, but we made cookies," she said.

I looked up then, straight into the eyes of desperation.

A small grin tugged at Milo's lips. "Hey, Jem."

"Go," I told Lou when I heard Beau's truck stop a few houses down.

She waved goodbye to Milo, then raced down the grass, and I turned my attention back to Milo before he could step outside and make things worse. "What were you thinking?"

"I would never hurt a child, Jem. Come on." He had the audacity to half roll his eyes. A pair of handcuffs were tugged from his back pocket. "But I'll need to take you in to ask you a few questions about the well-being of Miss Lou Lou Verrone. You know, being that you're her teacher and all."

I hissed, "Now? You're interested in her well-being *now?*"

I stepped away as he came forward, reaching for my wrist. "You know why I'm taking you in. Please, don't make this harder than it needs to be."

"You're not cuffing me," I spat. "I'll get in the damn truck myself."

As I walked over and opened the door, I quickly glanced down the street. Beau's truck was nowhere to be seen, and my stomach sank as I climbed up into the cab.

"Jem." Milo got in, and the truck grumbled to life. "Talk to me. What the fuck happened there?" His eyes looked me over.

"Do I look like I spent the past month with a killer?"

His jaw clenched, then he backed out of the drive. "I just want to make sure you're all right."

"No, you want to use me to get to a man who's done nothing wrong." It was easy to lie, I discovered, when to do the opposite could destroy your heart. Mine couldn't handle any more damage.

"You know that's not true."

I said nothing as he drove through the suburban streets, then followed the main road into the city. And I resolved to do just that.

Until he started talking about us.

"You don't even know"—he laughed out—"how fucking worried I've been, Jem. If something were to happen to you ..."

"What?" I asked. "You'd what, Milo? Don't you have a broken marriage to repair?"

His mouth snapped shut and remained that way until we arrived at the police station and he led me inside, straight past the desk attendant, and down a gray painted hall to an empty room.

Approaching the table, I dropped into a seat, the cool air causing the hair on my arms to stand as I watched Milo flick switches on a recording system by the wall, then leave the room.

It was surreal to see him do a job I had no idea he was even capable of.

How easy it was to forget just how hurt I'd been by his lies, when my heart now hurt worse, and for different reasons.

For a different man.

Milo returned with a small file, and I shoved down the emotion desperate to crawl out of my throat and eyes.

"Is that it?" I raised a brow.

He frowned, tugging out a chair opposite me at the table, then taking a seat. "What's with the attitude?"

"What's with kidnapping a kid from a birthday party just to get me to talk to you?" When he shot a worried glance at the recording device, I grinned. "Whoops. Stealing kids isn't okay? Even for a federal agent?"

"Jemima," he warned.

"You know, I could forgive you for upending my life and breaking my heart with your lies, but taking her?" I lowered my voice, pushing the words through clenched teeth, "That I'll never forgive."

I could tell when the Miles I knew became Milo, his mask slipping away. "Why do you care about her so much? Isn't she just a student?"

"I want a lawyer," I said.

He guffawed. "Jem, what?"

"You heard me." I glared. "I won't answer any questions without a lawyer present."

"You don't need one."

I pretended to look interested in my unpainted nails. "I've decided I'd like one anyway."

His hard stare threatened to flatten me to the seat, and I might've caved some months ago. But that was then. Before my world turned upside down. For the better, no matter how much my chest was on fire. "You're serious."

"Deadly."

He blinked, then laughed and roughly scrubbed a hand over his stubble-coated chin. "We're not the bad guys here."

"We?" I asked, pretending to look around. "Funny, the only other person here who's even remotely interested in me is you."

"Jem, I want to make sure you're okay." His eyes pleaded, but his eyes were carefully trained liars too.

"And as I've said, I'm fine."

"You were kidnapped by a hitman. A criminal with strong familial ties to the Sicilian mafia. Someone who enjoys killing others for a living." He said the words slowly as though my trip away from home had cost me more than a few brain cells.

"No," I said, then drawled back, "I spent half the summer at my boyfriend's home. There's a bit of a difference."

He slouched back in his chair, spearing a hand through his hair. "Jesus, fuck. You're joking, right?"

I just looked at him.

"Jem, no." He leaned over the table, face paling and jaw hardening. "This is so far from okay, it's not even funny." Remembering we were being recorded, his voice lowered to barely a whisper, as he accused, "How fucking could you?"

"There's nothing else you really need to know, so until I get a lawyer, I'm done talking."

We sat in silence, well, I did, for another ten minutes. Milo shot question after question, accusing look after pleading look, but he eventually gave in and left the room.

I watched the clock, wondering how long Lou had been home. If Thomas was okay, or if, at the very least, he'd calmed down.

Milo returned when the clock struck three. "Come on."

I stood, the chair almost falling back in my haste to get out of there. "I'm free to go?"

"No," he said, not looking at me. "You're in a cell tonight for impeding a federal investigation. But don't worry, I'll make sure you get one to yourself."

My throat closed when he grabbed my purse from the table, but I croaked, "Gee, how chivalrous of you."

His touch made me want to reach around and punch him, maybe knee him in the balls again. But too shocked by the unexpected, it was all I could do to breathe properly as he shut me in a tiny cage that reeked of ammonia and sweat.

The green gate rattled as he locked it, then he leaned his forearms on it. "Holler when you're ready." After pointing up at the small black camera in the ceiling, he walked away.

I refused to cry, but holy mother of should've kicked him in the balls, it was hard.

I looked over at the stained mattress that was no thicker than my thumb and sank down to the concrete floor, my head resting against the patched-up wall behind me.

With nothing else to do, and no chance of sleeping, I sat, and I waited.

He was mad, but maybe he'd come for me.

But after eating a bread roll and ignoring the sludge pile they called soup for dinner, I woke myself up from naïve dreaming yet again.

He couldn't even if he wanted to.

That was probably also part of Milo's plan. Though who knew what he'd be able to do if Thomas walked into the precinct. I'd bet a whole lot of nothing, or he'd already be in custody, but that small file suggested otherwise.

At the very least, he could end up where I was, and the thought of him here, pacing the cell with fury lighting his blue eyes made me smile, even as I pleaded with whoever would hear my thoughts to make sure that didn't happen.

Footsteps clipped toward me. "Jem-Jem."

My head rolled to face Milo as he lowered to sit on the floor. "Can I go yet?"

He shook his head and grabbed the bars. "I can't do that. I want to, but I can't." He blew out a rough breath, eyes meeting mine. "Please, just … give me something. What did you see? What did he tell you? Something."

I turned away and resumed staring at peeling paint. "What was in the envelope you had me collect from the grocer?"

"Keys to a car he wouldn't know to follow. And directions to a hotel."

I spoke again before he could. "You knew what happened to my mom."

His silence was answer enough.

A few minutes ticked by before he started talking. I didn't know if his plan was to talk until I said something I shouldn't have, but if it was, I was ready. "I couldn't break your heart like that, even if I was allowed to. I'm sorry." He sighed when I said nothing. "I've missed you, Jem. Forget all the bullshit for a minute. You know I miss you, and that I love you. Or else, I wouldn't still be here, trying to make sure I didn't blow my life to hell for nothing."

"If you're expecting me to feel sorry for you, that won't happen."

He huffed. "I'm not, but I am hoping you'll believe me when I say I just want this to be over. So we can go back to being us."

"There's no us to go back to." My voice was flat, bored.

"I don't believe you. You loved me—"

"Exactly," I said. "Past tense. I loved you once, but that time has now passed."

"What? This isn't you, Jem. You can forgive me. I know you can if you—"

Fed up, I spoke over him. "I can forgive mistakes, *Milo*. I can forgive betrayal. Maybe even of this magnitude." I met his gaze, and my voice softened. "But I can't just do that. It's not that simple. You forced me into loving you, forced me to hand over parts of myself that I'd never shared before, all the while you were feeding me scraps. Enough to gain my love and sustain it, but not enough for me to grant you forgiveness should the day come that you'd need it." A bitter laugh left me. "Funny, how I never realized just how little you gave until I'm faced with what I might lose."

He cleared his throat. "Lose what, Jem?"

With tears threatening, I looked away. "Do your parents even live two hours north? Where is that anyway?"

"Lambton, which is three hours north."

"And your last name? Is it really Fletcher?"

"It's Carlson. I'll tell you anything you want to know. Just tell me you're not in love with him."

A shallow laugh was my only response. I knew enough.

He kept trying, kept apologizing, but I pretended to fall asleep, and eventually, he left me alone. In a disgusting cell, on the cold, hard ground, and with renewed vision.

Milo Carlson was a spineless, self-serving dick.

CHAPTER
Thirty-Nine

Thomas

LOU RUBBED HER EYES. "WHEN WILL JEMMA BE HOME?"
Pulling her duvet up to her shoulders, I bent low and kissed her forehead, my eyes squeezing shut as I whispered, "Soon."

"It's getting late," she said as if I didn't know.

"She's just busy."

Lou rolled onto her side, peering up at me. "Is she with that man who made me cookies?"

My stomach revolted at the reminder.

"Yes, he's an old friend. Did you eat them?" Thoughts of the many different poisons he might've laced them with flashed through my mind.

Lou laughed at my expression, then pouted. "No, when Jemma arrived, I forgot to take one."

My next breath was ragged as I told myself to calm down. He wouldn't poison a child, but he apparently had no issues taking her and my Dove hostage.

Running a hand over my hair, I said, "Good night, Lou."

"G'night, Daddy."

It never got old, hearing her say that. The first few times had been jarring, to say the least. Considering I was so far from a paternal figure when she came to live with me, it was ridiculous. But over time, she wormed her way beneath my skin and slithered inside my heart. Tenacious little thing.

Eventually, I went from being confused to cringing to smiling so hard my face hurt.

Back in my room, I paced quick strides over the rug, my mind whirling with what-ifs.

What if she didn't forgive me when I saw her again? What if he was hounding her for information? What if he was begging her for another chance? What if she was so upset over my irrational actions, she took him up on the offer? Or, worst of all, what if he'd touched her, and she'd let him?

It was a mistake to instantly place the blame on her slender shoulders. I saw that now, but then, all I could see was rage and every worst-case scenario.

Forgetting the way someone touched you, laughed with you, and loved you was as easy as flicking a switch when part of your heart had been momentarily ripped from your chest cavity.

Over and over, thoughts twirled and overlapped, each becoming worse than the one before, until Murry appeared before me, shaking my shoulders. "Hey, hey." He slapped my cheek.

I growled, shoving his hand away.

He stepped back, raising his hands. "I was worried. You've been in here for an hour, mumbling to yourself"—his eyes shot upward—"and ruining your hair."

"She hasn't called. Beau hasn't called …" I turned and strode to the French doors, staring unseeingly to the dark depths beyond. "He said he'd call."

"I know," Murry murmured.

Beau was waiting in the city, not far from the precinct where she'd been taken in for questioning.

"I have to go."

"You don't. What can you do? Charge in there and demand they release her?"

I didn't answer that, and Murry soon left me to my anxiety-laden thoughts, for which I was thankful. One glance at the bed she'd made the morning before had me wanting to set the sheets aflame. Her scent was in my pillows, the hurt look in her eyes everywhere I turned.

Murry's last words came back to me, and I grabbed my phone, scrolling until I saw the last unknown number Jemima had dialed, and hoped to god it wasn't her father who picked up.

"Hello?" a sleepy voice greeted.

"Hope?" I asked.

"Yes, who is this?"

Breathing a sigh of relief, I said, "Thomas Verrone. Your sister's … boyfriend." The word boyfriend sounded empty. The title nowhere near the realm of suitable for what we were.

Immediately, Hope went from tired to alert. "Where is she? What's happened?"

Pinching the bridge of my nose, I asked, "How much has she told you about me?"

"Just that you were weird when you first met, and that she'd been staying with you over the summer. Why?" she asked. "What's going on?"

Weird. I shook that off and steeled myself, ran a lie through my mind, then confirmed it'd do. "I can explain quickly, but then I need your help."

She listened, and ten minutes later, she said she was on her way.

I hung up and inhaled a deep breath, the tension in my body loosening for the first time in hours as I slowly set some of it free.

My Dove. My Little Dove.

I'd sent her away, discarded her like she hadn't even mattered. Threatened her life knowing I could never take it. No
matter what she did or didn't do.

But I was too taken by anger and fear to remember that she
and Lou … one wasn't more precious than the other. I needed
them both for different reasons, and I loved them both for different reasons, but ultimately, I couldn't survive without both.

They were the only things that kept me sane.

They were all that glittered in a world of dark gray.

They were all that mattered.

And so I waited, and then I got my keys and decided I could
wait closer.

CHAPTER
forty

I MUST HAVE FALLEN ASLEEP BECAUSE WHEN I AWOKE, WITH my neck and back aching and my ass numb, the sun was creeping through the smeared miserable excuse for a window at the top of my cell.

"I don't give a fuck who you are, let her out before I call my dad and he speaks to your superior."

My heart stalled, then thumped hard.

Hope.

"Ma'am," someone said, "with all due respect, what exactly is your daddy gonna do?"

"Oh, Doug Clayton?" Hope laughed like a maniac. "That's right, what's Doug Clayton, the guy who used to miss my volleyball games and dance recitals every weekend just to run this cesspit, gonna do?"

Cursing was followed by, "I'll get the keys."

"Wait," someone said. "Agent Carlson said to hold her until he comes back."

"You mean to tell me that joke of a man locked her up, then went home to sleep in a *motherfucking bed?*"

Oh, shit.

The fact he probably did do that was the only reason I didn't let the laughter that was sitting in my throat free.

"Give me my sister before I call a lawyer and my dad."

A minute later, a young cop opened the gate, and Hope was hauling me to my feet, fury creasing her forehead and pinching her lips.

"How'd you know I was here?"

"Explanations later." She shoved my purse at my chest. "Let's go."

Exhaustion and soreness made walking those first few steps excruciating, but as I passed the front desk attendant, who was talking quickly to who I guessed was Milo or their superior, it vanished, and I strode fast for the doors.

Hope removed her hand from mine to unlock her SUV and open the door. I climbed in and gave her directions to my apartment.

Five minutes later, we walked inside the stale, dust-covered one-bedroom home I'd barely lived in, and I nearly wept with relief. "I need a shower, stat."

"Hang on a minute." Hope shut and locked the door. "You need to explain what that asshole did to you."

"Hope," I whined. "Give me ten minutes, 'kay?" I needed the time to come up with some muddied version of the truth. She knew Milo was undercover, but she didn't know he'd invaded my life to get closer to Thomas.

She huffed, stabbing a finger at me. "You have as long as it takes me to find some decent coffee and breakfast."

I nodded, and she locked the door behind her.

I'd taken most of my clothes to my dad's when I'd intended to stay there for the rest of summer, but I'd left behind a few pairs of jeans, some tanks and T-shirts, and a cocktail dress.

After brushing my teeth with a spare toothbrush I kept beneath the sink, I nabbed a pair of cotton panties, a bra that'd seen better days, then a tank and light denim jeans. In the shower, I scrubbed until I felt my skin burn beneath the hot water.

I hadn't left any shampoo, so I settled for wetting my hair and spraying some leave-in conditioner once I'd gotten out.

The tank was tight, too fitted, and the jeans scratchy and a pain in the ass to tug on. I'd just buttoned the fly when a light tapping sounded at the door.

My stomach roiled, and my hands shook, but I walked to the door, asking through the wood, "Who is it?"

"Your monster."

I wrenched open the door, my eyes tingling as I took in the sight of Thomas in a crumpled white T-shirt and jeans. He looked behind him, then gazed back at me with bloodshot eyes. "Let me in?"

I nodded and stepped back, his boots heavy over the old hardwood floor.

As soon as I shut the door, he grabbed me and hauled me to his chest, hands tight against the back of my wet hair, and his chest heaving beneath my cheek. "I'll kill him. I'll cut open his chest and bring you his heart. I—"

"Shhh," I laughed out, trying to gaze up at him, but he wouldn't release his hold.

"I'm sorry, Little Dove. I wasn't thinking straight. You have to know I would never be able to …" he trailed off, his lashes closing briefly over his bloodshot eyes.

Drawing in a long breath, I pushed away, and Hope opened the door, almost knocking us over as she barreled in with coffee cups and a large brown bag full of things that smelled incredible.

"Oh," she said, her lips shaping around the word. She shut the door and looked Thomas up and down. "You must be the evil drug lord."

I coughed. "What?"

She waved a hand and marched to the kitchen. "He called me and explained why your ex is being so crazy. That he was after Thomas because his family has ties to some drug trade."

I arched a brow at Thomas, who lifted his shoulders.

Shaking my head, I thanked her for the coffee as I took a seat on a stool at the small bar.

Thomas strode forward, eyes on me as I looked away, then he pressed his front to my back. The weight and his warmth were comforting enough to ignore the pinching pain in my chest when I remembered the way he'd looked at me, accused me and forsaken me without a second thought yesterday.

"So, he called you?" I asked Hope, then took a long sip of coffee.

She shoved a clump of muffin into her mouth, chewing around it. "Uh-huh. Late last night. I drove until I couldn't see straight, then stopped and refueled." She laughed. "I couldn't believe it; my baby sister ending up behind bars. Never ever would I dare to even imagine such a crazy idea," she stopped, smirking, "but there you were. Asshole," she added.

"Thank you."

"Don't mention it. I needed a mini vacay." She grinned above my head at Thomas. "And it was worth it to meet this tall, dark, and apparently naughty, creature."

Trust Hope to find the idea of a drug dealer sexy, I thought with a smile.

"You have a daughter?" she asked Thomas. "We should totally make sure our kids hang out, you know, considering they're practically cousins." She licked her finger and took a sip of coffee.

I tried not to choke as I lowered my to-go cup.

Thomas obviously had no qualms about humoring her. "I do; she's almost seven."

Hope's eyes lit, dropping to me. "Perfect."

Jesus. "Stop scaring him."

Hope flicked her long, dark hair over her shoulder. "He doesn't look scared to me."

Thomas squeezed my shoulders reassuringly in response and continued to humor her as I dragged a muffin to my mouth and demolished it.

She left half an hour later, needing to get home before nightfall so Jace didn't have a coronary looking after the boys on his own.

"She's …" Thomas tapped his chin after the door slammed shut on Hope's sashaying hips.

I headed to my room. "My opposite in every way."

"I don't think you're as different as you think."

I wanted to ask why he thought that, but my eyelids drooped alongside my heart as he took a seat next to where I was lying on my bed.

Thomas moved the blankets from the end of the bed to cover me, then sighed as he looked around my room. "You're upset with me." He looked down at me. "And rightfully so."

The temptation to lie, to have him lay down next to me and make the past twenty-four hours disappear, was strong. "I am," I admitted. "You don't trust me or didn't. I don't even know." I yawned. "I just need some space. Some sleep, probably, and then we can talk about it."

Thomas stared a long moment, ice-bright eyes tugging at my resolve. Then he ran a hand through his unnaturally mussed hair, strands falling around his face.

"I don't want to leave you. Can you be upset with me at home?"

Home. The way he'd said it made my lips and heart twitch. "I could be, but I'm not ready to yet."

His brows furrowed. "You mean to say you'll still be mad if I leave you, like you've asked, when you come home and we've talked about it?"

I couldn't help it. I laughed, tears leaking out of my eyes. "Maybe. I'm sorry," I whispered.

"For what? Why are you apologizing?" He scooted closer. "Explain. Are there stages of anger for women?"

Sitting up, I took his face, pressing my lips to his for as long as my heart could bear, then released him. "I know you were scared, and angry, but you hurt me." His head lowered, lips seeking mine again, but I slumped back to the bed. "A lot worse than he ever did." I let that sink in. "Do you understand?"

"Dove." The name was a pained sound.

I did my best to ignore the harsh swallow he took. "Go home, Thomas."

"Thomas?" With a frustrated groan, he stood. "Fine. But I'll be back tomorrow."

"I know," I said.

He still stood there, his feet unmoving and his beautiful face creased with indecision.

"Time, Thomas."

"Time." He blew out a breath and nodded. "Okay."

Yawning again, I watched him walk toward the door, the thread that tied me to him growing taut, urging to be gathered.

Thomas stopped, turning back. "Dove, I know you trust him to a certain extent, but a man like him clearly doesn't do well with losing. And he's lost a lot." Pulling out a gun from his waistband, he set it on the dresser. "He's spiraling. I know you know how to use it, so don't hesitate to. It'd be in self-defense."

I didn't even blink at the weapon, just met his gaze, then let my eyelids flutter closed when the apartment door shut.

The sound of a gunshot had my eyes flashing open, and my legs hauling me across the room to the gun on the dresser as my heart pounded.

I flung open the apartment door, and seeing Thomas slumped against the wall on the landing below the first set of stairs, blood coloring his white shirt crimson, I didn't think.

Clicking off the safety, I raised the gun at Milo, whose gun was still trained on Thomas, ready to pull the trigger again.

"Don't you fucking dare," I called.

"Dove," Thomas wheezed.

Milo's eyes widened, swinging up at me. "Don't be foolish, babe. Put it away."

The metal was cool against my steady fingers, fear and anger slowing my breathing and clearing my vision as I pressed my finger against the trigger and shot him in the shoulder.

CHAPTER
forty-One

RACING DOWN THE STAIRS TO THOMAS, I SCREAMED FOR help at the top of my lungs, knowing no one else came into this stairwell besides the landlord who owned the building. But someone had to have heard the gunshots from out on the street.

Milo cursed, folding over and almost falling down the stairs. He caught himself on the railing, but his gun clattered down the steps.

I set mine down and forced my eyes to what they didn't want to see. The sight was enough to send my shaking knees to the harsh concrete and rip off my tank.

I pressed it into the wound in his lower abdomen, and Thomas groaned, his eyes struggling to stay open. "Tom, look at me," I urged, then screamed for help again.

"For eternity," he rasped, lips tilting.

"Don't be cute right now."

"Holy fuck," I heard someone say, followed by the sound of them talking into a phone. "Yes, two victims and one, ah, almost naked chick."

Thomas cursed as I pressed harder on the wound that wouldn't stop gushing, then mumbled, "Dove, I think I'd rather die than have strangers see you half naked."

I laughed, a sob catching in my throat. "Then it's too bad

I'm not going to let you. So deal with it."

He smirked, then whispered words that made my heart soar and plummet, for I knew why he was saying them now. At that very moment. "I've been waiting for you." He coughed. "And whatever happens, I'll gladly wait for you again."

"Don't," I warned, tears drenching the word.

"Look at me," he demanded.

I did, and my entire existence seemed to hinge on seeing those blue eyes.

"I love you. We are the after you search for in those pages, Dove. There …" He stopped and winced. "There is no end for us."

I sniffed, glaring at him as tears stormed down my cheeks.

A defiant smile shot me straight in the chest. "I would've said it tomorrow anyway after you were done …" He coughed again and swallowed, and I knew, I just knew he'd swallowed his own blood to keep from scaring me. "With being upset."

"A monster indeed."

I heard the stranger helping Milo, and by the time the police and paramedics arrived five minutes later, Thomas was barely conscious and so pale I feared I'd soon be able to see through his skin.

It wasn't until the ambulance doors closed and I was being maneuvered into the back of a police car that I realized the scariest thing wasn't that I could lose him.

It was that I could lose him without him knowing I loved him too.

With blurred vision, I stood on the sidewalk for untold minutes after the police had finished taking my statement at the station.

Once the paramedics and police had arrived, I'd raced upstairs to grab a shirt, shoes, and my purse, then raced back down before being told they were taking me into custody.

Now that my brain had cleared enough to shift my feet, I looked around the street, and remembered I didn't have a car. It was in the barn at the castle.

I hailed frantically for a cab, spewed the word hospital when one pulled up, and clung tight to the plastic covering the back seat.

City buildings sped by in unrecognizable patches. The only thing my eyes searched for could forever be out of reach.

No.

The driver pulled up in the drop-off zone, and I tossed a twenty at him and jumped out before he could worry about the change. "Keep it, thanks."

He shrugged as I slammed the door, and I raced toward the automatic doors, almost barreling over an elderly couple.

My frantic hustle was in vain, considering the sour-faced nurse told me to take a seat in the waiting room. If I wasn't family, they wouldn't disclose anything.

After a half an hour of feeling as though my heartbeat was going to burst through my skin, I walked back over and tried not to growl. "He has no family. Please, make note of that."

The nurse sniffed, then after staring at me for an eternity, she looked down at her computer. "What's his name again?"

"Thomas Verrone."

She chewed her lip, then looked around. When our eyes met, she said quietly, "He's in surgery right now. Come back in an hour."

Nodding, I tried not to let that overwhelm me. It meant he was still here, so I'd take it.

After taking a seat again, I powered on my phone and

began stewing over how to contact Murry. Beau. Sage. Anyone who wasn't family but may as well have been. But I didn't have anyone's number.

Only Tom's.

Just as I was about to head over to the nurses' station for another update, my phone rang, and despite not knowing the number, I knew it was Murry. "Murry?"

"Where is he?" His voice was calm, but an undercurrent of concern lingered.

"Hospital. He's, um"—I drew in a trembling breath—"he's been shot."

A beat passed. "How bad is it?"

I shut my eyes, falling back into the hard plastic of the chair. "Bad, he's in surgery."

Murry cursed. "That fed did it?"

"Yes, he's here too."

"What do you mean? With you?"

Ignoring the accusation in his question, I said, "No, I shot him."

Silence.

"Damn, Jemma."

Tiny needles of guilt pricked when I remembered Milo was probably in bad shape. "It was in the shoulder, so he'll survive."

"Still," he said. "You okay?"

"No."

"Honesty, that's good."

I relayed as much as I could of what'd happened. As if I were speaking with the cops again, my voice and explanations were clinical, my brain too afraid to entangle itself with my heart.

He quieted for a few seconds. "Let me make some calls, and I'll get someone there with you soon. Hang tight, okay? Tom's not about to let some wannabe action hero take him out."

Murry laughed. His laughter broke, and so did the smile that'd started to nudge my lips.

Unable to stop the sob from climbing higher up my throat, I hung up, and hung my head in my bloodstained hands.

∞

A firm hand landed on my shoulder, and I startled, lifting my head.

Daydreaming of better times in his bed, in his library, in the park, in the parking lot, in my old room, in the classroom, hell, even in his dungeon was better than staring at the scuffed white floor and listening to the hospital's repetitive hum of activity.

Useless.

Sitting was useless. Anything I could do would be useless, and so I escaped the only way I knew how.

Then Beau took a seat, his knee bouncing into mine. "Heard you had a busy day."

I sniffed. "You could say that."

He stuffed his hands into his hoodie pockets, watching as a kid chased a basketball across the waiting room floor. "Any news?"

"He was still in surgery half an hour ago."

Beau glanced over at the nurses' station. "You got nurse surly over there to tell you that?"

"She's probably just tired."

"You're too nice," he said. "And the cops? What happened with them?"

"I was questioned but have no priors." I blew out a breath. "Self-defense."

He whistled at the sight of my hands and grabbed them.

His skin was calloused and warm, and even though it wasn't the touch I needed, I was grateful for it all the same. "Look at you now, Jemima Jolie."

Snorting, I yanked them away, and stood. "I'm going to go wash them."

"Nah, it's a good look on you." Judging by his grin and the wild look in his eyes, I figured he was serious.

My nose crinkled. "Be right back."

In the bathroom, I was pulled up by the sight of my reflection. A light dusting of blood smeared my cheek as though I'd rubbed my face before it'd dried on my hands. My pupils were dilated, the whites of my eyes bloodshot.

No sleep, shooting someone, and potentially losing a love you never saw coming would do that to you.

Red water circled the white porcelain, and transfixed, I stood there, watching Thomas's blood swirl into the drain.

The thought of washing him away had my hand reaching out to shut the tap off, and I stared at my almost clean hands in dismay.

I wasn't about to question my rational thinking capabilities, so I patted them dry, combed my fingers through my tangled hair, and wiped the blood off my cheek.

Walking past the nurses' desk, I heard a, "Pssst."

I stopped, backtracking as the nurse, who I discovered was named Jacky, said, "He's out."

I nodded, forcing those words down, then forced myself back to where Beau was sitting, his hands clenched together as he watched me approach.

After passing on the information, we waited, and thankfully, he didn't pry for more questions.

He just sat there, waiting for the return of a friend, while I waited for the return of my heart.

It was evening before we were finally able to speak with his doctor, and he allowed us to visit because Thomas had apparently been asking for me during short periods of wakefulness.

Beau took a step forward as though he'd charge to the elevator without a second thought.

Then he had that second thought and turned back to me, grimacing. "Go."

"Are you sure?"

He chuckled, his hand scraping through his tousled blond hair. "You think he wants to wake up to my mug instead of yours when he's been asking for you?"

I smiled, then took a step forward, and wrapped my arms around him, squeezing as I murmured, "Thank you."

It took half a minute, his body tense and his heart thundering beneath my cheek, but his arms squeezed me back. "Welcome."

On the third floor, I stepped out of the elevator and charged down the hall, almost skidding as I saw the room number. A nurse pressed her finger to her lips, scowling at me.

Ignoring her, I peered into the small window on the door, my forehead meeting the cool glass as I saw everything my heart needed to survive. Thomas's sleeping form in a bed.

He was still so pale, and monitors lit up the dark around him, but the doctor had said he was breathing on his own. They needed to monitor him closely, wait for more test results, and let him rest.

I opened the door, closing it with a quiet snick behind me, then pulled up a chair close to the bed and took his cold hand in mine.

"Little Dove." A croaked whisper, fingers twitching in mine.

Sunlight coursed through the room, and I blinked, bleary eyed as I took in my surroundings.

The beeping of the heart monitor and one look at Thomas brought it all rushing back, and it took everything not to throw myself over him and hold him tight.

I settled for squeezing his hand and grinning. "Hi, Monster."

"Shot anyone lately?" he asked curiously.

I shook my head, bringing his hand to my lips and brushing them over his skin. His thumb snuck out, rubbing my lips as I stared up at him. "You scared me."

"More than when I kidnapped you and locked you in my basement?"

I laughed. "Yes, way more than that."

His brows rose. "You mustn't be too upset anymore, then." He shifted, then groaned. "If I scared you that much."

"No," I said, gesturing for him to stay still.

Thomas frowned. "You were right to be."

"We don't need to talk about this now."

"Time, Dove. It's painfully evident, wouldn't you agree, that it's not always on our side."

He was right, so I nodded.

He licked his lips, and then murmured, "I'm not well versed in apologies, or admitting when I'm wrong, but I was wrong to lose faith in you, to think the worst, and to say and do what I did. Incredibly wrong and idiotic, and I'm sorry."

"You love her, and so do I. I get it. But what you did, the way you so easily …"

"I know," he said as I trailed off. "Emotions do strange things to people, and I suppose, despite feeling as though I was different, I'm not. Not as much as I'd like to think." He smiled, and the whiteness of it lit the dark pits that'd opened in my heart. "But do you get that I love you?" He shook his head. "I don't like the word. Too inadequate." Emotion—sweet, brutal emotion—saturated every word and every perfect detail of his face. "You're the reason my heart fell, the reason it falters constantly with barely a glimpse at you, and the reason it fucking hurts when you're not near. You've colored my entire world, and if you leave it—*leave me*—you leave me in black and white all over again."

His words wrapped around me like a warm blanket on a cold night, covering cracks and bumps left by the cold. A trickle of wetness cascaded down my cheek, dropping to my chin at the sight of water beading in his untamable eyes. "You don't need to worry or threaten me into loving you, Monster."

He gestured for me to come closer, his hand gently reaching up to tuck hair behind my ear as I carefully leaned over him. His breath feathered my lips. My heart. "I'll do whatever it takes to keep you with me even if it means getting shot again, Little Dove."

"No," I rasped, my fingers trailing over his cheekbones. I dropped my nose to his. "You can't threaten me because I already love you."

"Even knowing what I am … what I do?" His breath hitched as his eyes searched mine, desperate, hopeful, and scared.

My monster was scared, and seeing it only made my heart crack further. It crumbled into his hands, surrendered to him completely.

My lips met his, whispering, "Every dark and light hue. Every piece. All of you."

CHAPTER
forty-Two

Six months later

"THREE BUMPS, NOT TWO," LOU SAID.

She giggled as I dropped my head to bump my nose with hers. I kissed it, then tugged her duvet higher. "Love you, little Lou."

I blew a kiss to Funshine Bear next to her, my old rag-dolls in the corner of her room on the bookshelf. "Love you, Jemma-poo."

Smiling, I switched out the light and headed to our room to find Tom.

"Are you ready?" I called, grabbing my brush from the dresser and tugging it through my hair as I walked deeper into the room. "We need to ..." I trailed off, noticing he wasn't even there.

My shoulders fell, and I sighed as I trudged to the bathroom to quickly swipe some mascara onto my lashes. I'd changed into a yellow and black polka dotted sundress and spritzed perfume on before I realized he was obviously held up.

I was nervous enough as it was, given our family's history, and therefore kind of pissed he was going to make us late.

Thomas couldn't work for a few months after his surgery, and although he didn't need the money, I knew he was itching for the return of what he deemed as normality.

After we went to court, where Milo was sentenced to twelve years, he'd settled some, but I knew it was only a matter of time before we had a new visitor, or he was gone for days or weeks.

Milo was arrested before he could leave the hospital. Attempted murder and kidnapping charges were brought against him by me, and the witness in the stairwell of my apartment solidified his guilt.

We'd locked eyes a few times as he sat on the stand. His burning with a million questions and obvious accusation. Mine just looking. Taking in the man who'd changed my life in unforeseeable ways. Seeing him again, knowing that my statement would help put him behind bars, wasn't what wracked me with guilt. It was seeing Shelley, his wife, as she sat stoically in the back of the courtroom, barely a hint of emotion on her beautiful face that did that.

I'd wished I'd had it in me to walk away. To not say a word, for I didn't know. I wasn't responsible for ruining their lives. They were.

Yet once Milo was taken away and most of the room had emptied out onto the street, I'd stopped her outside on the sidewalk. A quiet apology was ready on my lips, but her smile, even as it wobbled, told me all I needed to hear.

She didn't blame me.

And as Thomas walked over and stood at my back, all she did was nod, then walk away.

I didn't know if that would be the last attempt to bring Thomas down. All I knew was that if and when they tried, we'd be ready.

Grabbing a pair of ballet flats from the walk-in closet, I slipped them on and then raced downstairs.

"Oh, hey," Murry drawled, halting below the stairs when he

saw me. "You look lovely."

"Where is he?"

Murry's eyes danced anywhere and everywhere to avoid meeting mine.

"Murry," I warned.

"He said he'd just be half an hour."

"Let me guess, an hour ago?"

He shrugged, then wisely walked away.

A minute later, I entered the code and pushed open the door, making sure it shut behind me.

"That's not an answer, Gregory."

"It is, I swear—fuck." The words were cut off by screaming as I rounded the stairs.

I waited, hands on my hips, until Thomas dropped the molar into the silver tray behind him. "What's wrong, Dove?"

"What's wrong?" I repeated.

The guy in the chair, blood gushing from his mouth, stopped moaning, and bounced his eyes between us.

"Excuse the intrusion, Gregory. I'll just be one moment."

"No, we need to go."

Tom blinked up at me, then stood from the stool and plucked the crimson-colored gloves from his hands.

"You forgot, didn't you?" I asked.

The middle-aged man, with sweat beading on his forehead, clenched his hands as he studied me.

"Hi," I said, for lack of anything else to say to someone who might not live.

Understandably, he didn't respond, but his fingers wiggled where his hand was strapped to the armrest.

"Dove, what have I told you about talking to my visitors," Tom said beneath his breath.

I rolled my eyes, and his jaw twitched.

His visitor, Gregory, smirked, and I wished he hadn't as more blood oozed from whatever crater Tom had created in the man's gums.

"And I didn't forget," he said, brushing by me to the bathroom. "I merely lost track of time."

Walking after him, I hissed, "We've put this off for months, and you merely lost track of time?"

He scrubbed his hands while I glared at the back of his head. "If they're talking, Dove, they're talking. It's easy to lose track of time."

I sighed. "Whatever. Please, just hurry up."

Thomas patted his hands dry on a towel, then snatched my wrist as I went to leave. "No need for sass, Dove. I know you're frustrated."

"If you know, then you need to hurry it up already."

He didn't move a beat, and I groaned, trying to wrench out of his hold.

His laughter made me pause and had my frustration curling into a tiny ball. A tiny ball that exploded into dust as he lowered his head, his nose skimming my cheek. "When you get mad, all I want is to devour your pretty mouth." Lips met my skin, leaving a trail of goose bumps as they dragged to my ear. His teeth gently took my lobe, then released it. "Until you're nothing but pliant flesh, all mine for the taking."

Moaning from the chair in the next room had my libido checking itself, and Tom sighed.

"Let me put him to sleep, and I'll be right up."

With a kiss to my forehead, he left, and I headed upstairs to wait.

"It would seem you have the rest of the evening off, Gregory. You can thank my Dove for that."

Smiling, I closed the door and shook my head.

Did his occupation, for lack of a nicer word, still bother me? In some ways, yes, it still did.

I wasn't immune to that kind of violence. I didn't think I ever would be. But I respected that part of him, and I knew he got more than financial gain from it.

Perhaps one day, his need for that kind of release would fade some more. Maybe even completely.

But if it didn't, I'd still be there, shining what light I could on my dark prince.

My dad set two beers down on the table with a thump, foam exploding from the top of the bottles as he eyed Thomas, then took a seat.

"How's the new job going, Jem?"

I took a sip of water. "Good. It's only part time, but …" Thomas took my hand in his and squeezed a little. "I think I can see myself staying there a while."

Three months ago, I started a new job teaching third graders at a small school in Minnen, a neighboring town of Glenning. The very same school Hope and I had attended as kids.

There were only twelve children in my class, and I was job sharing with a woman who'd just returned from maternity leave, but I liked it.

And so did Lou, which is how I came to apply for a position there in the first place. Thomas had transferred her at the start of the new school year, and although she was upset over not seeing Rosie as often, the change was good for her, and she adjusted quickly.

"It's gotta be like taking a trip down memory lane every day," Dad commented with a smile. "Much nicer than that uppity place in the city anyway."

"It is," I agreed.

Dad set his sights on Thomas. "So what is it you do for a living again?"

"I run my own business," Thomas said. "Dental surgery."

I sawed into my steak, taking a bite and chewing slowly.

"How was the parade, Dad?" I asked to steal his glare away from Thomas.

Thomas didn't seem to care and cut into his food with measured precision.

"The kids loved it. Raised a lot of money this year." He took a sip of his beer. "It'd be great to have you attend once in a while. You don't need to be a kid to enjoy it."

"We'll take Lou," I told Thomas.

Thomas paused with his fork halfway to his mouth, then nodded.

I guess attending a parade thrown by local police departments wasn't exactly high on his list of fun things to do. But reaching under the table, I squeezed his thigh for at least acting as though he'd do it.

"Lou? Is that the daughter Jem was telling me about?"

I grinned as a smile transformed Thomas's neutral features. "It is." He paused, seeming to weigh his next words. "She's excited to meet you."

My dad stammered around the smile he tried to hold back. "She … yeah? Bring her over next time."

Lowering my grin to my plate, I focused on eating, all the while wondering how Thomas could win my dad over, even just a little bit, without even trying.

Word never got back to my dad about my visits to Lilyglade's police department. I suspected the employees were told to keep their traps shut, and I knew Beau had his friend hack into their database to wipe any evidence.

The conversation turned to Lou, Thomas telling Dad about her upcoming piano recital, and then turned to football as it just so happened a game was on in an hour. Thomas wasn't interested in sports, other than swimming, but he knew enough to humor my dad.

I could tell he'd reached his limit when he placed his cutlery down and gently pushed his plate away. "Thank you, it was delicious."

My dad nodded, acting as though he thought nothing of it. But even though he knew his steak was always overdone and his mashed potatoes too runny, I knew he appreciated it.

"While I'm here, I'd like to ask your blessing for your daughter's hand in marriage."

My hand almost missed the table as I set my glass back down.

My dad's eyes widened, his brows gathering as he rubbed his chin. Seconds dragged into a minute. Then finally, he said, "Are you going to ask her anyway?"

"Of course."

Dad bobbed his head side to side. "I like your honesty." He looked at me. "You want to marry this one? For real this time?"

I looked at Tom. "Yes."

"You're sure?"

I gave my eyes back to Dad. "Yes."

"Has he asked you?"

"At least once a month for the past six months."

Dad's eyes bulged even more, and his gaze swung to Thomas before he shook his head in disbelief. "Right. Well, shit. Don't let me stop you."

I took our plates to the kitchen and scraped them clean as Thomas listened to Dad prattle on about some of the livestock he'd had trouble with lately, and some more about the previous week's game.

Spying on them through the little window, I saw Thomas nod and heard him say one-word responses at all the right moments.

It wasn't until I was stacking plates in the dishwasher that I heard Dad say, "Say, what's your last name? I could've sworn I'd met you before."

"Verrone."

Shit.

"Huh." A pause, then, "Were you related to the family who used to live here in Glenning?"

Thomas didn't hesitate. "Yes. I'm their son."

Double shit.

I ditched the plates and raced back into the dining room where the sound of crickets could be heard above the two men staring at each other. "It's been so great to see you, Dad. We need to go—"

"Wait a damn minute," he said, pushing his chair back and standing. "You live at the abandoned place next door?"

"It was never abandoned," Thomas said, rising slowly and buttoning his suit jacket.

My dad's mouth opened and closed, and I knew it was due to him not knowing what to say. If he said too much, he'd have to admit too much to me and possibly to himself.

So, he snapped it shut and let me kiss him on the cheek. He even shook Thomas's offered hand before we raced down the porch steps and headed for the trees.

"Dove, the car is back that way."

"We'll get it later."

We made it to the tree line before I couldn't hold it in anymore, and I doubled over, laughter pouring out of me. The sound of Thomas letting his own free had my head rising, and I took his hand, dragging him inside the woods. "He liked you."

He grinned. "For a few minutes."

I swiped beneath my eyes, still smiling. "That's longer than he's given anyone else."

Thomas shrugged, pulling me in the other direction. "I don't care."

"No?" I frowned.

"No. Because now"—he stopped and dropped my hand to retrieve the ring I knew he'd been keeping in his jacket pocket for months—"I can finally see you in this."

Three clustered diamonds shimmered beneath the glow of the moon and stars. Small, elegant, and … "It's stunning."

"Marry me, Jemima Dianne Clayton." Our eyes locked. "Marry me because even though it will be hard at times, I promise you'll never once regret it."

"Put it on, Thomas Antonio Verrone," I whispered.

With gentleness that set every nerve ending aflame, he took my hand and slid the ring into place.

His lips stretched into a satisfied smile, and pulling me closer, he lifted my hand to kiss it. "It's not worthy of your finger, but I'm starving to see you wearing this and this only."

I hummed and took a step back.

With curious eyes, Thomas watched me lift my dress over my head.

When I unclipped my bra, dropping it to the dirt, he found his voice. "What are you doing?"

"Wearing the ring only," I said while shimmying my panties down my legs.

He looked around at the trees, then snapped into action.

His jacket was first to go, and he didn't even get his pants all the way down before I hauled him to me and took his mouth.

His hands were everywhere as his tongue slid over mine. Up my back, holding my breasts, framing my face, and then finally, they settled on my stomach, and he carefully spun me around.

He moved my hair aside, his hardness pressing into my lower back. "So not only does our baby make you feisty, but he makes you daring, too."

We'd found out I was pregnant two months ago when I'd made plans to go back onto the pill and taken a pregnancy test first. It was early; I was six weeks along at most when we'd found out, but the look of pure, unbridled joy on Thomas's face erased any worries I had.

He'd already ordered nursery furniture and informed his clients he'd be taking a leave of absence for six months after he or she arrived.

"He?" I sighed as his lips moved down my neck, sucking and licking.

"He," he stated with that unnerving confidence.

Before I could press him more, a hand snuck between my legs, and my thighs shook as they opened.

"I love you," he murmured, lips hot on my shoulder as he slid his fingers through me, then raised them to his mouth.

My legs almost buckled, my need for him too strong to keep standing.

And with the stars, the trees, and the glowing eyes of wildlife watching us, he lowered me to the ground and settled between my thighs.

"Monster," I said on a sharp inhale when he pushed inside.

"Mmm?" He moved my legs behind him, then cradled my head in his hand.

"Give me your eyes." The day I'd almost lost something I never knew I'd need so fiercely was permanently etched in the center of my heart, and on bad nights, the memory turned dreams into nightmares.

After a few nights of Thomas holding me to him as I woke drenched in fear and sweat, I'd told him about it. That I feared what might happen if I couldn't see them, see him.

"After," he'd murmured to me then, just as he did now. "No end, Little Dove. Only always."

In the place where I first saw him with the eyes of a girl, in the place where fate first threaded my soul to his, I took his face. I took it and held it with the hands of a woman as he made love to me beneath a blanket of winking stars, and I wished for nothing.

Regretted nothing.

Not when every step I'd taken, every good and bad decision I'd made, brought me to him.

To my dark prince, my monster, and my after.

The End

Also by
ELLA FIELDS

Frayed Silk

Cyanide

Corrode

GRAY SPRINGS UNIVERSITY:

Suddenly Forbidden

Bittersweet Always

Pretty Venom

ABOUT THE

Ella Fields is a mother and wife who lives in Australia.

While her kids are in school, you might find her talking about her characters to her cat, Bert, and dog, Grub.

She's a notorious chocolate and notebook hoarder who enjoys creating hard-won happily ever afters.

Connect with
ELLA

Facebook
m.facebook.com/authorellafields

Website
www.ellafields.net

Instagram
www.instagram.com/authorellafields

Acknowledgements

I almost didn't write these. I worry I sound like a broken record every time, so I'll keep this short.

My husband and children. Thank you for putting up with a crazier than usual wife and mother while I battled crippling indecision over this book.

My beta readers. Michelle, Allie, Lauren, Brynne, and Serena. Thank you for the encouragement, your time, feedback, and love for this story. I love you all.

Brynne. You needed a paragraph, and you know it. I can't thank you enough for the time, care, and every slice of information and feedback you gave me. The fact you beta read this book like a boss while you were insanely busy and most would've said no, including myself, makes me want to weep with gratitude. Anything you need, I'm all yours, baby.

Michelle. Thank you for reading this story countless times and still loving it just as much, if not more, than me. Even if you didn't, you'd still be one of my greatest loves. Thank you for all you do for me.

Lucia. Thanks for being the Lucia to my Ella and fact checking mafia stuff with your hubby. Here's to being the best kind of assholes.

Allison. Thanks so much for being an extra pair of eyes.

The rest of my amazing team. Sarah Hansen, Jenny Sims, Stacey Blake, Nina Grinstead, and Sarah Grim Sentz. Thank you, thank you, thank you. I couldn't have asked for a better group of women to work with.

And my readers. Writing these quirky and kinda crazy stories is so much of my heart, and therefore, you guys are the ones who help nourish it. Thank you for taking a chance on something different and for following me wherever I take you. You'll never know how much that trust means to me.

Made in the USA
Las Vegas, NV
17 February 2021